# SHADOWS OF ASCENSION

## HEATHER HARRISON

Foster Embry Publishing, LLC
244 Fifth Avenue, Suite E148
New York, New York 10001
www.fosterembry.com



This is a work of fiction. Names, characters, places, and incidents are
the product of the author's imagination or are used fictitiously. Any
resemblance to actual persons, living or dead, businesses, companies,
events, or locales is entirely coincidental.

Printed in the United States of America

First edition, 2019
Second edition, 2020

*For my Family*

*"I don't believe in true love. If it existed, we would die in pairs."*

- Tyler Reed
  *The Darkening.* Dir. Jason Colt. Columbia, 2011. Film.

"I'm picking up ingredients for chicken parmesan," Kiara said, phone propped on her shoulder as she tossed a bag of tomatoes into the cart.

"I see," the voice on the other side of the line replied. "Why do I get the feeling you're volunteering me to cook?"

"Would you rather I cook for us?"

"Dear god, no! I'll cook, I'll cook!"

Kiara laughed out loud, startling a young child who looked to be dozing off. A woman, early thirties, with blonde hair in a messy ponytail and dark circles under her eyes glared at her, before spinning on her heels and pushing her cart toward the other end of the aisle.

*Good lord, it's not like I meant to wake the kid,* Kiara thought.

The young mother gave a curt glance over her shoulder, narrowing her eyes. Kiara responded with an innocent smile and focused her attention back on what Tyler was saying.

"Ugh . . . this day is passing too slow. Just three more hours and I will be on a plane. I can't wait to get there."

"What time do you land? Are you sure you don't want

me to pick you up?" she asked, leaning over to place garlic in the cart.

An elderly gentleman approached from the side. His wool-lined jacket carried the odor of stale cigar smoke. He leaned in close and grabbed an onion out of the bin beside her. She froze in place. The man tipped his hat and smiled. She looked away and shut her eyes. Kiara counted under her breath, lips twitching slightly. *One. Two. Three. Four. Five. Six. Seven.* Her hands gripped the bar of the cart.

After what seemed like an eternity, the smell of smoke dissipated, the man's footsteps nothing more than a faint echo in the distance.

"Earth to Kiara?"

*Crap.* She hadn't heard a word Tyler said. "Yeah, sorry. I kind of zoned out." She let out a slow, deep breath, peeled her hands off the cart. They were stiff and swollen, deep impressions crossed the center of her palms.

There was a momentary pause on the other line before Tyler lowered his voice and said, "You know I can take you shopping when I get there. You didn't have to go by yourself."

She looked around and sighed. Long rows of pop-up cardboard signs depicting fresh fruit were soaked in florescent light. Here and there, produce lay stacked in wooden bins, while the aroma of fried chicken permeated the shopping center. Other than a few customers, the place was empty. Most of the items she needed were already in the cart, and until a moment ago, she felt like she was holding up extremely well.

"I know. I'm fine, really. Plus, I'm dangerously low on alcohol."

"Well, I can see the necessity then," Tyler laughed. "Anyway, my plane lands at six so I should be there by eight or so. I've already arranged a rental, so don't ask. Your driving scares the crap out of me."

"You could drive on the way back," she complained, feeling both relieved and guilty. She knew her driving wasn't the only reason he didn't want her to pick him up.

The lady with the child passed by giving Kiara a clipped look while her small, very awake toddler smiled and waved with his chubby hand. She waited until the mother wasn't looking before giving him a tight smile and waving back.

"I guess I didn't phrase that last sentence well enough. What I *meant* is even thinking about you driving scares the crap out of me."

She brushed off his criticism and made her way to the checkout. He was still harping on her driving when her attention wandered to the cover of a magazine. Tyler's crooked grin and blue eyes stared back at her.

"Seriously Ki, you don't have to be on the phone with me if you don't want to."

The caption under his name caught her eye, and she chuckled. "Tyler, you never told me you were gay."

"What?"

Picking up the magazine, she flipped through the pages. "Well according to the latest issue of," she turned it over to get the name, ". . . *National Star*, you are. Let's see, it says," *'A reliable source tells us Tyler Reed has been struggling with his sexuality for some time.'*

"Oh, dear god, throw that crap away."

"Oh no." She tossed the magazine in her cart. "I'm buying this. I'm just dying to hear about your sexual struggles."

"Are you now? I don't know where they get these so-called *sources* from."

"Oh, I email them something every few months."

"Nice one."

Out of the corner of her eye, she saw the gentleman with the flannel jacket heading to the checkout. She ducked behind the rack. "If it was anyone else, I don't think they would have noticed your time off. You do have quite a reputation for being a man-whore."

"A well-deserved reputation, too," he boasted.

"You're such an ass." Plucking the magazine out of the cart, she placed it back on the rack. "Still, I can't wait to see you."

"Me neither. Hold on a sec, okay?" There was a muffled voice in the background. She tapped her foot as she waited. After a moment, he got back on the line. "Hey, I got to go, but I'll see you later tonight."

"Sure. See you then."

"Ki, wait a second before you hang up. I just . . . uh . . . I wanted to let you know I feel really bad about being so busy lately. I promise when I get there, I'll make it up to you. We'll make this week extra special, okay?"

There was something in the tone of his voice that made her anxious, but she shrugged it off. "Of course, we'll have the best time. I already have the Jell-O shots chilling in the fridge."

"That's my girl. Bye, Ki."

"Bye."

~

KIARA KICKED OFF HER SHOES, propped her feet up on the leather sofa, and focused on picking at a loose string hanging from the sleeve of her sweater while Dr. Henry Alverez finished his phone call. Her cell buzzed, and she glanced down. Tyler had sent her a picture of an American Airlines plane.

*On schedule*, was the accompanying text.

The strand she was tugging at refused to detach so she tried gnawing it off. Dr. Alverez turned around and raised an eyebrow as he hung up the phone. He walked over to her with a grin on his face. "I usually tell my patients to make themselves at home, but you may be getting a little too comfortable here."

Giving one last tug, she pulled the string loose. Kiara took the tissue Henry offered her and wrapped the string in it. "I get special treatment considering I'm your favorite patient. You're the one who keeps making me come back, anyway."

"Perhaps it's because I enjoy having you around. *Aclara mi día.*"

"You better not be insulting me. You know I will look that up later."

Smiling, he said, "It means 'brightens my day' dear, which you do." He sat in the chair across from her. "You seem to be in a fine mood."

"Tyler's coming tonight. It's our fifth, 'Gee, I'm glad you didn't kill yourself that day' anniversary."

Henry chuckled. "So, I guess a Happy Anniversary is in order. I should have bought flowers."

"No need, Doc. Just take it off my bill."

The doctor shifted in his seat and she struggled not to cringe. The chair had to be older than Henry himself, and the smallest of movements caused it to groan and squeak as though it was screaming in pain. For as much as he loved his chair—which he named Bob—she could not suppress the desire to set it on fire one day when he was out of office. The thought of trying to explain to the cops why she was breaking in wearing a ski mask and carrying a can of gasoline nearly sent her into a fit of giggles.

"Has it been five years already?"

She nodded instead of answering, afraid that once she opened her mouth, the giggles would escape.

Henry clapped his hands together. "Ah, you are such a pleasure to have around. I hadn't even noticed the time passing."

She could have said the same thing. Other than Tyler, Henry was the only person she could stand to be near. "In any case, we need to work on getting me well soon, or people will become suspicious of us."

His laughter filled the room, a bellowing voice which contrasted his thin frame and gentle nature. "You're killing me here, Kiara!"

"No, your stress is killing you," she replied, worried about his labored breathing and flushed cheeks.

Henry shifted in the chair and pointed at her. "It's rude to nag."

"I worry about you."

"Hush now. Today's not about me. It's about you. Anniversary and all good stuff, remember? Now, let's get started."

As per usual habit, Henry waited, giving her a chance to gather her thoughts before the real appointment began. Her green eyes wandered around the room. Thick mahogany bookshelves lined the walls, holding journals with an array of mental health studies. Here and there a knickknack sat—a small glass frog, droves of marbled paperweights, and feathered pens in decorative ink pods.

"So, I wanted to talk to you a little about these dreams you've been having lately. Have you had any more?"

Nothing in his demeanor changed; he sat in the same relaxed position, used the same charming tone in his voice, but there was no doubt of his authority. Something in the intensity of his gaze was different when he was in psychologist mode. Regardless of what it was, she was never prepared with a lie. "Yes."

*Dammit.*

"You weren't going to tell me?"

Kiara picked at her sweater. The room became quiet. A minute passed, maybe two. Sighing, she closed her eyes and took a deep breath. Upon opening them again, she faced his scrutiny. "I hate it when you do that."

Henry raised his brow, but a slight twitch at the corner of his mouth suggested he was trying not to laugh.

"Fine," she said, drumming her fingers on the sofa's arm. "I wasn't hiding it from you. I just wasn't going to mention it. I didn't think it was important."

Henry didn't respond.

"Honestly, I would have fessed up next week. I just didn't want to talk about it today. You know, celebrate my successes, not my failures, as you like to say."

"Yes, I can see why you wouldn't want to bring it up, today of all days." He tilted his head as in deep thought before focusing on her again. "Do you think you would have done it? Would you have jumped off that balcony if Tyler didn't stop you?"

"Yes."

"It never struck you as odd that you were talked out of committing suicide by a complete stranger?"

Kiara took a deep breath. "I know you're thinking I wouldn't have done it, but trust me, I would have. He saved me that day and I'm glad he did."

"Me, too." He gave her a faint smile and shifted in his chair. "So, back to those dreams. I think they are more memories than nightmares and that's a good sign. It means you're finally ready to fill in the gaps, your mind is ready to accept what happened."

"Sorry to be negative here, but I don't care to fill in the

gaps. Especially if it requires me to re-live the worst three weeks of my life. Anyway, if your theory is true, then why are the nightmares restarting *now*? If I was going to accept what happened to me, which I'm not, wouldn't I have done it years ago?"

"Which leads us to the big question. What have you done differently in the last six months that you haven't done before? Something to bring this on?"

She shifted in her seat. Shook her head. Henry challenged her with a slight frown, his gaze locked on her.

He sighed. "I wish you would tell me what you're keeping from me."

"I'm not keeping anything from you."

She got off the couch and walked to the window, peeking through the wooden blinds at his miniature garden out back. The doctors suggested it as a way to relax and Henry took to the hobby passionately.

"Are the Marigolds new?" she turned to ask him.

He nodded.

"They're pretty."

Giving her attention back to the garden, Kiara focused on the different flowers, not blinking until her eyes watered and the colors swirled together. She hated lying to Henry, especially when he knew she was doing it, but it was better than the alternative.

She walked back to the couch and sat. "The nightmares aren't a good thing. I don't want to remember. I want to put it behind me."

"You finished your autobiography. Maybe that has something to do with it?"

Kiara shook her head. "I don't think so, but maybe."

"Are you giving a copy to Tyler while he is down?"

She studied her nails, pretending to clean them. "Yes. I wrapped it and everything. I don't know if he will care, but it would be rude if I ended up publishing it and not letting him read it first."

In truth, she was nervous to give it to him, but she could always hold on to it until she was ready. More pressing was how she was going to keep her secret without Tyler noticing. So far, she'd kept it from Henry, but she only saw him for one hour, while Tyler would be with her around the clock for an entire week.

Henry chewed the inside of his cheek. After what seemed like an eternity, he leaned back. "And what about the dreams, have you talked to him about those?"

"Not yet." She narrowed her eyes. "And I would appreciate it if you didn't either."

He furrowed his brow. "You tell Tyler everything."

"Not everything. I kept the book a secret," she argued. "It would just worry him."

"I don't think Tyler worries much about anything."

"He worries. He just does it in his own Tyler way. Are you taking a jab at him? I thought we were past that."

"No, I was not taking a jab at him. He's gained my respect." Although he spoke with sincerity, there was a trace of doubt on his face.

"I need him."

Henry sighed. "I know and that's what worries me. I need you to be dependent on yourself, too. If something were to happen . . ."

He let the words drop and Kiara didn't need to ask why. This wasn't a new subject between them. She couldn't blame him for feeling the way he did. Yes, Tyler used to be a heroin addict. *Used to* being the key phrase. He'd been clean for over five years.

Henry cut into her thoughts. "Tell me about your last dream. Anything different?"

She crossed her arms over her chest. "No, it was the same one."

"So, you're tied down, and Andrew is there, talking to you. Is that correct?"

"Yes."

"Can you tell me what he said?"

"He asked me if I was ready to ascend," Kiara mumbled.

"Nothing was different?"

"I don't know."

"Yes, you do. What was different?"

She tried to respond but she couldn't find the words. Henry spoke to her in a gentle voice. "You can tell me anything, Kiara. There is nothing to be ashamed of. No judgment here."

Casting her eyes to the floor she whispered, "Tyler was there."

"And what was Tyler doing?"

"Watching."

"And how did that make you feel?"

Her cheeks colored. "I don't know."

Henry didn't respond. He rested his chin on his hands and peered at her. She tried to keep her expression passive.

"Is that the only dream you had this past week? The only thing that is bothering you?"

*No,* she thought, the word threatening to slip past her lips. The daily torture she had been going through was overwhelming. Hiding it was her refuge. Tears pooled at the corners of her eyes.

"What is it?"

Close to her breaking point, she nearly told him everything, but fear of the consequences kept her holding her tongue. "I'm just tired of being sick."

She heard him exhale. Henry walked across the room and sat beside her.

"Kiara, you're one of the strongest people I've ever met. What you went through, most people wouldn't have survived, and I can't think of many who would come out as well as you have, especially in such a short time."

"Short time?" Kiara brushed her hands against the wetness on her cheeks. "If by a short time you mean five years. And I didn't come out of it well. I've been hospitalized, institutionalized—a ward of the state. Not to mention I can't be touched without flipping out."

"Yes, you can." He reached over and put her hands in his. "Five years ago, I would not have been able to do this. You're a beautiful, strong woman, a successful writer, and a good friend. You are getting better. These nightmares will pass."

Henry squeezed her hand before moving back to the other side of the room, giving her time to process. Kiara wished she could piece together her mind the way he did.

She knew this was a bad time to bring up the next issue but couldn't see a way around it. "Have you thought about my request?"

Henry rubbed his hand across his mouth and sat up straighter. Between that and the way he was breathing through his nose, she knew he wasn't going to concede. "Kiara, I can't do it. You're just not ready."

"That's not fair. I can take care of myself. You just finished telling me how okay I was, how I've made so much progress, how I need to depend on myself."

"And I meant every word I said, but there is still a lot we need to work on. You can barely be around other people. You become irrational if someone touches you. Who would make decisions for you if you ended up in the hospital?"

"I can do this Henry, please."

"Have you talked to Tyler about this?"

"He won't care. He's my best friend, not my caretaker."

Henry tapped his fingers on the table. "That's where you are wrong. He is your guardian. You two have always acted like this is some game, like you're playing house, but it's not. He is legally in control of every aspect of your life, and now you want me to say you don't need a guardian? It makes no sense. You and I both know you're not well enough." He let out a deep breath. "If this has something to do with Tyler, then we can see about appointing you a state representative."

"No, I don't want the state. I want to be on my own. Maybe you're just doing this because you're pissed he got guardianship of me against your wishes." She regretted the words as soon as they came out.

Henry shook his head. "No, I'm not, and you know that. This isn't about some grudge. This is about your health and safety. Tyler's done a good job. He reads the reports, signs off, asks questions if he doesn't understand, and to be honest, I didn't expect that from him."

The doctor raised a couple fingers in the air. "There are two reasons I will not recommend you to be released. First, you're not ready. I know you're okay with the fact you can't be close to others, but I'm not. Secondly, there's something else going on. In the five years I've known you, I have never seen you work so hard to keep something from me. Whatever is bothering you, it's bad enough you refuse to talk about it."

"I'm fine." She resigned, lowering her eyes.

"I'll make you a deal, though."

Kiara lifted her head.

"If you tell me what is bothering you, and I'll know if

you're telling the truth, then I will consider recommending release."

She bit her lip, hope evaporating from her system, and shook her head.

"Yeah, I didn't think so."

HER PURSE SLID across the counter and hit the wall. Its contents spilled all over the marbled surface. Kiara murmured a curse word. It wasn't her purse's fault she was in such a bad mood. Henry cheered her up before leaving by taking her out for Italian food, all the while boisterously talking to anyone nearby in a horrible Italian accent, but on the drive home, her thoughts turned back to the conversation in the office. Henry had done a good job of trying to needle information out of her, but this new issue was something she wasn't ready to talk about. Maybe he wouldn't have her institutionalized again, but she wasn't going to take the chance.

Frustrated, she grabbed a book off the shelf, planning to read and take a few hours to wind down before Tyler showed up. Passing through the dining room, she caught sight of her reflection in the window and stopped.

*I look like hell. No wonder Henry doesn't believe me.*

For a long period in her life she dreaded looking in the mirror, the white-lined scars across her thighs and hips only serving as a reminder of what she went through. Her figure was small but curvy and her skin normally had a healthy glow to it, but lately she'd become pale, the dark circles under her eyes impossible to conceal. Slumping her shoulders, she headed in search of caffeine.

In the kitchen, Kiara started a fresh pot of coffee. With the book in hand, she leaned on the counter and watched it brew, eyes sliding closed as her mind drifted into a fog. The last rumble of the percolator startled her, and she jumped. With shaky hands, she poured herself a cup, taking several sips as she headed to the couch.

Despite the caffeine, she drifted off within minutes. As her mind ebbed in and out of awareness, a low-tuned keening like that of a thousand crickets drifted into the darkness of her developing dream. At first, she ignored it, mixing it in with the other background noises, but the volume grew, overwhelming her senses. Kiara opened her eyes, blinked several times to clear her vision as the noise came closer.

*Please, no.*

Trembling, she sat and turned in time to see a large black mass slither underneath the coffee table beside her, its inky skin pulsating and shifting. Shadows collected under the bulky piece of furniture, leaving a dim impression of the creature which resided beneath it. The thing turned its bulging head toward her, its piercing gaze holding her in place.

She stared into its milky eyes and whispered, "Go away."

2

Tyler dropped his duffle bag on the ground and stretched out the stiffness which set in during the long drive. He'd rented a luxury Sedan for the trip. At the time it seemed like a good idea but having not slept much over the last few days, the silent engine and leather interior left him falling asleep behind the wheel more times than he cared to admit.

Walking toward the front door of Kiara's house, Tyler felt a sense of homecoming. The blinds were parted, light illuminating the walkway, but a quick peek through them showed an empty room which meant she probably wasn't aware he'd arrived. Reaching into his pants pocket, Tyler wrapped his fingers around the house key. The damp wind flattened his light brown hair across his forehead causing it to stick there. Even though it was only September, the air had a bitter chill to it and the warmth from the car heater was evaporating quickly. Crickets sung in unison and somewhere in the ten acres of woods surrounding the house, he heard an anguished howl. With his fist gripped around the key, he leaned his head against the door. He'd been looking forward to this trip since they planned it months ago, but Henry's call had been an unexpected burden.

*"I need you to keep a close eye on her, watch for anything odd."*

*"Like what?"*

*"I'm not sure. There's something wrong and she won't tell me what it is. It's been this way for months. I can tell you, whatever it is, it has her spooked. She's been antsy, pulling at her clothes and playing with her bracelet. I haven't seen her do that in years. Sometimes she looks around like she's watching something I can't see. I think she might be hallucinating again."*

*"She hasn't done that in years. I don't know, Henry, she hasn't said anything to me that seemed off at all."*

That was a lie though. There had been several occasions over the last few months where she seemed distant. A few times she even called him drunk in the middle of the night, which was unlike her. One of those conversations, which he was unsure if she remembered, was part of the reason he was stalling outside her door.

*"I think it's because she's afraid. I'm worried about the direction she's headed. And honestly, it concerns me thinking about her being all alone. She's avoiding sleep, there are dark circles under her eyes, and she's losing weight."*

Henry suggested a nurse, but the thought of putting her under someone else's care disturbed him. He felt guilty about Kiara being alone out here, but she was perfectly capable of taking care of herself. The only reason he took guardianship was so she could use her money as she wished. The state had appointed a guardian for her when she was released from the hospital, but they didn't allow her to make decisions without having to jump through hoops.

*"You can't watch her all the time Tyler. You travel too much."*

*"I'll take her with me."*

*"And how would you do that? Get her on a plane? Take her on set*

*with you? People would become obsessed with her. She would be worse off than she is now."*

"It's not going to come to that Henry."

Could he be sure though?

*Yes, damn it. She's fine. She's stronger than that.*

He shoved the key in the lock and walked into the foyer. "Hello?"

Soft music played somewhere in the background and he could smell her perfume, a mix of honeysuckle and vanilla, but his voice echoed in the empty entryway. Tyler grabbed his bag from outside and tossed it on the floor, kicking the door shut with his foot.

"What, no welcome committee to greet me?" he yelled.

A blur of wavy black hair raced around the corner of the entryway before she came to a stop in front of him, socks sliding on the floor.

"You would get a better welcome if you knocked on the door instead of using your key." Kiara grinned at him.

He looked down at her full, pouty lips and large green eyes. Her face was lit up in a smile and she bounced lightly on the balls of her feet. She was tiny, and fragile, and beautiful. It pissed him off that Henry thought there was anything wrong with her. Before he could get a word out, she shoved a package in his hands.

"What's this?" he asked, the thick paper crinkled under his grasp. "Oh, crap! Was I supposed to bring you a gift? You didn't say we were doing gifts."

"Nope, just me. Plus, it's kind of, sort of, homemade," she said, motioning him into the living room. "How was your flight? Did they lose your luggage again?"

"Not this time. I left them in the trunk. I'll get them later."

"So," she rose on her heels, tilted her head at him,

"what do you want to do first? Eat? Drink? I'm all for drinking."

"Ki, you are a mess. How much coffee did you have before I showed up?" He picked up his bag and followed her into the living room.

"One, no, maybe two pots. I wanted to make sure I didn't fall asleep before you got here."

Her tone was light-hearted and playful, but her eyes slid to the floor as she fidgeted with the pillows on the ottoman. There was a sinking feeling in the pit of his stomach. Something was off, but he couldn't place his finger on it. Once again, his mind rolled back to their conversation from a few months ago. He didn't think that was it though. If anything, he was beginning to get the feeling Henry might be on to something.

Tyler slumped down on the couch and propped his feet up. The living area was large, designed like a small resort with huge bay windows and high arched ceilings. Kiara had the electric fireplace running. The room felt warm, cozy.

Between jobs, he stayed at his house in Los Angeles, but it was here he felt at home.

She plopped down beside him, scrutinized his expression. "Is something wrong?"

"No, of course not. I was just thinking about how nice it is to be here."

Kiara furrowed her brow. Did she know Henry called him? Tyler smiled, and she returned it, but as her gaze fell on his eyes, the smile faltered.

*Crap, she must know.*

He opened his mouth, not even sure what he would say, but she interrupted before he could start.

"I'm so sorry!"

*Huh?*

He ran his eyes briefly over her face. She didn't seem defensive or upset. Maybe it wasn't about the call.

"For what?" he asked, tension pulling his shoulders taut.

"You look exhausted. I shouldn't jump on you like that when you walk in the door. Do you want to go to bed?"

Tyler relaxed. "Ki, I think that's the first time I have ever heard those two sentences together without meaning anything sexual."

"Don't be vulgar." She wrinkled her nose. "I'm just excited to see you, but if you're tired, we can save the partying for tomorrow."

He leaned his head against the back of the couch, shut his eyes. He'd been awake since four in the morning. His body was demanding sleep. Still, he didn't want to let her down. Ignoring the exhaustion, he opened his eyes again. "Did you say party?"

She nodded.

"I'm always ready to party."

Kiara walked over to the music player, turned her back to him, but not before he saw her smile. Tyler ran his fingers across the gift he held in his lap. The paper was thick with a red and yellow paisley design sketched between rows of diamond shaped patterns. It quite possibly might have been the ugliest wrapping paper he'd ever seen in his life.

"Is it okay if I open this now?"

"Only if you promise not to tear the paper. I'm saving that beauty for your Christmas gift, too."

He chuckled. Finding a seam on the paper, he tore it open and pulled out a bound manuscript. It had Kiara's information on the front but no title. It appeared to be one of her stories. He saw her turning around out of the corner of his eye and assumed a grateful expression.

"Thank you. Is it a book?"

She giggled. "I guess I should have explained it to you. Open it to the first page."

Although she had instructed him to do it, Kiara waltzed over and opened it, pointing to a paragraph on an otherwise empty page. Tyler read what was typed.

*This book is dedicated to Tyler. You are my best friend, my savior, and my reality. I am thankful every day for the moment you came into my life.*

"You dedicated your book to me?"

She nodded.

"Wow. I don't know what to say. Thank you."

He read the inscription again. "This is the best gift ever. I really mean that."

Kiara tugged her bottom lip between her teeth, a small flush highlighting her cheeks. Not wanting to make her uncomfortable, he closed the book and asked, "Do you mind if I go shower and change before we party?"

"No, go ahead. That will give me time to start dinner."

Tyler raised his eyebrows.

She cocked her head, eyes narrowed. "Let me reiterate, I'm going to throw some frozen pizza in the oven. I can do that much."

"Whatever you say, ma'am." He threw the duffle bag over his shoulder and headed toward the largest guest room, the one she referred to as his room. Tyler shuffled the manuscript to his other hand. Stopping in the middle of the hallway, he turned back to her. "So, is this the book you've been keeping secret from me?"

She nodded.

"Care to give me any spoilers? What's it about? Monsters? Ghosts? A self-help cooking book?"

Kiara picked up a magazine and flipped through it,

keeping her eyes down. "No, it's about what happened to me."

The manuscript slipped out of his hands and hit the floor with a thud. She jumped. Her eyes grazed his before looking back down. "I wanted you to read it first."

Tyler picked up the book, taking longer than necessary, as he gathered his thoughts. This would explain why she seemed so edgy. They rarely talked about what happened to her and then it was only in short reference. When he stood back up, he didn't bother to hide his sincerity. "I'm really proud of you."

He turned and continued down the hallway, not giving her time to reply.

3

"I'm sorry about dinner," Kiara apologized as Tyler took a bite of the pizza.

She'd done everything the box instructed her to; double checked the temperature, made sure she placed it on the correct rack, but somewhere between setting the timer and checking for doneness, her mind had wandered off. When the smell of burnt crust permeated the house, she'd realized her mistake. While she was still staring at the blackened pizza, Tyler walked into the kitchen, and laughed. She'd offered to make another, but he insisted it was still edible.

"Quit apologizing," he replied, shrugging his shoulders. "It's not that bad."

She watched, horrified, as he took another bite. He chuckled at her incredulous look, causing him to choke. Kiara stood to pat him on the back, but he held out his hand to stop her. After choking down a few sips of water, the coughing fit stopped, and he tossed the pizza slice on the plate.

"You're right, this sucks. How do you even feed yourself?"

She pointed at the microwave. "If it has to be heated in anything other than that, I don't even bother."

Her cooking capacity consisted of TV dinners and soup.

Tyler stood. "Grab your drink. We're going to the kitchen so I can cook you a decent meal."

Picking up her glass and the bottle of rum, she followed him. Jumping up on the granite counter, she watched as he searched through her cabinets, giving her a look of mock surprise if he found anything he considered to be *decent* food. She screwed the lid off the rum and drank straight from the bottle. When she set it down, Tyler shook his head, grinning. "You're hitting it hard tonight, kid."

He sat some items on the counter. "I would cook the chicken parmesan, but it takes too long, so tonight we will have pork chops and salad." He glanced around the kitchen for a bowl. "Did you remodel in here? It looks different."

She made a noncommittal noise, and he didn't repeat the question, so she let it drop. She felt guilty letting Tyler cook, but not enough to stop him. He was a joy to watch in the kitchen. She put the bottle back up to her mouth, but he grabbed it away.

"If you get too drunk, you won't be able to learn." He took a swig from the bottle before replacing the lid and setting it on the counter.

"I didn't know I would have to participate."

Tyler handed her a cutting board. "Wipe the pitiful doe-eyed look off your face and grab a knife."

She scoffed at him but jumped off the counter and took the cutting board.

"You have to learn to cook sometime and I happen to be a good teacher."

She picked up the celery he handed her and looked at him doubtfully. His obsession with cooking was one she never hoped, nor wanted, to understand.

"I already know how to cut vegetables," she replied, chopping the celery into jagged pieces.

"Whoa! Slow down there, young Padawan." He placed his hand on hers. Tyler moved behind Kiara, his grasp tightening over her hand and knife. She could feel his warm breath on her neck. "Do it like this; slow, precise cuts, otherwise they'll cook unevenly."

He removed his hand and moved back beside her. Kiara stared at the celery. Her chest was tight, legs weak. She hadn't been expecting the intimacy. Tyler never touched her unannounced. She counted to five and let out a deep breath. "We're not cooking the salad, are we?"

"Nope." He popped a piece of celery in his mouth, smirking, but his eyes seemed intense. "A good cook always uses the correct technique, though."

*He did it on purpose.* The thought came out of nowhere, but she didn't doubt her instinct. *Why?*

She glared at him before continuing to cut as he'd instructed. The celery still came out jagged, but it was an improvement. She cut another piece, then stopped. "Weren't you even a little afraid I would freak out and stab you?"

"Very." He finished seasoning the pork chops and put them in the oven. After he shut the door, he wiped his hands off on the dish towel and grinned. "But I take my cooking seriously."

"You must."

"Tomorrow we will teach you how to cook. Maybe start with the chicken parmesan."

She cringed at his comment. "Why don't I just watch you make food for me?"

"Because you won't learn that way."

"Cooking is too difficult." She grabbed a piece of cucumber out of the bowl and popped it in her mouth. "Besides, you cut ten times faster than I do."

"You don't know that until you've tried. Honestly, I don't know how I would have survived rehab if it hadn't been for the cooking classes. It was the best therapy I had, except for you, that is." He winked at her. "Plus, don't think I didn't notice the new stove and hood. Can I assume they were damaged in a fire?"

"Maybe it just stopped working. Did you ever think of that?"

"That was my first thought until I noticed the wall had been replaced and repainted. What were you trying to cook that nearly burned the house down?"

"Chicken parmesan."

He shook his head, chuckling. "Maybe we should start with grilled cheese sandwiches then."

DEAD PINE NEEDLES scraped against the broken window, the sound doing nothing to dispel her terror. Kiara pulled on the ropes, ignored the pain. A wet trickle slid down her wrist and she laughed maniacally. Twisting them back and forth, she tried to lather the ropes with her own blood.

*I only need one hand. I can do it if I just slip one hand out.*

She pulled with all her strength, but the nylon rope caught on her palm, refused to budge any further. Kiara cried out in frustration, but nothing louder than a pale whimper passed her dry, cracked lips. A noise reached her ears; the sound of footsteps echoing on rotten wood.

*No, please no.*

She tugged harder, the muscles in her shoulders and back screaming. The door opened and Andrew walked in, a sweet smile plastered on his face. When he saw what she was doing, he frowned. Strolling over, he sat beside her on the bed and she recoiled.

"Shh . . . ," he whispered, running his hands through her hair. "It'll be okay."

Tears filled her eyes and the taste of vomit collected in the back of her throat. She turned her head and saw Tyler approaching from the other side of the bed, his eyes glossy black and focused on her face.

When he was within inches from touching her, she whispered, "Help me."

"I can't." His voice was hollow, unnatural.

"Why are you here then?"

"Punishment." As the words left his mouth, his skin began to sag, to melt away. Flesh dripped from his face, chunks of it landed on her chest.

She bolted up in bed, screaming.

THE SOUND WOKE him from a deep sleep. Before he knew what he was doing, Tyler was across the hall, standing outside her bedroom. His fingertips grazed the knob, but as he turned it, the screaming stopped. He paused, listening to see if it would start again but the house was silent.

He knocked softly. "Ki?"

"Come in."

In the dim light, he could barely make out her silhouette on the bed. A quick movement suggested she was wiping her eyes. She dropped her hands to her side and tugged the blanket over her lap. Leaning against the doorway, he waited until she regained her composure. This wouldn't be the first time her screams had woken him.

*She looks so fragile.*

"You okay?"

"Yeah." She wiped her eyes one last time and turned on the lamp. Her face was pale, drawn, but she gave him a weak smile. "Just a . . . a bad dream, you know? I'm sorry I woke you."

"No, don't be. Do you want to talk about it or anything?"

Kiara surprised him by laughing. "Oh, good god no, that's a horrible idea."

"Sorry," he chuckled. "I had to ask."

"I like the Tyler version of making you feel better anyway."

"You mean the one where I ignore conflicts and instead suggest we drink our feelings and dare each other to do crazy shit we won't remember the next day?"

"That's the one." She trailed her fingers over the white sheet. He waited for her to speak instead of interrupting. Maybe zoning out was a writer thing, or maybe it was just a part of her personality. He could never tell for sure.

A minute passed before she looked back up. "I'm glad you're here. It's nice."

The sincerity in her voice was hard to miss, and he felt a pang of guilt. He was surrounded by people constantly, to the point where all he wanted was to be alone. Kiara had no one except him and Henry. For years now, he'd been working up the nerve to talk to her about staying with him, but that would bring up a lot of issues he was sure neither of them was ready to deal with.

"So, is drunk truth and dare on the menu or are we heading back to bed?"

"I'll take a raincheck. You wouldn't be much competition with how tired you look. I'm pretty sure I could have you naked and running around the yard in less than twenty minutes."

"Ki, you could have me naked now if you wanted."

"I'm going to ignore that statement. Now go to bed."

"Fine. Wake me up if you change your mind." He caught a shadow of a real smile on her face as he stepped out. When he got to the room, he shut the door and threw himself on the bed, exhausted. His last thought as he drifted to sleep was how he hadn't heard her scream like that in years.

4

They were about a mile out behind her house. Thick brambles led to an empty field of deep grass surrounded by creeks and riverbeds. Kiara shut her eyes, engrossed in the rhythmic cadence of the woods. A warm breeze brushed past. Having been raised by several rounds of foster parents, nothing in her life was ever concrete, ever stable, but nature never changed. It bloomed with the seasons, passing on when it was time.

She figured that was the reason she chose her home. The countryside gave her a much-needed sense of security she never received as a child.

*I need to remember to tell Henry that. He would be impressed by my self-psychoanalysis.*

Lining her gun up, she squeezed the trigger. The sound echoed through the field and the coffee can flipped several times in the air before falling to the ground. Placing the safety on the pistol, Kiara set it down. "I totally just kicked your ass."

Tyler gave her a dirty look and aimed at the cans, missing his shot again.

"Damn," he said, pointing his gun toward the ground. "You do realize that, unlike here, they don't allow shooting practice in my back yard."

"Whatever you need to make yourself feel better." Kiara winked at him.

"Did you just wink at me? You know that's an invitation for sex, right?"

Strolling over, he put his arm around her shoulders, but she pushed it off. "You think everything is an invitation for sex."

"I'm usually right."

"For you, I imagine that's true."

He grinned and picked up the cooler they'd packed earlier that morning. "You know that's why I love you, right?"

"Because you can't have sex with me and lose interest?"

Tyler's mouth fell open, and she giggled. It was a rare treat to catch him off-guard.

"I was going to comment about your honesty, but now I'm thinking that's not your best quality."

"You do look pretty hot standing by that cooler of sandwiches." Her stomach was rumbling, and the temperature had risen several degrees under the cloudless sky.

"Are you wanting to play *the game*?" he whispered, dragging out the last word.

"Not a chance, I always lose. Plus, I get grumpy when I'm hungry."

"By all means then, let's get you fed. Lead the way."

The warm sun radiated on her bare shoulders. Although the breeze was cool, the tingling feeling on her skin hinted to the beginnings of a sunburn.

"Let's head down by the creek." She pointed to the alcove of trees about a hundred yards away.

The knee-high grass brushed against her jeans. Using a

long branch, she checked the ground ahead. High grass meant snakes, but she was too uncomfortable to have anyone out to brush hog it. All the gardening and lawn care around the house she did by herself. As for the rest, she let nature run its course.

As they reached the trees, Kiara squinted to see beyond the collage of dappled shadows. The temperature beneath the shade was several degrees cooler and the smell of damp pine needles permeated the air. A peaceful gurgling emitted from the creek as it cut through a mixture of rocks and clay. When her eyes adjusted, Kiara found a spot by the water and laid out the blanket.

Reaching into the cooler, she threw Tyler a beer. "Catch."

He caught it at the last minute and gave her a disgusted glare. "That should be considered a felony. You don't throw a beer. It ruins it."

She responded by throwing a sandwich to him and opening her own beer. They ate in silence, listening to the sounds of rushing water. She glimpsed at Tyler. He was staring at the creek, lost in his own thoughts. Although he rarely showed his serious side, she knew he was brooding over something. Propped halfway up on one elbow, his plain white t-shirt and black dickies made him appear casual and laid back, but she knew better. He had an intensity most people weren't aware of. She'd seen him crying in the bathroom, holding a needle in his hand, shaking. She had talked him out of suicide, begged him, screamed at him, and he had done the same for her. There was no hiding from each other.

"You realize you're staring at me, right?"

She blinked, pulled out of her thoughts. He had just finished his sandwich and was rolling the wrapper into a ball. Realizing she hadn't touched hers, she took a bite, ignoring his raised eyebrows.

"So, it's fine to just stare at someone and not acknowledge them?" He stood and walked over to the cooler, pulling out another beer.

She shrugged, mouth full.

"Creeper," he teased, grinning over the foaming can.

Kiara put her sandwich down and reached for him, putting the most adoring look she could muster on her face. "You're just so pretty."

"Okay, now you really are creeping me out." He laughed and threw the sandwich wrapper at her.

She caught it and threw it back, nailing him in the middle of his chest. "For your information, I was wondering what you were brooding about."

"I wasn't brooding," Tyler said, pulling out another beer out and handing it to her. "I was man-thinking. Two different things. Mostly I was thinking about how I don't want to go back."

Confused, she tried to remember how long he'd told her he was staying. "You're still here for the week, right?"

"Longer than that."

Before she could ask what he meant, he continued, "I'm not looking forward to going back to real life. I like being out here, it's peaceful."

"And this whole time I thought you came to see me." She took her shoes off and rolled up her jeans, scooted to the edge of the blanket and dipped her heels in the creek. The water trickled over them, cooled her hot skin.

"Nah, you just come with the package." He smirked and took his shoes off, following her lead. "How's the water?"

"Not bad considering it's nearly fall. If it makes you that unhappy, why don't you just move or take a hiatus?

You have plenty of money." Secretly she wished he would take a break and stay longer. Although she liked being alone, sometimes the loneliness was unbearable, but she would never tell him that. Especially not now, with all that was going on.

"I've thought about it. I guess I just want to hit that big role first. I don't know, maybe prove to myself that I'm more than just a pretty face." Tyler traced his finger in a circle around his features and grinned.

Kiara concentrated on picking up a pebble between her toes so he wouldn't notice her frown. After three tries she gave up, frustrated with both the pebble and him. "I wish you had more confidence in yourself."

She knew part of the reason for his addiction was because he believed he wasn't good enough, that people only *pretended* they liked him. Tyler explained to her that the drugs made him not care, that people couldn't get inside his head. He used to call himself a 'pretty Hollywood whore' until he realized it upset her.

"You don't see the scripts they send me. Most of them are about some mindless pretty-boy. It's sickening."

"Yeah," she said, reaching over and patting him on the shoulder. "It must be awful to be so hot."

He chuckled, but then his smile faltered. "You don't know what it's like to have people snapping pictures of you when you're trying to buy a roll of toilet paper."

Sighing, she took her feet out of the water. "Yeah. I do."

For years, the press hounded her. They broadcast her ordeal for the entire world to see, photos of her face covered in bruises and blood, crime scene details—images for people to feed on and forget once the next sensational news story came out, images she fought daily to erase. Over the years, it had died down, but now and then she would get a call or request for an interview. She changed her number every six months and ordered most of her supplies online, only going to town as needed.

"I'm sorry, Ki. I wasn't thinking. What I meant is you don't see me the way they do. All they care about is my looks and who I'm dating."

"That's true. I find you absolutely repulsive."

He grinned. "You're the best."

It occurred to her it had been a very quiet visit so far. *Too quiet.*

"Are you really not dating anyone?" She hadn't believed what she saw in the magazine, but there had been a definite lack of phone calls.

"Nope. I'm officially single." He lay on the blanket beside her, his blue eyes shining with humor. "I guess that makes me available."

"When did you decide this? And why?"

"Don't sound so put out. Are you living vicariously through me or something?"

"If I were, we might have to switch the word vicariously with vigorously. You date like twelve different girls a year."

"True."

She grabbed another beer out of the cooler and opened it. "Okay, no more jokes. Why?"

"It's simple. I'm trying to take my career seriously and nagging, jealous girlfriends get in the way. It's hard to focus on acting when your phone is going off every five minutes with someone who is upset because you have a love scene that day." He turned to look at her. "Plus, I got sick of dealing with the jealousy every time I came to see you or talked to you on the phone."

She took a moment to consider his words. "Yeah, I was

wondering about that. I figured that was the problem anytime you took your calls outside."

"You noticed, huh?" he asked, brushing his unruly hair off his forehead and giving her an apologetic look. "Sorry."

"No, I get it. I wouldn't be too happy if my boyfriend spent weeks at a time with his female best friend. Even if said best friend was some kind of jacked up freak with a weird physical contact issue."

He stretched his arms above his head and yawned. "Nah. I never told them that part."

Kiara stared at him, shocked. "What? You can't be serious. What did you tell them then?"

"That I was going to spend a week with my best friend," he answered, shrugging his shoulders. "If they couldn't handle it, then that was their problem. If they called too much while I was here, I just turned off my phone."

"Wow, that's kind of an asshole thing to do." Tyler had a reputation for being uncaring, but that was his other life and she hadn't seen that side before.

"Don't look at me like that. I'm as nice as I can be about it and I try to be supportive of their feelings, but I can't tell them about you. Every day I count myself lucky the media hasn't gotten wind of us. I don't keep it a secret because I'm being a jerk."

A part of her wondered why people hadn't put them together in the news. She always assumed they were lucky. Realizing Tyler had a big part to do with it made her feel guilty for thinking the worst. She wondered how many times she had caused his relationships ending.

"I'm sorry, I hadn't thought of that. Thanks," she said, sincerely.

"Don't worry about it." He looked up under his lashes

and she sensed his discomfort. Kiara felt a pang of sadness. The fact he showed so much aversion to being treated like a decent guy let her know he still suffered from his self-esteem issues.

"So, what about you?" he asked.

"Oh, you know, all of my relationships are going great." She downed her beer, dramatically, and he chuckled.

"Do you ever miss it?"

"Not really. I guess once you've been platonic for so long it's hard to feel anything else." She propped up on her elbow facing him. "I'm sort of like a female eunuch."

"So, the idea of never dating again for the rest of your life is fine?"

"No, but that's how it is." She picked up some pine needles and tossed them in the creek. "Occasionally, I think about what it would be like to pick out a wedding dress and walk down the aisle, or what it would be like to have kids, but usually it just makes me sad. It's hard to explain."

"I understand it better than you think." He was quiet for a moment. When he spoke again, she could tell he was trying to lighten the mood. "Who do you see when you imagine yourself walking down the aisle?"

"Sometimes it's Porky Pig, sometimes it's you," she joked.

"What are you trying to say here? Am I interchangeable with Porky Pig? Ouch, Ki."

She shrugged her shoulders and grinned at him.

Tyler chuckled. Raising his eyebrows, he asked, "So, you fantasize about marrying me, huh?"

"Only because you ask me about once a week."

"Yeah, but you always turn me down," he pouted. "You would be the perfect wife. You're easy to look at, you're fun, make a good living, and you would let me sleep with other women."

"Maybe there's another reason I'm able to think of pigs and you at the same time," Kiara replied.

THEY STAYED OUT UNTIL DUSK. It was Tyler who suggested they go before it got too dark to find their way back. As they approached the house, Kiara remembered what she meant to ask him earlier in the day.

"Tyler, what did you mean when you said you were here for longer than a week? Did I miss something?"

"I extended my trip until the fifth. It's kind of my anniversary surprise."

She did the math in her head. "That's like three weeks. How did you forget to tell me?" Excited he was staying for that long, she tried to ignore the nagging doubt in the pit of her stomach. It had been years since he could manage more than a week off with his work schedule. It struck her as odd he now had a gap.

Tyler looked at her face and frowned. "I thought you would be happy, but you don't look happy."

The overly casual tone of his voice sounded fake, and she stopped mid-stride, having figured out what was upsetting her. Tyler was horrible at keeping anything from her, especially something he was excited about.

"Did you extend your trip after you got here?"

"Is something wrong with me wanting to spend more time with you?"

He pretended to act offended, but she wasn't falling for it. There was another reason, and he was trying hard to hide it from her. Yes, she had been acting a bit off, and maybe he had noticed, but that still shouldn't be enough to make him rearrange his schedule.

*Unless . . .*

"Henry called you, didn't he?"

"Yep," he said, keeping his tone light.

The fact he was staying because he was concerned left her feeling ashamed and angry. It was unfair for Henry to call and there wasn't a damn thing she could do about it. Yes, she was hiding something and yes, there were the nightmares, but that didn't seem serious enough to warrant a phone call. For Henry to do that pissed her off.

Kiara stomped off toward the house. The steady crunching of leaves and dead sticks under her feet was the only noise other than the continuous chirping of crickets. She didn't look over her shoulder to see if Tyler was following. Lost in her own thoughts, she startled when he grabbed her hand, pulling her to a stop.

"Ki, please, he's just worried about you. So am I. If there's something bothering you, I wish you would tell me."

Kiara tried to pull away.

Tyler held on tight, unwilling to let go. "Look at me."

Doing as he asked was a mistake because the worry and concern on his face dissolved her anger, which was the only thing holding the tears at bay.

"You don't have to tell me anything. But if there is something you need to talk about, I want to be here for you."

The stubborn refusal to let him or Henry in on her secret began to waiver, and she wanted to tell Tyler, but there was a lump in her throat, and she couldn't make the words come out. The fact he wasn't pushing her to tell made it even harder.

"Look, ever since we left that hospital, we promised to

take it as it comes. That's all this is. If you're going through something, then I want to be by your side," he said.

She stared into his eyes, a dark obsidian blue, and remembered that she trusted him for a reason. "Okay."

"Good," he said, holding his arms out. "Can you handle a hug?"

At first, she hesitated, but it was only habit that provoked that reaction. Taking a few steps forward, she leaned in. Tyler wrapped his arms around her.

She took a deep breath smelling him, a mixture of woods, sweat, and cologne. She was rarely close enough to someone to pick up on their scent and had forgotten how appealing it could be.

This was their typical hug; her leaning her head in but keeping distance and Tyler careful to touch her as little as possible. It took years for them to get to where she was comfortable with it. Sometimes she thought about how much effort he'd put into making sure he never touched her without making her aware first, to the point where it had become natural to him. She knew she needed him in her life. He was her only real contact with the outside world, but most of the time she forgot it was a two-way road. She wasn't naïve enough to believe she was as important to him as he was to her, but she didn't think they were too far off.

He shifted, his body language signaling he was prepared for her to pull away, which she usually did long before this. For months now, Kiara suspected she no longer feared physical contact with Tyler. Feeling secure with herself and perhaps a little smug, she leaned in, pressing against him. One second passed, maybe two, but not long enough for her to find out if she was right before Tyler let go and backed away, putting several feet of distance between them. He was staring at her like she was a stranger.

*Did I make him angry?*

"I'm sorry, Tyler."

"Don't be," he replied, giving her a tight smile. "That was my fault. I was just caught off guard, that's all."

"Um, okay then."

What else could she say? Tyler was studying his hands like he was unsure what to do with them. After a second, he shoved them in his pockets, a weak smile on his face.

"Let's go in. If I don't feed you soon, you're going to get grumpy."

She tried to smile at his joke but couldn't manage. In the back of her mind, she couldn't ignore the thought Tyler was disgusted by her.

Walking toward the house, Kiara wondered if things would get back to normal before she fell completely apart.

TYLER CONTEMPLATED TAKING a shower but decided it could wait until morning. Instead, he slipped off his jeans and changed into sweat pants. He pressed his ear to the wall and heard running water. Confident Kiara was in the shower, he pulled the gray box out of his duffle bag and opened it. A small silver ring stared back at him, light glinting off the red rubies and white diamonds. He pinched the offensive piece of metal between his thumb and finger and pulled it out.

*How can one tiny, little thing be so frustrating?*

Two years ago, they'd visited a flea market down in the village. Kiara was so taken by the ring that he went back to purchase it the next day, intending on surprising her. The jewels were fake and after giving it some thought, he decided to replace them first. One thing led to another and somehow it ended up costing him a small fortune. That's when he began to doubt giving it to her at all. For birthdays and holidays, they exchanged small, thoughtful items, not expensive, useless ones. Last year, he found an original Snoopy Snow Cone Machine on Amazon that she reminisced about one drunken night. When he gave it to her for Christmas, she squealed in delight. Every time he thought about giving her the ring, it felt wrong, inappropriate somehow, yet he carried it on him when he visited.

*Just in case, that's all.*

Tyler let out a sigh and mumbled under his breath, "Lost my fucking mind."

He pushed the ring back in the box and shoved it under the mattress. Laying down, he thought back to their hug. Not for one second had he believed the hug was sexual in nature, but he reacted to her anyway. The look of hurt and embarrassment on her face was enough to make him want to kick himself, but what could he say?

*Sorry, I only pulled away because you turned me on? Yeah, that would have gone over well.*

Still, he had never been that close to her, never thought it was possible, yet there she was, testing the boundaries. That had to mean progress.

*It would be nice to hold her, to touch her more often, wouldn't it?*

For the first time in five years, he questioned whether that would be a good thing. Grabbing some clothes and a towel, he headed to the other bathroom. A cold shower wouldn't hurt after all.

5

ou going to bed?" Tyler yawned and sat up.

She glanced at his hooded eyes and laughed. "Yes. You've been snoring for the last five minutes."

"I did not fall asleep on you, Ki."

"Okay, fine then, what was I talking about?"

"Um . . . how awesome I am?"

Kiara grabbed a small pillow off the couch and threw it at him. It hadn't bothered her he'd fallen asleep. It was nice watching his eyes flutter, listening to his gentle breathing, knowing she wasn't alone.

If she was truthful with herself, Tyler wasn't the only one exhausted. A good night's rest wouldn't hurt either of them. On the way to her room Kiara stopped to check the thermostat. It registered seventy-two degrees. She rubbed her hands up and down her arms. Tyler's footsteps echoed down the hall behind her.

When he came into sight, she asked, "Is it cold in here?"

He shook his head.

Leaving the temperature alone, she continued to her room. The house came with three large bedrooms, two across from each other, and one on the opposite side of the house. Originally, Tyler started off staying at hotels but one night he got too drunk to drive and she offered for him to stay. After that, it just seemed silly for him to do anything else. She couldn't remember why he moved from the far bedroom to the one across from her, but she imagined it had something to do with her nightmares. Even though he wasn't around much, Tyler tended to be overprotective when they were together.

"I'm sorry I fell asleep on you."

"No, really, I was just teasing. You've been running around and putting up with me since you got here. You slept, what? Four hours last night and who knows the night before. Plus, you look like shit."

He laughed and pushed her shoulder playfully. "Guess I better get my beauty sleep then."

"You sure you don't want to join me?" Kiara motioned to her bedroom.

"Bed. Now. Go."

"Wasn't that what I was offering to do?"

Tyler laughed. "Go to bed already."

"Fine," she pouted at him. "I'll go. I'll go right now. Alone. In the dark . . ."

She didn't have to turn to feel him rolling his eyes. She'd missed this. Missed him, the way he could always make her smile, make her feel alive. When she got to the bedroom door, she stopped. "You sure you won't change your mind?"

Tyler rolled his eyes. "How about I take a rain check on that one?"

There was a pause. He stood, hands shoved in his pocket, lazy grin on his face. Her invitation had been a joke. Just as it had been every other time she'd said it. So, why did it seem to strike a chord now?

*Because a part of me isn't joking.*

"You promise?" The words slipped from her lips, light and soft.

Tyler took his hands out of his pockets, stood straighter. His eyes narrowed. Fixated on hers. Then he laughed. "Your acting skills are really coming along. For a second, I thought you were serious."

She cast her eyes to the ground. "Yeah. I, um, I've been practicing that one for a while. Goodnight, Tyler."

Damn her stupid mouth and damn the stupid tremor in her voice. She gave him a weak smile and turned away so he wouldn't see the blush creep up her cheeks.

"Hey, Ki?"

"Yes?"

"I would give you the world if you asked me to."

"I know. That's why I love you." Kiara turned the doorknob and stepped into her room.

Her shadow disturbed the pouring moonlight seeping in through the panes of the window. It cast itself upon the floor.

*Floor?*

She no longer stood on wide planks of oak, but instead upon an edge of jagged stone. Water wept from an unseen ceiling above, dripped down the walls and wet the bottoms of her feet. There was a breeze that came up from below, from what seemed to be a chasm. It carried with it a noise, a rhythmic beating that sounded like a heartbeat. She turned to run back into the hallway, back to where there was gentle light from a distant living room, where there was no jungle rhythm of faraway drums, but the warm sound of Tyler's laughter. But the doorway was gone. There was no door. No way to escape this chasm, this void.

Only black granite, polished to some unnatural gleam by the slickness of water. Gone too was the window, only for some reason, flashes of light permeated the space. A jolt of white light forked from within the cavern. That's when she saw them. Humanoid in shape. Abominations. Thousands of them, all with black unseeing eyes, climbing, up, up from below, to where she was standing. Something touched her shoulder. She screamed so loud the sound bounced off the granite and made it seem as if there were a multitude of women screaming in whatever Hell this place was. Kiara turned, scream still stuck in her throat.

"It's just me."

Tyler stood in front of her. Kiara wanted to scream for him to run, to tell him the monsters were coming, but nothing came out. Nothing but a whimper. Those monsters were coming to take them away, to drag them down into that cavern, and she could do nothing to stop them. She could only watch. Kiara looked over her shoulder. She gasped, then blinked. Blinked again. There was no looming black pit. No monsters. Her room was exactly as it had been this morning; duvet tossed on the floor, books scattered in the corner.

Tears burned in her eyes, blurring her vision. At a loss for words, she slid to the floor, hung her head between her knees. Her heart still pounded, even though in the back of her mind, she understood whatever she saw wasn't real.

"Hey," he whispered, his fingertips brushing her hand, "are you okay?"

*Oh god, how can I explain?*

"I'm fine, I just . . . I don't know. I just thought I saw something." Taking a breath, Kiara lifted her head.

Tyler squatted, his face only inches away. She desperately searched for anything she could say to explain what happened, but came up blank. He was staring at her, concern hanging on every feature. "Do you want to sleep in my room tonight?"

"Um, no. I'll be fine."

Tyler held out his hand to help her up. She took it, surprised when he let go and stepped across the hallway to his room. He kept his back turned, reached into his closet and pulled out a shirt.

*Okay, leave already before he asks more questions.*

She was crossing the threshold to her room when he called out to her.

"Ki?"

She turned.

He was leaning against the closet, t-shirt in hand, intently staring at her face. "When you're ready to talk about what's going on, I don't care if it's three o'clock in the morning, come get me, okay?"

She bit her lip, nodding as she closed the door.

## 6

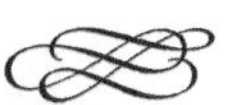

Just as the sun fell below the distant mountains, Tyler finished his three-mile run by racing up the balcony steps. He wiped the sweat from his brow and tugged the earbuds from his ears as he plopped down on the lounge chair. Today had been rough. Kiara overheard him canceling his return flight. Although she said nothing, he saw the hurt and embarrassment on her face. Neither spoke about the prior night's episode, but it hung in the air all day.

Running helped to clear his mind. He needed to step away to grasp the situation. Kiara was mentally ill. He knew that. She'd been that way since they'd met, but since it was brought on by extreme trauma, he'd always assumed she would heal. She still cringed anytime someone tried to touch her, but progress was steady if not swift. He truly believed someday, maybe another five years down the road, she wouldn't have haphephobia, or whatever the hell Henry called it. All it boiled down to was; she feared being touched, but who could blame her after what she'd been through?

So, there it was, she had a phobia that was manageable, maybe even curable, and they would both live happily ever after. At least, that's what he'd thought until last night. Concern was edging its way into fear. There were notable changes in her anxiety level since his last visit, but that hadn't worried him too much. Last night, she was terrified to the point of being damn near catatonic. Then, she'd refused to tell him what was going on. He wanted to let her keep her secrets, but he wasn't sure how long that would last. To say they hadn't weathered worse times in the past would be a lie. This, though, this was different. Something about the way she was acting made him nervous.

Tyler's cell rang, breaking his reverie. Night had fallen while he had been sitting there thinking. Henry's name showed up on the caller ID and his finger hovered over the answer button before letting it roll to voicemail. He would deal with Henry later. Gathering his phone and earbuds, he went inside. Tyler walked by the library and saw Kiara hunched over, engrossed in whatever she was writing.

He went to his room to grab some clothes for the shower, tossing his phone on top of the manuscript lying on the dresser. Tyler reached down and rubbed his fingers over the coarse cover. It surprised him she'd written about her ordeal and given it to him. Not that he thought she didn't want him to know everything, but because the gesture meant she was no longer shielding him from her past. For Kiara, not discussing the past was the way she preferred to move on from the trauma and abuse. Henry thought it was an unhealthy way to deal with things, and so did the rest of the doctors, but Tyler didn't. If she got through by not focusing on it, so be it. It wasn't like she closed the door on her past completely. She had let him know little bits and pieces here and there, he just never pressed her for more. Tyler figured that was one reason they worked so well together.

He opened the manuscript. So far, he'd read six chapters, and each page was gut-wrenching. By chapter two, he'd wanted to punch something, and by chapter four, he'd thrown it across the room, suppressing the urge to vomit. To read the words from her point of view and to see it through her eyes was too much for him. Still, he owed it to her to try.

Leaving the room, he made his way to the bathroom and started the shower. At some point, he would need to call Henry back. Before then, he was hoping to have a better handle on the situation. Kiara thought the world of Henry, and Tyler didn't believe she would have made as much progress if it had been a different psychiatrist helping her. That being said, there was still some bad blood between them over the guardianship thing. They had talked on four or five occasions before that point, and he even sat in on two of the appointments. He liked Henry. He thought the feeling was mutual, therefore it came as a surprise when Henry not only disapproved of the guardianship, but wrote a letter opposing it. Trying to be cordial about the situation, Tyler requested a meeting between the two of them to discuss the issue. To this day, he wished he'd never done that.

∿

Three Years Earlier

"Glad to see you, Tyler." Henry reached out and shook his hand. "How was your trip?"

"It was fine."

Henry's demeanor unsettled him. He'd expected him to be stern, perhaps even angry. Not acting like they were old friends going out to dinner. Tyler knew he was being defensive, and it showed in his clipped tone.

*Cool it. Don't blow this.*

His lawyer didn't think Henry's opposition would amount to anything because he had no basis for his claim that Tyler would be an inappropriate guardian for Kiara. Still, he didn't want to take any chances, so he put on his best smile, trying to pretend this was nothing more than a casual conversation.

"Have you been to see Kiara yet?"

"No, not yet. You were on the way, so it made more sense for me to stop by here first."

"Have a seat then."

Tyler did as he was asked, taking a seat in one of the recliners instead of the sofa. He felt sitting on the long leather couch would give Henry the upper hand. Henry walked over to the mini-fridge behind his desk and opened it.

"May I offer you a drink? A soda maybe?"

Tyler bristled. He didn't want to go through an hour of cordialities before they got to the point of the meeting, but instead of speaking his mind, he took the offered soda. He opened his drink as Henry settled in his own chair. It was time to get this over with.

"I wanted to talk to you today because of your opposition to my guardianship request." He set his soda down and leaned forward. "Honestly, I don't understand it Henry and neither does Kiara. This gives her a chance at being in control of her own life, a chance at happiness, and I know you want that for her as much as I do. So, why would you be against it?"

On the flight over he had worked on this speech, coming up with several ideas on how to broach the topic, finally settling on the straight forward approach. He was impressed it sounded as good out loud as it did on paper. Henry didn't look impressed, though. Henry looked as if he'd expected him to say that exact thing.

"Can I ask you something, Tyler?"

"Sure."

"How many friends do you have?"

"Plenty. What does that have to do with this situation?" Despite starting the conversation and trying to remain in control, he was feeling defensive again.

"I mean *real* friends. Friends you tell all your secrets to, that you share all your thoughts with? People who truly know you? Other friends you would do this for?"

"Where is this going, Henry?"

The doctor stood and walked over to his desk, picked up two files and set them in front of Tyler. He reached forward and opened the first one. Kiara's bruised, unconscious face stared back at him. He flinched but tried to gain his composure before Henry noticed. Flipping through the rest, he saw police records, detailed descriptions of what was done to her, pictures of the site.

He shut the folder. "What's the point of this?"

"How much do you know about what happened to her? Has she told you herself, or does most of what you know come from the news?"

"She's told me plenty. I don't press her for details because I understand what she wants."

"Do you? How many friendships have you kept in the past?" Henry nodded to the second folder.

Irritated, feeling like he was in a losing battle, he opened the second folder. This one shocked him, but differently. Pages upon pages of his own psychological and criminal history.

"How did you get these?"

"I have a friend."

Tyler shut the folder. "So that's what this is all about? My heroin addiction? A few arrests for bar fights? Those are all way behind me, Henry. My records are clean and so am I."

"That's not what this is about. This is about cycles."

Tyler raked his fingers through his hair. "Fine, why don't you explain it to me then."

He had to give Henry credit for looking grim instead of smug, even though he was owning the conversation.

"What I'm talking about is your addictive personality. We both know Kiara can't be touched—"

"I haven't, and I wouldn't." Tyler raised his voice, balled his hands into fists.

"I know." Henry put his hands up in the air. "I'm not saying this is about sex. I'll admit it worried me at first, but that was a long time ago. What I'm trying to say is, Kiara is different because you can't touch her."

"So, what? If it's not about my past heroin addiction or trying to sleep with her, I fail to see what this is all about and honestly, you're starting to piss me off."

"Please just listen. We both know despite my opposition, the guardianship will still go through."

This time Tyler couldn't keep the shocked expression off his face, but Henry continued, ignoring it.

"I wanted to meet with you because Kiara is a very sick girl and guardianship of someone like her isn't a game. It's a very serious situation, one which I don't think you are prepared for. If you're going to go through with this, for her sake, please think about the motivation behind it."

"I already know the motivation—her happiness. I'm

not an idiot, either. I've done my research on the subject and met with several advisors. I plan on helping her in every way I can."

"Just please keep an open mind. Kiara is in a very fragile place in her life and if something goes wrong and you walk away, she might not survive. Do you remember when we first met, and I asked you, 'Why her?'"

"Yeah."

"You answered, 'Because she makes me happy.'"

"So, what?"

"You told me about how she makes *you* feel, not how you feel about her. If you open that second folder again, you'll see you've said the same thing about heroin, sex, bar fights, and numerous other cycles of addiction you've had."

Tyler's stomach sank. The full impact of Henry's words hadn't hit yet, but he was getting the picture.

*He can't be right. He's just messing with my head.*

Tyler didn't open the folder to check, nor did he respond.

"Tyler, look, I like you, I really do. I can see all the effort you're putting into trying. I think this is a bad idea. Part of the reason she makes you feel so good is because you can take care of her without having to worry about any physical or romantic contact. But what happens when she gets better? What happens when you *can* touch her? What happens if she wants you to? I think you're addicted to the way she makes you feel and when that feeling goes away, so will you."

"That won't happen."

"I pray you're right."

~

Tyler stepped out of the shower, dressed, and wiped the steam off of the mirror. In sweats, with a two-day-old five o'clock shadow and un-styled hair, he felt like any other normal guy. The press played him up as *"naughty but sophisticated, successful with a bad boy edge."* Nobody bothered to get to know him.

*If they did, would they be that far off?*

Kiara insisted he wasn't the asshole he viewed himself to be. The truth of the matter was, he wanted to be the man she saw him as, and he tried his hardest, but he was constantly afraid of falling off that pedestal.

*"I think you're addicted to the way she makes you feel."*

He dried his hands and threw the towel in the corner. That thorn had been in his side for too long. It was time to let it go. She was his best friend, and he loved her, but there were boundaries. Was he attracted to her? Yes, of course he was, but he had never acted on it, never thought about her that way, or at least hadn't until she called him a few months ago.

Kiara had been drunk and crying. There was nothing worse than answering a phone call and listening to her suffering when he was on the other side of the continent. It was rare for her to break down, though. He hadn't known what to do except say he wished he could be there with her.

*"I wish you were here, too. I don't want to be alone anymore. I'm scared."*

*"There's nothing to be scared of. Just pretend I'm there, my arms around you, protecting you. Can you do that?"*

*"Yes, I just wish it wasn't pretend."*

*"It doesn't have to be pretend. I can take time off, come down."*

*"I was talking about you keeping your arms around me."*

*"You're getting better, Ki. It will happen one day,"* Tyler said,

his heart beating in his chest. She had never expressed a desire to be held by him before.

*"Your touch doesn't bother me. You could hold me now."*

As drunk as she was, her speech wasn't slurred. She seemed very sure of what she was saying.

*"Ki, if that's true, I'll be on the first flight out."*

*"It's true. I think it is, at least. Anyway, don't come down. I just need some sleep. I'll be better by the morning. Thank you for listening to me. I'm sorry I woke you."*

*"Wait, why haven't you mentioned that you thought I could touch you before this?"*

*"Because I didn't think you would care."*

*"Why would you think something like that, Ki?"*

*"Because you don't see me that way. I think it's important to you to think you can't touch me like that."*

*"Touch you like what?"*

She had evaded the answer, and he didn't press her. So here he was, one drunken conversation she probably didn't remember, torturing himself trying to decide how to deal with the situation. After five years of working diligently *not* to think about her romantically, he couldn't seem to stop the thoughts from popping up. Frustrated, he grabbed the dirty laundry off the floor and stepped out.

He glanced in several of the rooms but there was no sign of Kiara. She wasn't at her computer, but the cursor was flashing at the end of an uncompleted sentence. Assuming she was pacing around, he wasn't *too* worried. Kiara liked to use the library because it had no windows, no television, and no distractions, but when she was stuck on something she would roam, lost in thought. He would wait until she came back.

In the library, books were stacked along the shelves on the West wall. There were two mismatched vintage chairs with colorful pillows and a light gray loveseat in the center of the room. Her computer sat on a mahogany desk covered with sheets of printed paper, most of them scribbled with notes.

He went to a shelf and pulled out *The Awakening*, one of her novels, and settled himself on the couch. Half an hour passed, according to the clock on the wall, and she had not returned. He was thinking he needed to find a hobby to take up if she was going to spend so much time writing every evening, when a loud chime blared through the speakers, followed by a robotic voice announcing the back door was open. Kiara must have forgotten to turn the alarm off before going out.

At least he knew where she was.

He set the book down and left to join her on the balcony. Her house was large, built in the 90s and settled in a valley with a view of the mountainside. Before this, they had confined her to a small apartment even though the sales from her books were exponential. She was wealthy, but the state held her funds because they didn't think she was mentally competent. She found this place and fell in love. He didn't blame her. It was gorgeous, open, built with mahogany and stone, complete with high arches and floor-to-ceiling windows. Then, the state denied her request to purchase it.

Listening to her on the phone, broken-hearted, he became unraveled and took the matter into his own hands. He visited a lawyer, asking if it was possible to take guardianship given his past. When he was told yes, he asked Kiara what she thought. She hesitated at first, not wanting to burden him, but eventually she agreed. Unfortunately, it would be tied up in court for a while, so he purchased the house and when they granted him guardianship, she paid him in full.

He walked into the central dining and sitting room

combo, his eyes drawn to the balcony. His stomach did an odd flip. Kiara was climbing over the edge of the railing. When she dropped a leg over the side, his paralysis broke and he tore across the room, throwing the door open. Time thickened. His movements felt sluggish, and yet his eyes took in every detail, from the slightest twitch of her hand to the tiniest grains on the surface of the wood beneath his feet. He watched in slow motion as she pulled the other leg over. He screamed her name as she hung off the opposite side, looking down at the ground, but she didn't respond.

In retrospect, he would have no recollection of how he made it from one end of the balcony to the other. One minute he was standing there and the next, he was grabbing Kiara by the shoulders, pulling her back over the railing.

"What the hell are you thinking?"

She didn't answer.

"Are you okay? Are you hurt?" His eyes trailed up and down, scrutinizing her for injuries. When they reached her face, he met a blank stare. "Ki?"

She didn't respond, didn't move and didn't blink.

"Ki?" He shook her by the shoulders and she still didn't move. His chest tightened, and he shook her again, hard enough to send her head rolling. It worked because she blinked, the dull, blank look leaving her eyes.

"What the hell is going on?" Tyler asked.

"Nothing," she stammered, her eyes wide and fearful. "I'm just writ—"

Kiara stopped mid-sentence and looked around. It was obvious she was realizing for the first time she was outside. Giving her a moment to take in the situation and himself some time to calm down, he waited to speak.

"I came out, and you were over the balcony, about to

jump."

"No." She shook her head, denial written across her features. "I wouldn't have. I was in the library writing."

"No, I've been in the library for the last thirty minutes. I thought you were off pacing around, so I was reading, waiting for you to come back. I heard the back door alarm go off and came out here to find you. Where were you the last half hour?"

He knew he should calm down, knew he was scaring her. Tyler took a deep breath and tried to rein control of his emotions.

*If I had been a couple of seconds later . . .*

"I don't know, I'm sorry," she said, her eyes glistening with tears.

"It's okay. I believe you." Tyler ran a shaky hand through his hair. "Everything's okay."

He wasn't sure which one of them he was trying to reassure.

"You're shaking."

"You scared me, Ki. It's okay, though. Let's go inside and we will talk about this in there."

Taking her by the arm, they stepped in. Kiara curled up on the sofa, hugging her knees, making herself as small as possible. He wanted a drink, needed one to calm his nerves, but was too afraid to leave her alone. Cutting his eyes back and forth between her and the kitchen, he decided that a drink could wait and sat on the couch.

Tyler listened to her story—what little of it there was. All Kiara remembered was being in the library, writing. She didn't remember getting up or leaving the room, nor climbing over the balcony railing.

"I haven't been sleeping well, so maybe I fell asleep and sort of, I don't know, sleep walked or something."

"That's the only thing that makes sense."

It would explain how she seemed out of it at times, might even explain her panic attack from the other night. It was better than the other option. During a stint in the hospital, Kiara had severe hallucinations. They institutionalized her for a while and eventually she got past them. Still, Tyler wanted to hold on to the sleepwalking theory more than he did the hallucination theory. Soon—tomorrow, if not tonight—he would have to force her to tell him, as much as he hated that. So far, he'd been patient, but the incident today changed everything.

"You're mad at me, aren't you?" she asked, twirling the ends of her hair around her finger.

"Not at all. I'm worried about you and scared. I haven't felt this way since I saw you on the balcony the night we met. Why would you think I'm mad?"

Kiara fidgeted with the pillow on her lap. When she spoke, her voice was low enough it was barely more than a mumble. "Because I've been acting crazy and I won't tell you why. Because you're having to rearrange your life to take care of me."

"Ki, I'm not mad or upset. I don't blame you for today, either. I couldn't tell if you were going jump. For all we know, you might have been climbing over the balcony daily."

Her eyes widened when she realized what he was saying. Having been alone for the past several months, she might have done this dozens of times and no one would have been around to notice.

"The point is, we can figure this out together. You're not alone anymore. I need you to tell me what is going on so I can help."

"I know." Her eyes were swollen, half closed.

*She looks so tired.*

"Look, we should be safe tonight. Let's just take

precautions, keep the alarms set and leave your door open so I can check on you. Tomorrow we'll sit down and figure this out, okay?"

SHE SHUFFLED TO HER ROOM, barely awake enough to walk on her own. Too nervous to sleep, Tyler went around checking the alarms, windows, and doors. As he turned from checking the side door, he noticed a light coming from the downstairs storage room. He went to turn it off but stopped, curiosity clawing at him.

*"Where were you the last thirty minutes?"*

*"I'm sorry. I don't know."*

Kiara hated the storage room, claimed it reminded her too much of the room Andrew kept her in. Tyler couldn't think of a single time he'd seen her enter the storage room. He walked down the steps into a small, dim space. The walls were unfinished wood and the lack of ventilation left a dank smell in the air. A few items leaned against the corner; an old desk, a couple boxes, and a pile of paper. As far as he could tell nothing seemed out of place. Tyler made a quick circuit around and was about to leave when he glanced down at the papers on the desk. He recognized her handwriting, even though it was messy and scrawled. He picked them up, one at a time until he got to the bottom of the pile. Each sheet carried the same identical phrase, hastily written.

*I watched him die.*

SWEAT DRENCHED THE SHEETS. Kiara bolted upright, tugging at the damp night clothes clinging to her skin. As her eyes adjusted to the dark, she pulled her arms into her chest, surprised to find they were not bound. The thudding of her heart suppressed all other noises. No matter how many times she told herself it was just a nightmare, she could feel his hands on her, taste the stale odor of clove cigarettes, could hear his voice.

*"Everyone underestimates the health benefits of cloves, Sugar Bear. The Indians knew. Such a fascinating culture. They understood the power that comes from pain, how the human body can ascend to another level. Are you ready to ascend?"*

She peered at the door to make sure she was alone. Although she couldn't recall screaming, she might have woken Tyler. The doorway stood empty, though. She ran her hands down her thighs and brought them up in front of her face, expecting to see blood. There was only a thin coat of sweat.

Most days, she could suppress the memory, but when she slept, her dreams brought him back to life. Henry prescribed medication to help her have dreamless sleep, but she rarely took it since it made her groggy.

The clock blinked on the nightstand. 2:38. If she took half of a pill now, it might wear off before she woke for the day. Wiping the last of the tears away, she left the room.

Tyler's door was open a crack, but the light was off. She wondered what he was dreaming about, if he was dreaming at all? Hell, she wondered a lot of things about him lately. Overhearing his conversation the other day, knowing he was staying because he was worried about her, made her feel guilty and ashamed. It wasn't his job to take care of her. At the same time, it made her love him even more. Kiara frowned at the thought. They tossed the word *love* around all the time and she knew they both meant it, but for some reason it seemed different lately. She knew what he looked like in the morning, how he wore his pants low on his hips, how one side of his mouth curved up farther than the other when he smiled, but suddenly, there was an *awareness* of these things. Her eyes were often drawn to his bare chest, the curves of his body. She wasn't blind to how attractive he was, it just never mattered before.

*Now, though . . .*

She shook her head. With everything that was going on, it was no wonder she couldn't control her emotions.

Tiptoeing past the room, she made her way down the hall. The wood floors felt icy on her bare feet. Kiara assumed it was her imagination until she slipped, nearly losing her footing entirely. Reaching down, she ran her fingers across the polished grain, and they came up wet. Tucking the hair that had fallen into her face behind an ear, she glanced down the hallway into the living room. The entire floor was covered with what appeared to be a thin sheet of condensation. Shivering, she walked back to the thermostat. The temperature registered 48 degrees even though it was set to 70. She would have to call someone to fix it in the morning.

Freezing, with sweat-damp clothes and bare feet, she stepped into the living room. A gust of cold wind brushed past her and she turned. The patio door stood wide open.

At first, her sleep deprived brain didn't register what she was looking at. Then her eyes were drawn to something else out of place. The keypad for the alarm system was pulled off the wall and hung loosely by two cylindrical white wires. Kiara approached the door as if in a trance, ignoring the voice in the back of her head screaming at her to stop. Reaching up, she grasped the small rectangular box. The two small screw holes on the top of the alarm pad were empty.

A June bug flew in and landed on her exposed hand, startling her. Its thin legs scratched her skin as it shuddered, tucking its clear underwings beneath its shell-like casing. She reached up with her other hand to knock it away. The June bug fluttered off, but Kiara didn't notice. In her hand was a small Philips screwdriver.

Kiara backed up, away from the door, her eyes glued to the screwdriver. She had no recollection of picking it up.

Her empty hand grazed the top of the dining room table, desperate to feel something real. She dropped the screwdriver and it clattered to the floor. As it rolled underneath the table, she noticed another set of footprints on the damp wood.

"Hello, Sugar Bear."

She flipped around and stared into the eyes of a dead man.

A set of dull brown eyes stared back. He looked no different than she remembered; a round baby face, colorless features, blond hair. The man standing in front of her could blend into any crowd; only Kiara knew the evil that lurked within.

"Andrew," she whispered.

He smiled, his lips parting. Droplets of dark ooze trickled down his mouth onto his chin. She stepped back, face frozen in horror, hands trembling. Andrew's cheeks began to swell until they were distended, the skin translucent, mouth stretched into a thin line. Something moved beneath the bloated flesh, pulsing and quivering. Bruises mottled his face. His eyes turned dark as the blood vessels burst. He opened his mouth, releasing a stream of black liquid. It splattered across her nightgown, pools of it ran in rivulets beneath her bare feet. The thick drops which landed on her squirmed. She screamed, beating at them, hands moving in a frenzied storm. They fell to the floor, twitching, slithering into the larger puddles.

A scuttling noise, the chirping of a million crickets

echoed in her ears and she looked up at the ceiling as a black mass hovered above her, its thick, obsidian hide pulsating as it shifted, un-forming and reforming back into an insectile creature.

Kiara cut her eyes back to Andrew but he no longer stood in front of her; instead, she stared at another creature, one of those that had been crawling up the pit.

The room took on a surreal quality. She could no longer feel the cold air coming in from outside and her heart smacked harshly in her chest. She was rooted in place, paralyzed, unable to scream. All she could do was stare at the thing. There were no eyes, no mouth, no skin, just an empty black void. The humanoid figure was dense, endless, like looking into the depths of an abyss. As she tried to peel her eyes away from the creature, she detected a shuffling from inside it, as if something was struggling to get out. She closed her eyes, too afraid to see what might escape.

*It's not real, it's not real, you're dreaming.*

She opened her eyes. Instead of the creature, Andrew stood in front of her again, close enough to touch, a joker-like grin spread on his face.

"It's time to ascend."

Kiara turned to run. Her feet slipped on the wet floor and her head smacked against the table.

Andrew grinned down at her as everything faded into blackness.

7

hey left the doctor's office and headed to the pizza place around the corner.

"See, I told you so." Kiara raised her bandaged wrist in front of his face. "Just a sprained wrist and a tiny bump on my head. Admit it, you were overreacting."

"Really? You think making you go to the doctor when you knocked yourself out cold last night was an overreaction? I should have brought you to the emergency room."

In truth, he felt guilty he hadn't. Seeing her lying unconscious on the floor was one of the most terrifying moments of his life. It took a lot of begging on her part to wait until morning. Had it not been for the fact he knew how horrible going to the doctor was for her, he wouldn't have waited. He was angry at himself. It must have shown on his face because her smile dropped, and she looked down at the ground.

"I'm sorry."

"Don't be. I'm not mad at you. I'm angry with myself for not taking better care of you."

Her eyes met his. They were swollen and dark from screaming and crying. Every time the doctor touched her, Tyler had to restrain himself from punching the guy. She was wrong though, he hadn't overacted.

"You don't have to take care of me. I shouldn't have climbed on the table. I could have waited until morning to change the batteries on the alarm."

He sighed and pushed a strand of hair from her face. "From now on you're grounded from having your feet anywhere but on solid ground, okay?"

The cobblestone walkway was empty. Small leaves crunched beneath their shoes as the sky dissolved their shadows under a misty gray cloak. The lightweight jacket he wore was enough to keep him warm from the chilly, damp air. Kiara was bundled in a thick black hoodie, her hands shoved into the pockets. He wasn't sure whether it was because she was more susceptible to the cold, or if she was hiding underneath the material. It hurt him that she lied about what happened last night. Instead of accusing her, he'd acted like he believed the story. He only hoped that eventually she would tell him the truth.

*Eventually being today. I can't keep putting this off. That's twice now she's been in danger.*

They entered the restaurant and chose a booth at the back. Since it was still early, only a few patrons were there, most hidden behind a newspaper, cups of steamy coffee grasped in their hands. Tyler picked up the menu while Kiara pushed the glass shakers filled with parmesan and pepper flakes off to the side of the thick table and placed them on the windowsill.

"Good morning, Jennifer." Kiara greeted the young waitress who approached the table. "How's Toby?"

"He's doing great." The waitress replied but then

scrunched her face. "Well, actually, he's a little pissy right now because I've changed his cat food, but other than that, we're doing well."

Kiara and Henry ate lunch at this restaurant often. Jennifer was one of the few people in town Kiara would talk to. Although Tyler had not met her, he knew of her.

"Oh," Jennifer said, nodding to Kiara's bandaged wrist. "What happened?"

Kiara gave her an abashed look. "I slipped and fell. Nearly gave Tyler a heart attack."

Jennifer glanced at him for the first time. It wasn't a surprise to see her eyes widen. He was used to people recognizing him. She stuttered at first but then gathered herself. "Well, um, I'm glad you were there."

He thanked her for her concern. After she took their order and left, Tyler asked Kiara if she had called Henry to cancel their meeting today.

"Yeah." She took a drink of her soda. "He wasn't happy to hear I was hurt, but he understood why I was canceling."

Tyler stared out the window, watched leaves fall in the plaza. Last night, partially to convince him not to take her to the emergency room, she had promised to tell him the truth about what was going on. He was hoping she would volunteer the information before he had to drag it out of her. Hell, he was sure he didn't want to hear it as much as she didn't want to tell it. There were other things he wanted to ask her about, too, things he wasn't sure how to bring up. When he was changing shirts before they left, he'd noticed her looking at him differently. Twice this morning she had brushed her hands across his back as she walked by. A simple caress, one which wouldn't feel out of place if it had been anyone else. Those questions would have to wait until after they resolved this first set of issues. That was *if* he even needed to ask them.

*I'm a sick bastard for even thinking about her that way.*

He clenched his jaw. Turning back to face her, he noticed she was staring. She blushed and looked down at her soda.

"What are you thinking?" he asked, the words slipped out before he could stop them.

"Nothing," she answered, a little too fast.

He raised his eyebrows, and she laughed.

"I was thinking about how everything seems to be changing. Something feels different. I feel different." She gave him an apologetic look, which he didn't understand, before continuing. "Henry thinks I'm facing my fears."

"And you don't believe him?"

Kiara bit her bottom lip and cast her eyes down. "I don't know. I've been having nightmares again, and he thinks the reason is because I'm facing my fear of being touched. He even used the term 'embracing my sexual nature.'"

"Well, okay then." Tyler struggled to keep a straight face. "What do you think?"

"I don't know what I think about that. I try not to."

"So," he paused, rolling the paper from the straw around his finger, "you never get, you know, turned on or any feelings like that?"

"Wow, okay, I can't believe you just asked me that."

He lifted his hands in defeat and shrugged his shoulders. "Hey, if you don't want to talk about it, it's fine. I have to admit it though, I am curious."

He leaned forward, whispering, "How does anyone go five years with no release?"

She laughed at him. "It's not like that. I have feelings and thoughts. I just can't stand *anyone else* touching me."

"Oh my, I have follow-up questions after that statement."

She realized what he was insinuating and blushed. "Q&A is over."

"Wait, come on. I'll move on to a different question." She was shaking her head, but he asked anyway. "What do *feelings and thoughts* entail, exactly?"

"You seriously don't want to know this stuff, right?"

Tyler shook his head and grinned. "Yes, yes I do."

"I can't believe I'm having this conversation." Kiara looked around to make sure no one was listening. "I read books and watch movies. I can still react to stuff. I'm a twenty-six-year-old woman, not a brick wall."

"By react you mean get turned on, right?" She flushed but didn't answer. Tyler pressed further. "So, do you ever fantasize about people?"

*Too far.*

He berated himself for not having dropped the subject already, but his curiosity had gotten the better of him. She was stirring her drink with the straw and not looking at him.

"I'm sorry, Ki, too personal. I understand." Tyler leaned back against the booth.

"No, I don't mind. I'll tell you anything, you know that. I ask you all the time so it's only fair. It's just hard to explain. I would say that, no, I don't fantasize about people, at least not in the normal sense. If I try, I just think about him and I shut down. Sometimes I feel achy, you know, lonely. It's usually something I can brush off, but . . ."

She stopped stirring her drink and became quiet, lost in thought.

*But what?*

He opened his mouth to ask but Jennifer brought their

order to the table before he got the chance. They both thanked her and started eating. He watched her chew her food, somewhat amazed at her ability to have come as far as she had, and somewhat terrified it was all about to fall apart. She glanced up at him between bites.

"Your turn. What are you thinking?"

"I was just thinking about you. What you've been through, what we just talked about. It never occurred to me you could still think about things like that. It makes me happy to know that part of you isn't completely destroyed."

"I'm glad it makes you happy, I really am, but it embarrasses the crap out of me," she said, laughing. "Also, I wouldn't hold your breath about me not being completely destroyed. Can't be touched, remember?"

He reached across the table and placed his hands on hers. "Yes, you can."

She grinned. "Yeah, but at this rate, I will be eighty before I let anyone get to third base. We both know the chances of me initiating a sexual relationship with a man are slim to none."

"You seem to be doing fine with me."

Kiara slid her hands out from under his, eyes locked on his face. "Was that a Freudian slip, or did you mean to say that?"

"I don't know what—," he began to say, then stopped.

He did know, he just hadn't realized. He'd meant to say she seemed to be doing fine *to* him, not *with* him. Tyler shook his head. "I wasn't thinking."

"Hmmm," she said, her eyes darting to the table before coming back to meet his. "Is that why you freaked out when I hugged you the other night? Because you thought I was trying to do something *with* you?"

"No, of course not." Tyler raked his hands through his

hair. "You caught me off guard, that's all. I'm happy you're wanting to explore your feelings. You just might want to warn me next time."

"Explore my feelings," she mumbled, eyes turning dark. "So, I got close to you and you freaked out because you thought I was trying to explore my feelings. Was that it? Or was it because you thought I was trying to explore you in general?"

"Ki—"

"I'm not a child, Tyler," she spat out. "I've had things done to me you couldn't even imagine if you tried. So, no, I wasn't *exploring*. Your toy box is no different from any other mans."

"Jesus, Ki," he breathed out, hands trembling. "It was just a bad choice of words."

She faced away from him and stared out the window. Tyler cupped his hands over his face and took a deep breath. Her accusation was a little too close to the truth. Shocked, having never heard such vulgar words come out of her mouth, especially about him, he could only stare. His reverie broke when he saw a tear roll down her cheek.

*Crap.*

He walked over and sat down beside her, brushing the tear off. "I love you."

"I know." Her lips barely moved but when they did, he noticed them quiver. "I didn't mean to say that to you. I feel like I don't know who I am anymore."

Another tear rolled down her cheek and this time he grabbed a paper towel and handed it over. She dabbed at her eyes and turned to face him. "Please don't be mad."

Tyler placed his hand against the side of her face. "Ki, I'm not mad at you. It's not your fault. I'm more worried that you're mad at *me*."

"I'm not mad, just embarrassed."

"Do you want me to take off my clothes and streak through the restaurant so you won't be embarrassed anymore?"

"No. Then I would just be embarrassed of you."

He laughed, and she smiled along. After a few minutes, she became serious again.

"Tyler?"

"Yeah?"

"Today, I want to do fun and silly stuff," she said, but then yawned. "Okay, maybe a nap first, but then we can go out to a bar or something. And tomorrow, after the hangover wears off, I'll tell you what's been going on. I feel like things aren't going to be fun for a while after that, so do you think we can have a good day?"

"We can do better than that. We'll have an awesome day, might even go skinny dipping together in the hot tub." He smiled at her but inside her words filled him with fear. He worried about how she seemed to think whatever was going on would change things *that* much.

*Worse, I think she's right.*

"Would you like that?" she took on a serious tone, but her eyes lit up in humor.

"Oh, are we playing the game now?"

Her only response was to lift her eyebrows. He leaned forward so he could whisper. "What would you do if I said yes?"

"I might be willing to wrap a towel around my naked body and slip underneath the water with you." Her voice was seductive, but the blush on her cheeks let him know she wasn't going to win. "What would you do?"

He grinned. "I would ask you to show me what you meant when you said you couldn't stand having anyone else touch you."

"That is so not fair." She covered her face which had turned a shade of bright pink.

"Does that mean you fold?" He leaned back, laughing.

"Yes, and that I am never telling you anything about my private life again."

8

Closing her eyes, Kiara tried to ignore the rattling cage. She was numb from the cold coming in through the broken window. She supposed that was something to be grateful for. A cough racked her chest, searing pain radiated down both arms.

*Pneumonia? Good, maybe I will die.*

She'd accepted the fact she wasn't going to make it out of here alive. Having shed her tears and mentally wished the few friends she had goodbye, Kiara welcomed death. Nothing would make her happier than being able to stretch out her arms. Flexing her fingers, she pulled against the handcuffs to lessen the ache in her wrists.

Boards creaked; footsteps echoed down the hallway. She writhed against the bonds. As the door knob turned, she stilled, pretended to sleep. She did not hear him enter the room and after a few minutes, she could no longer bear the silence. Kiara opened her eyes.

She was standing inside a brightly lit store. Something about her new surroundings struck her as familiar. A woman walked up to her, older, petite, with strings of silver running through her raven hair. She reached her hand out and Kiara took it.

"Thank you so much for coming, Miss Moore. You made this such a success."

The woman waved her arms around, and Kiara realized why the place seemed familiar. She was in a book store she'd done a signing in many years before.

Kiara walked out the door, intent on heading home and taking a nice long bath when she heard a voice behind her say, "Miss Moore?"

She turned. "Yes?"

"Hi, I'm sorry to bother you. I was hoping to catch you before you left but I got held up." A young man smiled and held up one of her books. "I know it's a little late, but I was wondering if you would mind signing this?"

"Of course," she said. "You're that actor, right?"

"Yeah, I guess so." He ran his hand through his hair. "Tyler Reed. It's nice to meet you Miss Moore."

"It's Kiara. Nice to meet you, too." She shook his hand. Grabbing a pen out of her pocket, she opened the novel to the first page. Tucked inside was a receipt for the book purchased at 11:25. She glanced down at her watch. It was now 11:30.

"So, uh, you're a fan, huh?" she asked him.

"Yeah. I heard you were coming today so I grabbed my book and tried to make it in time, but I got stuck in traffic."

"I'm sorry to hear that." She tried to hide her smile while scribbling the message. She closed the book and handed it back to him. "Well, at least it all worked out in the end. It was great meeting you, Tyler."

She turned and walked away.

After a few moments, she heard him yell, "Hey, do you want to have a cup of coffee sometime?"

"Sure," she yelled back over her shoulder, "call me."

"I don't have your number."

"Yes, you do." Kiara stopped and pointed to the book he was holding. He opened it and laughed.

"The receipt, huh?"

She nodded. "Next time you want to ask someone out, you might want to have a better cover story."

Kiara walked away, smiling to herself as she headed toward the parking lot.

"I noticed you have a flat tire ma'am.? Do you need some help?"

Kiara turned to see who spoke, but no one was there.

*That voice. I recognized that voice.*

The memory came back. Him changing her tire, her offering to drive him to his car, pain followed by blackness.

Kiara screamed.

"Shh . . . it was just a nightmare, Ki."

She opened her eyes. Tyler stood over her. Tears fell down her cheeks and he wiped them off. "You're okay now. It wasn't real."

"It felt real," she whispered.

He caressed her face with the back of his hand. "That ship has sailed already. There is no need to worry about it anymore."

Shutting her eyes, she took a deep breath to calm herself. Something touched her stomach and she opened them. "What are you doing?"

He shook his head. "Nothing."

"I thought you just touched me?"

"No." He raised his hands up in front of her face to prove it. As she was looking at them, she felt the movement again.

"There it is again." She tried to lift herself up to look but couldn't.

"Oh, that?" Tyler nodded to her stomach. "Those are the rats. They were getting hungry."

Kiara screamed louder this time.

~

"Wake up."

Her eyes popped open. Tyler's face was hovering over hers. He was holding her arms down.

"Let me go! Let me go! I have to get them off." He released her. She kicked off the covers and jumped out of bed. "Oh god, Tyler, help me. Help me get the rats off."

"Ki, it was just a dream." He furrowed his brow and reached out to her. She backed away.

"No, it wasn't," she said, her voice shaking. "The rats are real."

"There are no rats here. I promise you, you're safe."

The cold floor underneath her bare feet combined with the look of sympathy on his face made her realize the truth. She felt her heart rate slow.

*It was a dream. Just a dream.*

When they came home from the restaurant, she'd shut her eyes for a few minutes. She must have fallen asleep. Kiara sat on the bed and leaned back against the head-board. "It seemed so real."

"But it wasn't. I promise."

She tugged at her bottom lip, sucking it in between her teeth.

"What are you thinking?" he asked, lightly touching her face.

She let out a sigh. "I didn't put it in the book, not that.

Henry doesn't even know. I think the doctors just assumed the bites were from something else."

"What are you talking about?" he asked, his tone hesitant.

"The rats. He kept them as pets."

She closed her eyes, remembering. "He liked to feed them my blood. He kept their cage in the room and whenever he hurt me, they could smell it. They would get excited and run around shaking the cage. Some nights they were so loud I couldn't sleep. It took months for me to stop hearing the sound of their claws scraping against the cage at night."

She opened her eyes again. Tyler was sitting Indian style on the bed with his hand covering his mouth.

*I might as well tell it all.*

"He hated women. He wanted to control them. When I got my cycle, he wouldn't touch me. Three days, three wonderful days he left me alone. He could tell I was happy and that pissed him off, so he let the rats loose on me." She stared at her hands. "I was too ashamed to ever tell anyone."

There was a moment of silence and then the bed shifted. Tyler crawled up beside her. "You have nothing to be ashamed of. I wish I could do something to take away your pain. I don't know what to say. I can't find the right words."

"I don't want to be sick anymore. I'm tired of these things in my head," she whispered.

"I know. We'll get there, okay?" Tyler smoothed the blanket out with his hands. Although he sounded calm, his hands were shaking.

She felt awful having upset him. "Come on."

"Where?"

"Let's get ready to go out. Nothing serious today, remember?"

9

"Hey Ki, have you seen my black button down?" Tyler walked into her room without knocking. As soon as he asked, he spotted the shirt hanging on a drying rack in the corner. Walking over, he grabbed it off the hanger. "You know, you don't have to do my laundry for me."

"I don't mind." She was kneeling in the corner of the room, searching for something. He could only see the top of her head. Her voice sounded cheery enough, though. "Oh, let's have shots before we leave, like a pre-party or something."

He laughed, happy she was excited about going out. After their conversation earlier, he found it hard to keep a smile on his face. There was this dark burning in the pit of his stomach, a sourness which refused to let go. His immediate reaction was to dull the pain with drugs, but years of therapy taught him it would only be a temporary relief.

The image of which she spoke slipped into his mind again, causing him to clench his fists. Every time he found out something new about her ordeal, he couldn't help but

80

wonder how she could be such a beautiful, loving creature. Then again, he always knew she was a much stronger person than himself. Initially, he'd planned on talking her out of this bar idea, thinking she couldn't handle it. After what she told him though, he didn't have the heart to tell her no, and so he tried to ignore his concern. At least, he did until he turned around and looked at her.

"What the hell are you wearing?" The words blurted out of his mouth before he could stop them.

Ignoring his outburst, she jumped off the bed and twirled around. "So, what do you think?"

She wasn't wearing anything too outlandish. The flowy black top came up to the neckline, but it was backless, and her jeans hugged her curves. The bottom of the shirt came up maybe a centimeter above the pants line, hinting at the smallest bit of skin. Her makeup was flawless, large green eyes behind a smoky black shadow played up her full pink lips and delicate cheekbones. He stared, keeping his thoughts hidden, considering his words.

"I mean, I know it's silly to dress up, but I thought it would be fun. You don't have to say anything," she said, wringing her hands together.

"You look beautiful." The words came out flat, uncaring. Apparently, he'd been trying too hard to hide his feelings.

"Oh." She looked away. "I can change. I didn't realize it would upset you."

*I'm being an ass.*

"Please don't. You can wear what you want."

She still looked upset, and he wanted to make her feel better, but he couldn't seem to think straight.

"It's okay. I think I want to change anyway."

She walked over to the closet and pulled out some clothes. He came up behind her, feeling like a jerk for ruining her good time. It wasn't her fault he was having inappropriate thoughts.

"I'm sorry if I made you feel uncomfortable. Please don't change."

"I just don't want to wear it anymore, okay?"

"I didn't mean to hurt your feelings."

She didn't comment, just continued digging through the closet.

"Ki, listen to me, you're absolutely stunning. I'm just worried others won't be able to keep their hands off you and sometimes I worry that if I say the wrong thing, I'll make you uncomfortable and I'll lose you. I'm sorry. I'm being extra cautious in what I say to you and I shouldn't be. Honestly, you're beautiful to the point it hurts to look at you."

Kiara stopped digging through the closet and turned to him, raking her hands through her hair. "I'm sorry, I guess I forgot what it was like to be girly and emotional."

"Forgiven."

"What's with the bad lines anyway? So beautiful it hurts? It's like some sort of conundrum—you're beautiful but I can't stand looking at you? Makes no sense."

"I guess it depends on how you look at it. I would think it's the perfect line for you. People like to covet beautiful things, to hold them." Tyler walked across the room to the mirror and pulled off his t-shirt. "There is nothing worse than seeing something beautiful you can't have. It's painful."

"Do they teach you this romantic bull in acting school? Is there a course on how to pull a compliment out of your ass?"

Tyler chuckled as he buttoned his top, not giving her the satisfaction of an answer. As he turned back to the mirror to roll up his sleeves, he glimpsed her reflection in the background. "Something wrong?"

Kiara was chewing her bottom lip. "No."

"Are you sure?"

"You're too good for me, that's all. I keep wondering when you'll realize that and go away."

"I think the same thing about you."

They both stood in awkward silence for a moment. He wasn't sure what he was thinking, but instead of fighting off the instinct, he walked over and kissed her on the cheek. When he pulled away, he noticed she looked more surprised than scared.

"Now, come on." He nodded to the door. "We have a date to go on."

## 10

They drove into the parking lot of a well-lit bar with a red neon sign boasting the name *Roosters Crow.* Gravel crunched under the wheels of the car as Tyler pulled into a space. Kiara unbuckled her seat belt and reached for the handle but stopped when she noticed Tyler hadn't moved. He was staring out the window.

"Are we going somewhere else?"

"No, this is fine." He tapped his fingers on the steering wheel. "It seems busy for a Tuesday night. Are you sure you want to do this?"

"I'm not the one who looks like they are going to freak out. That reminds me, though." She dug in her purse, pulled out two mini bottles of tequila, and handed him one.

His mouth dropped open. "You brought liquor to a bar? We already had shots before we left."

She shrugged. "I thought I might be nervous, so I wanted a few drinks to loosen me up before we got here."

"Let me get this straight—you needed to get drunk to go to a bar to get drunk?"

"It sounds like solid logic to me." Kiara twisted the lid off and downed hers. When she was done, she waved the empty bottle in his face. "We should throw the empty ones away, though. We don't want to be irresponsible and leave containers in the car."

Tyler laughed. "I don't know if I love you more because your logic is the most construed I've ever heard, or because it genuinely makes sense to you." It took him two tries, but he downed the bottle and handed it to her for disposal.

"Can it be both?"

"By your standards, yes. Now come on."

## 11

They walked across the parking lot. An unseasonably cool day had turned into a moderately warm night. Pebbles scratched against the bottoms of Tyler's shoes, the smallest ones lodging themselves in the grooves. Kiara was quiet. He sensed her anxiety as they approached the wraparound porch. The door opened and loud country music poured out, becoming muffled as it shut again. A young couple stumbled to their car, giggling. Kiara watched them go, her brows lowered into a V-shape. After a moment, she headed toward the door.

Tyler stopped her. "Hey, I told you I planned on keeping you close, and I need you to tell me right now if that will bother you. Since you wore something pretty much backless and since I can already see you tensing up, are you going to be comfortable with that?"

Her eyes were wide, but she nodded.

"Completely sure?"

"Completely. Now stop being a party pooper."

He frowned, but she stood her ground and opened the door. Entering the bar, Tyler blinked, trying to adjust to the dim lighting. Unpainted wood booths and tables were lined up against the closest wall, leading into a dance floor and stage. The overall ambiance was western. As far as he could tell, there were about twenty-five other people there and most of the tables were empty.

"Do we sit at the bar?" Kiara asked, sounding unsure.

"No," he slid his hand behind her back to steer her. Her skin felt flushed with heat, and she shuddered under his touch. "We go sit in that booth in the far corner over there."

She gave him a pouty look but followed along. A couple people, both girls and guys, turned and ogled them as they passed by. He pulled her in closer. As they sat down, he studied her face to see how she was doing. Her eyes looked a little glazed over and her breathing was quickened but other than that she seemed okay.

"How are you holding up?"

"I'm fine."

"We can always leave."

"No, really, so far no one's been close enough to bother me at all. Plus, I know they are here. It's the unexpected that makes it worse." She pulled a menu out of the condiment holder and flipped through it. "Oh my gosh, can we have fried pickles?"

He laughed at her enthusiasm. "Of course."

A young, dark-haired waitress approached the table. He ordered an appetizer of pickles and beers for both.

"You didn't order shots," Kiara accused.

"Ki, if you want shots, you can have shots. I, on the other hand, have to drive home and don't plan on getting us killed on the way."

"I can sober up and drive. I want you to have fun, too."

"First of all, hell no. We have a better chance of survival if I drive drunk than you drive sober."

"That was one time, Tyler—"

"—and," he cut back in, "I go to bars all the time and this is your first time in, what? Five years at least?"

"Actually, this is my first time ever."

He sat back. "Are you serious? You've never been to a bar?"

She laughed and shook her head. "Nope, never."

"How does that happen?"

"Well, I had just turned twenty-one when Andrew . . ." She paused and drifted off for a second.

*Dammit. I could've done the math and figured that out without asking.*

". . . anyway, I just never got around to it."

The waitress came back with their order and they ate in silence. He watched her enjoy fried pickles, which was something he would never get excited about, but she made it seem like they were a special treat.

"You're staring."

He realized she was right. "Sorry, ma'am."

She tilted her head to the side. "What were you thinking about?"

"You. How happy you seem and how you were when I met you." He picked up a pickle and ate it, the oil making him gag. Lifting his beer, he washed the taste out of his mouth. "Do you know what your first words to me were?"

She scrunched her face, thinking. "Do you mean on the balcony or after that?"

"No," he shook his head. He was sure she didn't remember seeing him before that moment, but this was the first time he confirmed it. "I saw you many times before that day."

Her mouth popped open.

"I was there when they brought you in. At that point, I had been in the hospital for a few weeks. A nurse was wheeling me down to do testing. I heard you coming from the other side, you were screaming something fierce. Right when they were rolling you by me, you pushed one nurse down and my nurse ran over to help hold you. You were thrashing. Someone ran up and gave you a shot. After a moment, you relaxed and turned your head, looked right at me. I'm not going to lie, Ki, you sent shivers down my spine. The way you were staring, I can't explain it, but it's like you knew everything about me."

Tyler took a deep breath. "Anyway, I couldn't tear my eyes away and then you spoke. You said to me, *'You're not real.'* And all I could think was, *'how does she know?'*"

"Oh no, Tyler, I'm so sorry. I don't remember that."

"No, no, don't be upset. There is a point to this story, but I don't want to tell you if it's going to upset you. I've thought about mentioning it a lot over the past few years and it just never seemed like the right time. I don't want to ruin your night, though."

She shook her head. "You're not, I'm having a great time. Please finish."

He waved the waitress over and ordered two shots for her and a coke for himself. "So, continuing on. A few days pass. I was stuck between obsessing over what you said and trying to convince myself you didn't know what you were saying. As you know now, I always felt like a fake, like I didn't deserve fame. You couldn't have known that then, though. It wasn't long before the news about what happened to you came trickling in. They already had me in the back wing, and they put you across from me since our stories were so sensational." He paused and took a drink of coke. "I listened to you scream for weeks, every time they touched you. I felt sorry for you. At some point, I even thought you might be an angel, but that probably had something to do with the withdrawals."

Kiara's eyes were wide open. "How come I never knew this? How have we not talked about it before?"

"Taboo, I guess? I don't think either one of us wants to relive that stint in the hospital." He set his drink back down. "So, like I said, I became obsessed with you, obsessed with the idea you knew the truth about me. I snuck into your room, looked through your things, tried to figure out who you really were. You weren't aware of much those first few weeks. You saw me sneak in once or twice, but you never spoke. I think I was waiting for you to wake, to talk to me, to find out what you knew."

He looked up, lips set in a grim line. "That's how I knew you were on the balcony. I was watching you. I saw you leave your room. Since you'd never gotten out of bed before, I knew something was wrong, so I followed you. After that day on the balcony, I realized you weren't an angel, that you didn't know me. I also realized you were the most remarkable and beautiful person I had ever met, and I needed to have your approval, to have you like the real me."

Kiara cut in, a grin plastered on her face. "I hated you so much after that night on the balcony. I couldn't figure out why you wouldn't leave me alone."

"If you hadn't refused to speak for two weeks after trying to commit suicide then we probably wouldn't be friends because I'm sure you would have banned me from your room. So, as you said, I kept bothering you. You wouldn't talk so I did all the talking and I told you things I never told anyone else. Then one day, I was telling you this story about a bar fight I had gotten into and I heard your voice. I remember being so shocked I nearly went catatonic myself and didn't answer. Then you repeated yourself."

"Why would you do something so stupid?" Kiara mumbled.

He laughed. "You do remember."

"Yeah, I watched you play chess by yourself, non-stop talking to me and I was so angry at you. Nobody ever told you no, was ever honest with you, and it was obvious you went out of your way to get in trouble."

"Yeah, I know, you spent the next hour lecturing me about it." He chuckled. "Do you remember the look on the nurse's face when she came in and her catatonic patient was giving her recovering heroin addict the fifth degree?"

She started laughing and he joined her, ignoring the people staring at them.

When they calmed down, he said, "Anyway, that was one of the best moments of my life, getting lectured about a bar fight from you and here we are, five years later."

"Ha, I guess that is ironic." She looked around. "Are you going to start a fight?"

"You never know, the night's still young. Probably not, though, I don't think I could bear another one of your lectures."

She chuckled. They sat in silence for a few minutes. He noticed her staring at a couple on the dance floor.

"Did you ever dance?" he asked.

"Yeah, I took classes in high school. Once upon a time I even daydreamed about being a famous dancer but then I found more joy in writing. What about you?"

"Yeah, but not at first. I was a horrible dancer but there's a dance scene in *East of Tarragon* and the director insisted I learn." Tyler hated all the experiences her captivity had taken from her.

"Come on, let's go dance." He stood and held his hand out.

She shook her head. "I can't."

"Yes, you can. There's only one couple out there and I promise, I will barely touch you.'"

"You don't bother me Tyler, it's—"

"Come on. It won't hurt to try."

She stared at him, bit her lip. Her eyes darted to the dance floor. After a moment, she stood. "Okay."

They walked to the edge of the floor, away from the crowd. He turned to face her, took one hand in his, and placed the other behind her back. He moved and she moved with him.

"Are you okay?" he whispered.

"Yes," she said, smiling.

For the whole song, the smile never left her face. He never imagined being able to do this with her. To dance. To hold her like this. It was simply amazing. The music changed; something slow and sensual. Kiara moved forward, closed the distance between them. Tyler faltered and missed a step.

"Are you okay?" she teased.

He gave her a dirty look. "Must I remind you to warn me before you touch me?"

"Are we switching roles now?" she asked, grinning. "Because I don't think I could be as gentlemanly as you."

"Hmmmm . . ." He slid his arm further behind her. "So, tell me, what would you do that was less gentlemanly if our roles were switched?"

"Tyler, I am not playing the game with you right now."

"Fine, I'll drop it. But be warned, you will have to answer to that statement one day," he teased, pulling her closer without thinking.

*I'm getting too comfortable with this. Five years of not touching her and it takes me less than a week to completely forget my boundaries.*

She stopped dancing and looked up; her eyes wide. Her breathing increased, her pupils became swollen, full. It wasn't fear reflected in her eyes, it was a look Tyler had seen on many other women's faces, but not Kiara's.

Attraction.

He heard Henry's voice in his head.

*"Right now, part of the reason she makes you feel so good is that you can take care of her without having to worry about any physical or romantic contact because you can't touch her."*

He stared at her, stuck in the moment, unable to look away, wanting to kiss her but knowing better. Her lips, wet and slightly parted, invited him in. Her hot skin sent jolts of electricity down his body. All his carefully controlled willpower was destroyed with one look.

There was a noise off to the left and she looked over that way, giving him a moment to rein in his emotions. Taking a deep breath, he shut his eyes, but opened them when he felt her face press against his chest.

"People are taking pictures, Tyler."

He looked over and saw a group of five people trying to inconspicuously take pictures of them on their phones. "Shit."

He turned and pulled her off the floor, waived the waitress down on the way, and handed her some money. Kiara bent to grab her jacket out of the booth, but before she could, two guys approached them.

"Excuse me?" A tall, dark-haired man asked while his drunk friend stared at Kiara, not hiding interest in what he saw. "Um . . . I'm sorry to bother you but you're Tyler Reed, right?"

Tyler nodded, but gave his friend a dirty look.

"Hey, my girlfriend's a huge fan and it would mean the world to her if I could get your autograph."

Tyler felt bad for the guy. He was obviously embarrassed to ask. At the moment, though, he was more worried about Kiara. Their eyes met, and she nodded slightly.

"Sure."

The guy handed him a napkin and a pen. While Tyler was signing it, he heard the friend ask, "Hey, you're that author, aren't you? The one that guy messed up? I kept thinking you looked familiar."

Tyler looked up as the dark-headed guy he was signing the autograph for smacked his friend on the arm. "Dude, not cool."

Kiara looked mortified.

"Oh, shit. I'm sorry. That was probably rude of me to bring up. You can punch me too if you want." The guy closed in.

"Get away from her." Tyler handed the napkin to his friend and stepped in between him and Kiara.

"Dude, it's cool. I'm not hitting on your woman. I'm just trying to apologize."

His words came out slurred, and he stumbled, grabbing Kiara's shoulder for support. She screamed. Before Tyler could stop her, she had slid across the booth and curled up in the corner.

"Dude, what the hell?"

"Go, just go." Tyler pushed the guy out of the way. "Ki, it's me. Come on, we've got to get out of here."

Out of the corner of his eye he saw people gathering around them, taking pictures and videos.

*Shit.*

"Ki." He reached out and touched her arm. She jerked away. "Listen to my voice. I'm going to put my arms around you and pick you up. We need to get out of here."

The guy he signed the autograph for spoke up. "Man, I'm sorry. Do you need help?"

"Don't. Please." Tyler held his hand up to ward him

off. "She doesn't like being touched, okay?"

"Man, that's messed up," the guys friend mumbled.

"Okay Ki, I'm going to pick you up now."

Tyler didn't want to rush, but he feared it would only get worse the longer they stayed. She didn't cry out, and he knew it was taking a lot of effort for her to stay quiet. As they passed by, people moved out of the way but weren't the least bit ashamed to take pictures. *Assholes.* He tossed her in the car, buckled her in, and left the parking lot in a hurry. On the way home, he silently fumed over how stupid he'd been to bring her there. She stayed curled up against the door, her body tense. Fifteen minutes into the drive, she finally spoke.

"I'm sorry."

"No. Don't you dare. I was stupid to think people wouldn't recognize us." He grabbed her hand. "It's not your fault."

"It's embarrassing, I'm ashamed of myself. Hell, I'm embarrassed for you. It's going to be awful."

"I'm not embarrassed or ashamed of you at all, nor will I ever be. I don't care what stories the press puts together or says, I only care that they leave you alone, so please, just let it go."

Kiara didn't respond for a few minutes. He was about to start in on another round of reassurances when she replied, "I did promise no seriousness tonight, only fun."

"Yes, you did."

"And you didn't start a bar fight."

"I was tempted to."

"That must have been one hell of a lecture I gave you."

"You're pretty persuasive. So, what do you want to do to keep tonight fun?"

"Get drunk and skinny dip in the hot tub?"

He laughed. "You're on."

12

"Ugh." Kiara turned away from the light, her stomach rolling and head pounding.

*I'm dying.*

She reached into her sleep fogged mind and tried to figure out why she felt so bad.

*Oh, yeah, we got trashed.*

The room spun when she opened her eyes, making the sour taste of liquor rise into her throat. She covered her face with the blanket and reached toward the nightstand, prodding around until she felt her cell phone. Grabbing it, she pulled it under the covers and squinted.

"What time is it?"

She pulled the blanket off her eyes. Tyler was lying beside her.

"It's seven in the morning."

"I'm dying, Ki." He covered his face with his arm.

"Me too." She closed her eyes and tried to sleep but her throat was parched. "Tyler?"

"Yeah?" His voice was hoarse.

"Do you have a drink?"

He turned his head, looking at the nightstand. "No, but I'd love one."

She sighed. "Okay. I'll go grab us some water. Ibuprofen, too."

"Yes, please."

WHEN SHE WOKE AGAIN, it was dusk. Having decided it wouldn't hurt for them to sleep the hangover off, they both took Xanax along with the headache medicine. Probably not the smartest idea, but effective. Tyler was still dozing beside her. It occurred to her they'd slept in the same bed all day, both having passed out while talking. Kiara knew that meant *something* but was too dopey to focus on it.

While debating whether to take a shower, she had a sudden sense of being watched. The room was cold, the sheet felt icy against her skin. There seemed to be no noise, not even the usual sounds of the air conditioner or creaking of the house. Along with the complete silence was an absence of color, the graininess of an old picture. Then, a faint noise from the far corner of the room. She turned.

A dark shadow crouched. Even though it had no distinguishable eyes, she felt its horrifying gaze and trembled in fear. The creature didn't move, but it seemed to pulsate and quiver, cloaking the air in a death cloud. A guttural sound came from the abomination. Unable to stop the thought, she envisioned its mouth torn open in an endless scream, blackness pouring out. Too terrified to move, she stared at it. The noise began to resemble words. She could not make them out, but it repeated the cadence over and over. Something crept in her mind, a memory so vivid she felt like it was forced. There she was, lying in a hospital room, IV's and wires hooked up to her arm. She turned her head. Tyler was in the corner of the room, sitting in a wheel chair, his eyes hollow, body bone thin.

"You're not real," she whispered.

"I know," he replied.

The vision faded. Kiara gasped as though she had been drowning. The shadow was still there, crouched in the corner, but now she could make out what it was saying. She heard her voice coming out of the abomination. *I watched him die. I watched him die.*

"No." She whispered, covering her ears to block out the creature, but she could still hear it.

*This isn't real. This isn't real.*

She rocked back and forth, the words emanating from the beast pounding in her head as she tried to drown them out.

*Please make it go away.*

Something grabbed her wrist, and she screamed.

13

yler opened his eyes. There was no sunlight streaming through the windows and the room was lit only by a lamp. They must have slept the whole day. Kiara was sitting on the edge of the bed, facing away, a sheet wrapped around her.

"Good morning, Sunshine." She didn't respond.

"Are you asleep sitting up?"

Still no answer.

"Hey, Ki?" He propped up on his elbow and looked closely at her. A feeling of dread formed in the pit of his stomach. Something seemed wrong with the way she was sitting. She was *rocking*, mumbling incoherent words.

Sliding off the bed, shivering when his bare feet touched the cold floor, he approached slowly. "Shit."

She had her knees tucked into her chest, hands over her ears. He still couldn't make out what she was saying, but he could make out panic in her tone.

"Hey, it's okay." He reached out and grabbed her hands. She screamed and he let go, backing up a few steps.

"It's me. It's Tyler." He knelt, their faces inches apart.

Her eyes were wide, glazed over. "No. You're not real. It's a trick."

He curled his hand around hers, squeezing. "No trick. It's me."

She stared at him, lips trembling. He pulled her hand away and placed it on his face. "See, all real."

"It's here," she whispered, eyes darting to the corner.

Chills ran down his body, the hair on his arms stood up. He turned. The corner of the room was empty. "There's nothing there. What do you see?"

She looked over his shoulder and then back at him, shaking her head. He gave her hand a squeeze and walked around the room, hoping it would convince her they were alone. The fear on her face was so genuine a part of him expected to see something. He made a pass around the room, checking all the corners and closet before coming back to her. "There is nothing here, okay? You're safe."

She dropped her bare feet on the floor, shoulders slumped. For the first time, he realized she wasn't okay, might never be okay again. He couldn't live in denial any longer. She laid a hand against his chest. His shirt bunched under her palm.

"Kiara?" he whispered.

"Are you really here?"

"Yes."

Her hand trembled and her green eyes pooled with tears. "I need you."

He wrapped his arms around her, pulled her into his chest. Warmth radiated off her small body. With her head nestled under his chin, he could feel her hot breath on his neck. He ran his fingers through her hair and closed his eyes. It was nice holding her, but he knew she only did it because she feared something else. Warm lips caressed the underside of his jaw as she nuzzled closer.

The thin fabric of her top shifted beneath his hands.

"I need you," she whispered again, but this time the words had a different meaning.

He stilled.

As if sensing his hesitation, she ran her tongue over the stubble of his jaw, trailing it down to the center of his throat. Heat, thick and wet, seemed to emanate from her, making it difficult to breathe, difficult to think. Slowly, almost sleepily, he slid his hands up to the back of her neck and tangled his fingers in her hair.

Kiara tilted her head back, her mouth full, needy, but the look in her eyes made his blood run cold. They were distant, angry. He tried to pull away, but she held on tight.

Grabbing her wrists, Tyler removed her hands from around him. She reached out for him again. Raking his hands through his hair, he backed away. "Kiara, I'm sorry. This isn't right."

Her eyes burned with hatred. "Why not? You'll fuck anyone who wants you, so why not me?"

The words stung, left him speechless. She jumped off the bed, approaching him like a predator ready to pounce. When their bodies were centimeters apart, she stopped. He remained still, heart pounding. She ran the tips of her fingers over his chest.

Tyler backed away again. "Stop. This isn't you."

She grabbed his wrist, nails digging in and drawing blood. A trail of red ran down his arm and she grinned. It dawned on him. Kiara *wanted* to hurt him, wanted to frighten him. She was enjoying this. Something deep and dark inside her had taken over. Something he didn't understand and couldn't fight.

She let go, and he dropped his arms to the side. Almost instantly, she put her hands back on his chest. He closed his eyes and took a deep breath as her fingers roamed his chest, sliding down to tug on the buttons of his pants.

"I love you, Ki."

She stopped moving. The room became eerily silent. After a few seconds, he felt her pull away.

"Get out." Her tone was quiet, angry.

He opened his eyes and reached for her, but she backed away.

"Get out, get out, get out!" She screamed, her face screwed in a grimace, finger pointing at the door.

"Ki—"

"Out!"

He pleaded with his eyes, walked backward to the door. When he got past the threshold, she slammed the door in his face. He heard a loud crash, followed by huge, wretched sobs. With his back pressed against the wall, he slid to the floor, and listened to her suffering.

14

Kiara swept her hand across the nightstand. The lamp fell to the floor and pieces of glass scattered across the room. She covered her mouth and sobbed into her palm. That wasn't her.

She couldn't have done that to Tyler. She'd never hurt him. A cramp doubled her over, and she crawled to the trash can. Vomited.

Several minutes passed, maybe hours. She heard the door open, felt the cold rag placed on the back of her neck. That simple act of kindness was enough to send her into hysterics.

"I'm so sorry," she gasped between sobs.

"Shh . . . it's okay," Tyler murmured. "I'm always here for you."

When the tears subsided, when she could catch her breath, she pushed herself into a corner. If someone had told her she would one day sexually assault her best friend, she would have called them a liar.

*I told him I wanted him to fuck me.*

"What can I do?" he asked.

She moaned and placed her head in her hands. "I want to die."

"Please don't say that."

She tried to find the words to explain how awful she felt, how sorry she was for what she did. At the same time, even though she knew better, she felt rejected. A shiver ran through her. Her room, normally a haven, felt like a prison.

"I feel like he's inside of me, making me think like him, want like him." She looked up. "I feel so dirty."

Tyler gave a sarcastic laugh and covered his face. "Is it sad that I'm a little offended by that last statement? I'm so messed up."

"True," she agreed, "but I'm pretty sure I'm way ahead of you. You've gotten over your drug problem. I seem to get crazier by the day."

Tyler sagged against the wall. "Not really. Once you're an addict, you're always an addict. The want never goes away. I still wake up in the morning, thinking I'm high, feeling horrible about myself. Then I realize I'm sober. It's hard to shake that feeling, though." He stood and paced the floor. "I've used three times since I've been sober. I didn't tell you because I was ashamed of myself. I'm an addict, even if I don't use. I'm addicted to sex, addicted to anything that makes me feel good. I throw away women, treat them like crap. Not a single one of them has meant any more than a one-night stand. I can't seem to make myself care about anyone else, other than you."

She was speechless. There had been a time or two when she suspected he was high when he called her, and numerous times when she heard a woman's voice in the background at three a.m. Kiara never understood what would possess him to call when he had a date in his bed, but she also never questioned it.

He stopped pacing and sat beside her. "I overdosed on drugs, Ki. I nearly died. I go out of my way to destroy myself, have been doing it for as long as I can remember. The things that happened to you, these things you are going through, aren't your fault. I chose my fate."

"Tyler, that doesn't—"

"Let me finish, please."

She nodded.

"After I fell down the stairs and ruptured my spleen, the doctors said I was lucky. That if I kept using drugs, my liver would have failed within the next few months. I listened to them, but the only thing I could think was how bad I wanted to get high. I planned on doing it first thing when I got out of the hospital." He reached over and held her hand. "Then I met you. When the desire to use gets bad, I think back to our stay in the hospital, to the first time I made you smile. You saved my life. I know you thought it was the other way around, but it wasn't. I don't remember what I was talking about, probably just rambling on, but I remember your smile because I had never seen it before. One moment you were contently listening and the next, your face lit up with a smile, and in that moment, I realized I had done something good for once and I wanted to keep doing it. I wanted to be the person who gave you a purpose, who picked you up off the ground and would always be there. At the time, I wasn't sure how I would accomplish all that, but I knew I couldn't do it if I was a druggie. So, I made two promises to myself, one that I would never use again and two, that I would never hurt you."

While she was still considering his words, he added, "Tonight, I knew you weren't okay. I knew to walk away and yet I struggled. You're the only good part of me. I came so close to destroying that and I feel bad about it, but most of all, I can't have you beat yourself up because you think you treated me wrong."

"Please don't blame yourself. Tonight was all me and even if it was hard, you had the sense to walk away." She shook her head, tears ran down her face. "I don't remember much, but I know a part of me wanted to hurt you. There's something so wrong with me I don't think it can be fixed and I know I should send you away. I should have Henry put me in an institution again, but I'm too selfish to do that. I'm not ready to let go of you, of living."

"I wouldn't go. I need you as much as you need me. We are both being selfish."

They sat in the silence for a few minutes, lost in their thoughts. Outside, a flash of light lit up the window, followed by large pellets of rain. Thunder shook the floor, but they ignored it, the storm inside had already broke. Kiara felt herself begin to doze off and saw Tyler's eyes drifting closed.

"Tyler?" she whispered.

"Yeah?"

"Was it good for you?"

They both laughed, a sad, painful laugh that only those who are hurting inside can understand. Under the blanket of thunder, their voices carried no farther than the dim corner in which they sat. When the last of their laughter disappeared, they shut their eyes and leaned against each other, too worn out to get up.

"I love you, Ki."

"I love you, too."

15

yler poured water into the coffee pot while she pulled down the mugs. After an entire night sleeping against a wall, they both needed a dose of caffeine. She set the cups down beside the blinking light on her caller ID. "What the hell? I've got twenty-two missed phone calls."

He took a deep breath as she pressed the play button. "Miss Moore, this is Lucia White. I write for LA Scene Magazine and I wanted to see if we could do a story about you, what happened, and how that led to your relationship with Tyler Reed? Please call me back. I promise to make it worth your time. My number is—"

Kiara turned off the machine and looked at him. "They're all going to be like that, aren't they?"

"Yeah, probably."

"You don't seem surprised." She brought the cups over and he filled them with coffee.

"I have sixty-seven missed phone calls, twenty of them from my agent, so I had a pretty good idea."

"What are we going to do? Is this going to ruin your career?"

He laughed and nearly spit out his coffee. "No, Ki, if anything, my career options just got bumped up. People are nosy, they can't help it. It will take a while for this to die down. Our best bet is to wait it out, stay out of the public eye. I'll call my agent and we'll go from there. I'm not worried about it. Right now, I want to focus on what's going on with you and what you haven't told me."

The way he said it let her know her impasse was over. It was time to tell the truth. She'd decided to do that a few days ago, so she wasn't upset about it. Last night proved to her that Tyler would not throw down the gauntlet and walk away. Plus, she was scared. She knew she could no longer handle this on her own. The only reason she hadn't told him yet was because she didn't know how to approach it.

"Can we talk about it in a bit? I need to think of where to start. Maybe you can make your phone calls and by then I'll have it figured out."

"Sure. I'll call Henry, too, give him a heads up in case the media gets wind of him."

Kiara shut her eyes. "Oh crap, I didn't think of that. He's going to be so pissed I went to a bar."

TYLER SPENT over an hour on the balcony, first with his manager, then with Henry. Daniel was respectful enough to try to hide his excitement, but it was there, nonetheless. The videos had spread like wildfire. Tyler shouldn't have been surprised about how much the media had discovered in such a short amount of time. Luckily, her property was guarded by a gate, far enough from the house where she wouldn't notice if the press began gathering out there. After agreeing to make a statement within the next few days, Daniel had let him off the phone. When he came back in, Kiara was just finishing straightening up the house. "Hey, I would have helped."

"No, I needed to clean. Keep busy, you know?"

She straightened a cushion on the couch and spread out a stack of magazines on the table. It was obvious from her body language she was nervous.

"Well, just expect a phone call from Henry later. He's not the happiest with me."

"I'm sorry. I didn't mean for you to go through that. I should have called him myself." She stopped straightening and sighed. Tyler was glad he made the phone call instead of her. Henry was more than unhappy, he was pissed. After realizing Tyler wasn't going to defend himself for taking her there, he'd calmed down, even admitting he understood how hard it was to tell Kiara no when she wanted something. When asked, Tyler admitted he'd noticed changes in her and extended his stay until he figured it out. He hadn't let on to his real suspicions though.

"Nah, he did well, considering."

"Thanks, Tyler."

"Of course. Are you ready to talk?

"I guess so."

They both took a seat on the couch and he waited as she seemed to struggle with what to say. Kiara stared off into the distance for so long he worried she might have gone into one of her fugues. Finally, when she started speaking, her voice was monotone, emotionless.

"It started with Rebecca. That's one part I will never be able to forget, never get past. Her dying and my living will stay with me forever. They said I was chained to that bed for three weeks, but to me it seemed like three years. I changed so much during that time. Within days, everything I thought I was, and everything I thought I knew crumbled. By the end, I was a shell of myself, something so evil and hateful that I stopped wishing for death and started to believe I was destined for Hell."

The fire crackled, but neither one of them stirred at the noise. In a way, Tyler could feel her suffering, could see what she saw as she was lost in the memory.

"When I came to the first time, I wasn't alone. She was shoved in a bed in the corner, far enough away that I never got to see her face, but to this day I can't forget it. He came to me that first night and she yelled for him to let me go. *Begged* him. He went to her and I could hear him beating her. She screamed so much . . ."

Kiara trembled. Tyler went to her side of the couch and touched her face, but she brushed him off.

"Listening to her was horrifying, but . . ." She stopped and looked him in the eyes. "You always talk about how you think you're a bad person, how I'm so good, but you're wrong. I didn't like listening to her suffer, but it meant he wasn't touching me."

"Ki, please don't. I don't need to know."

"Yes, you do. I tried to get Henry to relieve you as my guardian. Did he tell you that?"

"What? Why?"

"I know I'm crazy. I know I'm falling apart. I don't want to put you through this. I wouldn't blame you if you left. It might even be a relief."

"I'm not going anywhere."

"Please, before you make that decision, you need to understand that I'm sick. I'm no good for you. Other people can take care of me. Henry will make sure I am well taken care of. Go out and live your life."

"That's what I'm doing."

The grateful look in her eyes betrayed how desperate she was, how much she needed him. "Continue the story, Ki."

"At some point he left. I woke to her calling out to me and we started talking. She was in her thirties, a nurse, with a loving husband and five-year-old at home. One night, after a late shift, he grabbed her on the way to her car. She kept talking about how she never got to tell her little boy goodbye. She made me promise to tell him how much she loved him, how much she thought about him in the end.

"Three days later, I saw them for the first time. I was sleeping, but I heard a noise, something scratching around —it was awful. I opened my eyes and this creature was on the ceiling, above the bed, looking down at me. It's not human, it's black and its skin looks like tar, but it moves. You know how an animal's hackles rise?"

He nodded his head.

"It does that, but its movements are more liquid. It's hard to explain. Its long, about five feet and it lies on the ground on all fours, but when it moves, the arms and legs float out to the side, like its crawling on its belly. The eyes are the worst, they're milky, filmy looking."

She shuddered. "Then I noticed the other one, a figure of a man, no features, just this thick blackness and it's more terrifying than the first. Something about the way it makes me feel, I don't know, it's more than just fear. They crawled to Rebecca and hovered over her. At some point, I passed out and when I woke up, she was gone. Anthony said she *ascended*. I knew better, but still, those creatures . . ."

Kiara was looking at him, but he didn't think she was aware of him. "I never saw them again, at least not until several months ago. I woke up from a bad dream, thinking about you, wishing you were here holding me. That's when

I realized my phobia no longer included you. I felt strong, healed, and thought maybe it was time to put the past behind me. So, I went to visit her grave. As I was walking away, I saw a young boy, maybe ten and his father approaching. They both had their heads down, but I knew who they were. I remembered my promise, to tell her son what she said, but I couldn't, you know?" She begged with her eyes, pleading for him to understand. "I knew he would see it, see her suffering. It's inside me. I drove away instead, wishing I was a stronger person."

"Ki—"

"Ever since then, they've been haunting me."

"What do you mean?"

Kiara filled him in on the past few months while he sat there, mesmerized and horrified by what she had been going through. When she finished telling her story she was pale, a broken woman. He did the only thing he could think of and pulled her into him, holding her like she'd wanted that morning a few months ago.

IT HAD TAKEN hours for her to calm down enough before he felt comfortable leaving the room. When he came back carrying lunch and some Cokes, he thought she'd eat, but she only picked at the food. Tyler decided not to press her since he didn't have much of an appetite himself. When she complained about being tired, he took her full plate back to the kitchen and she went to bed, leaving the door open so he was free to check on her.

After waiting an hour, he stepped into the room. There was a light, rhythmic motion of her chest and her eyelids fluttered slightly. Tyler grabbed his laptop and settled down in an armchair. They were both exhausted from the last few days, but it still worried him how much she was sleeping. Having dealt with depression on and off throughout his life, he recognized the symptoms. Now he knew what was going on with her. He should call Henry and come up with a plan, but he held off, not wanting to chance doing something she might not forgive him for. He stared at the computer screen before typing in the phrase *haunting*. As he weeded through sites, he tried to ignore the little voice in the back of his mind telling him it was all in her head. Tyler wasn't one to completely dismiss the paranormal, but in general, he didn't think ghosts existed. There was a ton of information on the subject, but none of it seemed to entail the creatures she described.

*What the hell am I doing? Instead of calling Henry and giving him a chance to help her, I'm doing what, exactly? Looking up ghosts?*

He mumbled a curse under his breath and slammed the laptop shut. As he was halfway through dialing Henry's number, Kiara moaned and rolled over

Dark, silky curls swept across her face and he could see her eyes twitching under purple lids. His gaze moved down to her stomach which was partially exposed. A bruise skirted beneath the edge of her shorts and disappearing under the top. He leaned over the bed and pinched the bottom of the tank top between his fingers, lifting it up halfway to her ribcage. The bruise covered the entire area. Noticing a change in her breathing pattern, he glanced up to find her staring sleepily back at him.

"I'm sorry." He took his hand off her. "You have a bruise."

"I know." Her words were slurred.

"I didn't mean to wake you, Ki. I wasn't thinking."

Her eyes slid shut again, but she responded. "It's okay."

"How did you get the bruise?"

"I don't remember," she mumbled.

"Didn't it bother you when I touched you?"

"No…" Her eyes slid open a bit.

"But you were asleep."

She blinked at him twice before responding. "I still knew it was you. Your touch feels . . . I don't know. It's different."

She shut her eyes again.

"Different how? Ki?"

No response. *Oh, for the love of god.*

"Ki?" He shook her gently. "Different how?"

She blinked. "I don't know. It's familiar. Makes me feel good."

He waited for her to say more, but she slipped off to sleep. Tyler walked back to the chair. There was a lot of information to process and he didn't know where to start. Only three things were certain in his mind; the fact he loved her with everything he was, that she was comfortable with him touching her, and that this change happened around the same time she started seeing things.

## 16

Kiara hurt. She was sore and weak all over, her eyes heavy and swollen from crying. Tyler was lying on the other side of her bed. She wasn't surprised to see him there. Had he called Henry?

*Probably. I wouldn't blame him if he did.*

She knew that should upset her but couldn't bring forth any emotion. Staring at the ceiling, she tried to think of anything to break out of this numbness, but she was left empty, lifeless.

"You okay?" Tyler whispered.

He must have sensed her movement and woken. Although he was a light sleeper, she should have known he would also be hyperaware right now. She wished she wasn't putting him through this.

"I killed him, you know."

*Why did I say that?*

"I know."

"I lied, though." Her words sounded loud in the silent room, even though she whispered. It must be because she never expected to say them out loud.

Tyler shifted and propped up on his elbow, faced her. "About killing him?"

"No." She paused, waiting to see if the numbness had gone away. It hadn't. "About what happened *after* I killed him. They thought I had gone unconscious, but I was awake. I kept my eyes open the whole time."

Tyler didn't say anything.

"I didn't know how I'd gotten loose. One minute I was tied up and the next, I wasn't. Time was different in that room, though." Kiara shut her eyes and she could see it in her head. It was as though she was floating above, watching herself. "I remember untying my feet. It took forever. The pain of moving after so long was excruciating. I was so weak."

Tyler squeezed her hand. She supposed he was letting her know it was okay, that she didn't have to tell him, but she ignored it.

"I heard him coming, so I grabbed the knife. I think he liked to leave it on the bedside to torture me; knowing a chance for escape was so close yet I couldn't quite get there. Everything he did was like that. Intentional, calculated."

Kiara looked at Tyler but whatever he was thinking or feeling was hidden behind a mask. She wished there was some emotion he would show her. Maybe she could feel something if she just saw how. "So, I laid in bed and pretended to sleep. I thought for sure he would hear how loud my heart was pounding or see the untied ropes around my legs. For him to miss a detail like that was just not possible, but somehow he did. He leaned over me and I opened my eyes. I thought, *this is it, he's going to kill me now,* but he was smiling.

"He said, 'Good morning Sugar Bear.' I raised the knife, slammed it into his throat. It, it sank right in."

Tyler remained still.

"His eyes . . . they were so wide. I pushed the knife back and forth while it was in him. I didn't feel any resistance, but I heard this snapping and tearing sound, like a sheet being ripped apart, and the blood . . ." she took a deep breath, ". . . there was so much. I couldn't take my eyes off his and after what seemed like forever, they dimmed. He fell on me and I panicked. He was so heavy. It seemed like I pushed for hours but I'm sure it was only for a few seconds and then he slumped to the floor. The side of his head hit the dresser on the way down and I remember thinking how odd it was that his neck could twist like that."

She shuddered at the memory. Silence permeated the room. Tyler remained quiet. Finally, she pulled herself out of the memory and continued her story.

"I must have sat there, staring at his body for hours, afraid he would open his eyes. Blood covered the floor and seeped through the cracks in the wood, but I kept thinking maybe it wasn't enough blood. At some point, I noticed the noise. The rats were banging on the cage, going crazy over the smell. They probably had been doing it the whole time. I got off the bed and stepped over his body. That was the most terrifying moment for me. I was convinced he was just waiting until I got up and he would grab my leg as I passed. When I got beyond him, it shocked me to see him still lying there, not moving. I went over to the cage and opened the door. Then I ran to the far corner of the room. They scurried to his body and I could hear this smacking sound as they chewed on him.

"At some point I trusted he was dead, trusted the rats wouldn't hurt me and so I sat beside him, watching as they ate at his throat and eyes. I could feel their sharp feet cross my lap as they ran around, frenzied to get to other parts of his body, but I knew they meant me no harm. I reached over and tore open his shirt. One rat bit me in the process, but I think it was by accident. They didn't seem interested in his chest or stomach and I figured it was because they couldn't smell the blood. So I put the knife against his chest and cut him open."

"They went crazy." She laughed, a low guttural sound that didn't resemble her own voice. "When they slowed, I took off his pants and started cutting his legs. I did this repeatedly, for hours." She swallowed, and her mouth felt like it was full of molasses. "I watched as they tore into him and I laughed. I couldn't stop laughing."

She wailed as the numbness seeped from her body only to be replaced by complete despair. She reached out to Tyler, and he pulled her into his chest. And even as sunrise streamed through the windows, they remained together in the dark.

17

yler sat out on the balcony, sipping his cup of coffee. The mountain landscape behind him, highlighted in shades of pink and purple, signaled the beginning of another day. His focus was not on the beautiful sunrise, nor the taste of coffee, but on the darkened window.

She hadn't left the room in two days. Most of the time she slept. Twice she got out of bed and wrote on her laptop, *"I watched him die."*

A cold breeze swept across his skin and he shuddered. After what she'd told him, he couldn't shake the feeling of being watched. Taking a sip of coffee, he tried to push the thought away. It took him a long time to convince her he didn't think she was an awful person.

Secretly, he was glad she did it. A part of him even wished Andrew was still alive so *he* could kill him. Wishing for the impossible wasn't helping him, though. His focus needed to be on how to get her out of bed. Yesterday evening he tried to get her to eat and drink, but she was barely responsive, and refused. Finally, this morning, when he could no longer ignore the persistent voicemails, he returned Henry's phone call. Tyler didn't tell him about her hallucinations, but he let him know about the depression. Luckily, Henry was out of town until tomorrow morning, or else he would have been there in person. Instead, he instructed Tyler to bring her by the office the following day.

Stressed and exhausted, Tyler laughed, snapping back with, "Yeah, sure, if I can get her out of bed, that is."

In retrospect, he should have kept his mouth shut.

"So, what you're telling me is that you can't take care of her?"

The conversation which followed was unpleasant and Tyler was still fuming. In that dark room, a full breakfast tray still sat beside the bed, growing cold. He had coaxed, even begged, but no matter what he did, she either ignored him. So, he stepped out before trying again.

He needed to get his anger under control. Then again, maybe it would be better if he stayed pissed. When it came to Kiara, he bent over backward to make sure he dealt with her gently. Obviously, that would not work now. He shoved his chair back and stood. Taking a deep breath, he walked back into the house and entered the bathroom.

Although the house was older, she had updated the bathroom before she moved in. Stone walls and a marble floor led to a double wide shower. The frameless shower doors reflected an infinite sheet of clear glass from the floor to ceiling. Tyler reached in, turned on the water, and waited for the temperature to adjust. He placed a towel on the bar hanging outside and made his way to her room.

She lay under the duvet, folds of material hugging her small body. A gaunt face and swollen, purple lids enhanced her almond-shaped eyes, which twitched, lost in a dream state. Cracked lips parted slightly, trembled as the faintest exhale slipped through them. Had it not been for a light puff of breath, she would appear to be dead. Even at her worst, he thought she was a vision of ethereal beauty.

Tyler wondered what she was dreaming, whether he was in it. His breathing subconsciously slowed to match hers. She must have sensed him staring because her eyes slid opened.

"Hey." He smiled at her.

"Hey." The words were barely audible. "What's going on?"

"It's time to get up. I've already got your shower running." He spoke softly, hoping she would be more agreeable if he did.

Kiara blinked. "Why?"

"Because you've been sleeping for days, Ki. You need to get up, shower, and eat something. You'll feel a lot better when you do."

She frowned and pursed her lips. "Not now. I'm tired."

He sighed as she closed her eyes and rolled over, facing away. It was time to take this situation into his own hands. Twice now she had let him hold her, had insisted she no longer feared his touch, but he didn't know how far that trust extended, doubted she knew either. He was about to find out, though. They both were.

Tyler reached down, tugged the blanket off of her, and tossed it on the floor. She cringed and curled into a fetal position, her eyes wide.

"You need to get up, right now."

She seemed tense, expectant, but she didn't respond.

Tyler leaned down, putting his face close to hers. "Ki, get up, right now."

She squeezed her eyes closed, clenched her fists around the bedsheets.

A loud thrumming, like ocean waves filled his ears and

his head throbbed. Henry didn't think he could take care of her, Tyler even doubted it himself, but he thought Kiara trusted him. Until now, that was.

*She doesn't think I'll touch her, thinks I'm incapable of doing anything to upset her even if it's for her own good. That's why she's not reacting. She thinks I'll give up.*

The idea that she might use his kindness against him did nothing to squelch the anger already spiraling out of control. Tyler took a deep breath and let it out before reaching across the bed, grabbing her by the hips, and pulling her shorts down.

Kiara shot up as if he'd struck her. "What are you doing?"

"Taking you to the shower." He pulled the shorts over her feet and threw them on the floor. She scooted back on the bed, putting distance between them.

"Are you going to go take a shower now or do I need to continue?" Tyler was surprised how steady his voice sounded.

She pointed at the door and screamed, "Get out!"

He sighed. "I'll take that as a no."

With one quick stride, he crawled up on the bed. Kiara moved to escape, but he straddled her and grabbed the bottom of her tank top. "You can either march into that bathroom and take a shower, or I will undress you and drag you in there myself. Which do you choose?"

Fearful eyes stared into his and he faltered, loosening his grip. She used the hesitation to slip out of his grasp. He caught her arround the waist and pulled her back across the bed. Kiara screamed and lashed out with her nails, scratching his chest and neck. The situation had escalated in a way he hadn't expected, and he fought to gain control. Grabbing an arm, he trapped it between her body and his while struggling to secure the other above her head. Stuck and unable to strike back, Kiara twisted and squirmed underneath him.

"Ki, I need you to calm down."

She shook her head. With his one free hand, he worked the bottom of the tank top up to her shoulders. Realizing he would have to release her to get the flimsy fabric off, he let go and quickly tugged it off, his arms grazing her bra.

"Don't touch me!" she screamed.

*Fuck!*

He hadn't intended for this to become so physical. Guilt layered itself on top of the anger, but what else was he to do? Giving up now would make the whole ordeal a useless and painful waste of time. Grabbing her by the waist, Tyler threw her over his shoulder and carried her to the bathroom as she screamed and thrashed the whole way.

"Stop it! Please stop!" Her small fists pounded against his back, but he didn't notice. His vision blurred, dark around the edges, and a shrill ringing in his ears drowned out the noise. When they reached the bathroom, he slid the door open with his foot, allowing him to carry them both in. Steam billowed out, fogging up the mirror and making the floor slippery, but he didn't stop or slow down. Slinging her off his shoulder, he plopped her down in the far corner of the shower.

"I'm staying right here until you've showered." He reached back and turned the shower head until it sprayed directly on her. Kiara gasped as water pelted her in the face. Tyler picked up the soap and sponge and knelt. He ignored his wet clothes, ignored the look of terror in her eyes when he grabbed her wrists, pulling them away from her body, exposing her lacy pink bra and panties which were now see through.

"I'm naked," she shrieked.

"No, you're not. And do you think I give a shit? I've seen plenty of naked women. Now take this damn sponge and wash yourself or I will." Tyler flung the sponge down and it smacked against her thighs.

Her bottom lip trembled. "Don't do this to me."

"Don't you dare put this on me," he said through clenched teeth.

She glanced down at his hands and froze. Realizing they were balled into fists, he relaxed them, and she seemed to relax, too.

Tyler stood and caught a reflection of himself in the glass, face full of hate and menace. He glanced back down at her, curled in the corner as though she wished she could disappear.

*What have I done?*

Feeling numb, he stepped out of the shower and leaned against the wall. He would never hurt her. He knew that, he thought she knew it, too. Sliding down to the floor, he covered his face with his hands. This whole thing was a mess. He should have been more patient with her, should have admitted to Henry he needed help. Instead, he'd lost his temper.

*I probably lost her, too.*

Tyler kicked the cabinet door, causing it to slam it shut. With nothing else to focus his anger on, he kicked it a second time. Then a third. The wood splintered with a loud cracking noise. Kiara screamed.

He cursed and jumped up, his hands held out in front of him as he re-entered the shower. "I'm so sorry. It's okay, I promise. I would never hurt you."

She tucked her legs in, body shaking.

He knelt, his throat tight. "Ki, please?"

Water soaked through his clothes, but he ignored it. He

needed her to do something to let him know she didn't hate him. "Please look at me. I love you."

For the first time since they'd started saying that to each other, she didn't say it back.

"I've lost you," Tyler mumbled, placing his head in his hands.

18

$S$ilence. The only noise she heard was the steady sound of running water. She fought for the strength to raise her head. Tyler was a couple feet away, hands covering his face.

Kiara hadn't meant to do this to him, hadn't meant to put him in this position. She'd fought against him, broken him down, and her heart ached. Emotionally, she was drowning, submerged in water and unable to breathe. Now, as she watched her best friend, Kiara found a reason to keep her head above water.

Was she afraid of him? A little, but she couldn't let him know that. This was her fault, and she needed to fix it. "You're getting wet."

Tyler removed his hands, uncovered his eyes and mouth. He looked at her, eyes hesitant.

She repeated her statement. "Your clothes are getting wet."

"Yeah," he whispered. "I guess so."

She could tell he didn't trust the situation. He looked like he was waiting for the axe to come down. Biting her

126

lip, she dropped her arms, flushed as she realized how much of her body was exposed.

"*I've seen plenty of naked women.*"

She pulled herself onto her knees, scooting forward until she closed the distance between them. Even slumped down, he towered over her, and she had to lift her chin to look into his eyes. With trembling hands, she tugged on the bottom of his t-shirt. "You're getting wet."

There were a million questions reflected in his eyes. She tugged his shirt higher. He furrowed his brow but seemed to understand what she wanted because he lifted his arms above his head. Kiara's fingertips grazed his stomach and bare chest as she pulled the t-shirt off, tossing it out of the shower.

Tyler swallowed hard. "I will never forgive myself for hurting you."

"No, I hurt myself. You only did what you had to."

Reaching down, she grasped the button on his jeans. Before she had the chance to do more, he put his hands on hers.

"What are you doing?"

"I need to prove I trust you. I *want* to prove it."

He gave her a sad smile and shook his head. "Not like this. Come on."

Tyler stood and extended his hand to help her up. Kiara took it and as she got to her feet, staggered.

"I feel like a million pounds."

"You haven't eaten in days. You're just feeling weak. Let's go to the kitchen and I'll make lunch."

Kiara's stomach growled in response, but she ignored it. "After all this, you're going to let me get away without a shower? I don't think so." She grinned at him and he smiled back but it didn't touch his eyes.

"Okay. Sure. I'll go make lunch so you can bathe."

It took every bit of courage she had to say what she said next and it still surprised her when the words came out. "No, you promised to bathe me. I expect you to keep your promise."

"You're kidding?" Shock and disbelief colored his voice.

"No."

"I can't do that, Ki."

"Why not?"

"Because I can't."

"I'm telling you that you can. Like you said, you've seen plenty of naked women. I'm not even naked."

They stared at each other across the shower. Kiara tried to remain strong but there was a voice in the back of her head telling her he was disgusted. His face showed nothing but confusion and fear, though.

"I'm sorry. I just . . . I wanted to show you how much I trust you. I didn't mean to make things weird."

She grabbed the shampoo off the bar and began to wash her hair. Just the act of lifting her arms seemed to sap most of the energy she had. It wasn't the first time she'd been depressed, but this was the closest she'd come to losing her grip on reality. If Tyler hadn't been there, she might have stayed in that bed until she died. She was rinsing the shampoo out when she felt his hand touch hers. Startled, she tensed.

"Ki?"

"No, it's okay. I'm so tired that I was drifting off. It wasn't you." Kiara looked at him over her shoulder. "Really, you don't have to do this. I understand if you don't want to touch me."

Tyler frowned. "How am I supposed to respond to that? Tell you I don't want to touch you? Tell you I do? Which answer are you going to be happy with?"

*Oh, god, he's right.*

Both answers scared her, just in different ways. She swallowed. "I'm so sorry. That was wrong of me."

"It's okay. Now turn back around so I can help."

Tyler took his time as he washed her hair. Taking a deep breath, she shut her eyes and concentrated on relaxing. After he was done, he stepped away. She turned to see him pouring body wash on a sponge.

Without looking up, he said, "I do want to."

"Want to what?"

"Touch you."

Those two words seemed to suck the air out of the shower, rocking her on her heels.

He finished putting the soap on the sponge and held it out to her. "I just thought you should know."

His eyes burned with raw intensity and yet his words were vulnerable. Kiara looked down at the sponge he was holding. She knew he was giving her a choice. To take the sponge would be admitting she wasn't comfortable enough for him to wash her with it. Their friendship wasn't rational or normal, but having him bathe her might cross a line. Regardless, she had to choose.

Kiara reached out and took the sponge from Tyler. His eyes flickered to it, then her face. He nodded, his mouth set in a grimace. She shook her head and let go of the sponge. It hit the shower floor between them.

"I'll get it," Tyler said, leaning down.

"No, leave it."

He stood back up, one brow raised. Kiara grabbed the bottle of soap from the ledge. She took his hand and poured a small amount in his palm. "I don't want you to use the sponge."

Tyler shut his eyes and took a deep breath before opening them again. "Ki, you don't—"

"Please don't argue with me on this. My self-esteem can't take much more."

They stared at each other.

Tyler caved. "Okay. Turn around then."

She pulled her hair over her shoulder, exposing her back, and waited.

Tyler leaned in and whispered in her ear, "No matter what, if you get the least bit frightened, promise you'll tell me."

"I promise," she lied.

The first touch was gentle, hesitant. A tremor went through her. Tyler moved his hands in slow circular motions. They felt slick and hot on her tender skin. When he finished her back, he knelt, and massaged soap up and down her legs, stopping when he got to the apex of her thighs. Her skin seemed to smolder under his touch. Every rivulet of soap running down was like a gentle caress and she ached deep inside in a way she hadn't felt in a long time. She knew he was waiting on her to turn around, so he could finish, but she couldn't move.

"Do you want me to stop?" Tyler asked, his voice low, nervous.

"No. I'm okay," she said, looking at him over her shoulder. "I just—I didn't expect it to make me feel like this."

He bit his lip. She could see the question in his eyes, but he didn't comment on her statement. Tyler squeezed more soap in his hands. Kiara could feel the heat radiating off his body as he stepped closer. He reached around, placing his palm on her stomach. Slowly, he trailed his hands over her ribs and then back down, stopping as he came to her panty line. Kiara could feel his warm chest grazing her back with every move. The dull ache became a throbbing desire. Without thinking, she leaned into him, a moan escaping her lips.

Tyler buried his face into her neck and whispered, "Don't move."

She froze, eyes popping open. The length of him pressed against her lower back, hard and throbbing.

"Ki, baby, I'm going to step out of this shower and go make us lunch."

"You don't have to," she whispered. "I shouldn't have done that. I'm sorry."

"Don't apologize. This isn't your fault."

"Then stay," she argued. "I want you to stay."

"I can't," he said, backing away. "You don't know what you want, and I will not take advantage of that."

"Because I'm sick?" She turned, facing him.

"Yes. Because you're sick and you're depressed, and because I think I'm part of the reason for that." Tyler kissed her hair and stepped out of the shower.

19

Showered and hair dried, Kiara had no excuse to stay in the bathroom any longer. She wasn't sure if she was more embarrassed or ashamed, but she needed to face the aftermath of her actions, regardless. She passed by the library and noticed the fireplace emitting a crackling glow. It made the house warm and cozy. Just the fact he'd gone through the extra effort to make her comfortable left her on the verge of tears. How could she face him without becoming a sobbing mess?

Tyler was sitting at the table, sandwich in hand. She took the seat beside him, where he'd placed her lunch. She repeated the mantra in her head, *'just act normal,'* but still was not brave enough to make eye contact. If he sensed her discomfort, she didn't know. He was slumped in the chair, legs propped up on the table, eating as if nothing had happened.

She picked up her sandwich— turkey and pepper jack on rye— and ate. It tasted like a gourmet meal. She mumbled out garbled words of gratitude between bites, but that was all that was spoken between them for a while.

She nervously cut her eyes upward, to see if she could gauge his mood. He saw her glance and set his chips down, as if ready to talk, but she returned her focus back to the meal.

After finishing her sandwich, she took a drink of orange juice, choking on it when he said, "I like that pink bra and panty set you were wearing."

Kiara tried to clear her throat, but the pieces of rye bread refused to go down and the acid from the juice burned her esophagus.

He ignored her coughing fit and continued, "As a matter of fact, I was quite surprised to see you wear such sexy undergarments. Doesn't fit your personality. So, I took the liberty of going through your panty drawer. You have one hell of a lingerie collection, Ki."

Her mouth fell open, coughing fit forgotten, as she met his gaze for the first time. His eyes were lit with humor and one corner of his mouth lifted in a smile. She knew he was teasing, probably just trying to cheer her up, but her emotions were still reeling from earlier.

Still, she could at least try. "You did not."

"Oh yes." His grin spread to the other side of his mouth. "I'm particularly fond of that little red number. The one with the thong and studded garter."

"You went through my panty drawer?" Warmth spread over her face, the heat on her cheeks making her eyes water. Years after her captivity, when she'd come to terms with her self-esteem again, she'd decided she could quit hiding her body, at least to herself. She ordered a sexy bra and panty set online and when she wore it, it made her feel pretty. Since then, she ordered new sets regularly, not worried about what other people would think because no one would ever see them. At least, that's what she assumed.

"Yep. Then again, that black lacy getup with the slit up the stomach might be a front runner."

She was so embarrassed she forgot the reason she was upset. The lingerie collection was a secret of hers, one which she had planned to keep. Then, she realized what he was doing. Of course he would know she would be upset after the shower, how hard it would be for her to face him. He was teasing to cheer her up. He was still staring at her, a grin on his face, waiting for her to respond.

She set the glass she had been holding down and leaned over, giving him a hug. "Thank you."

He hugged her back, awkwardly from the position he was sitting in and laughed. "Jeez Ki, if I knew I would get this type of response for going through your underwear, I would have done it years ago."

"Shut up, you ass." Giving him one last squeeze, she returned to her seat, smiling.

"So, are we okay now?" Even though he kept the question light, she could see the worry and fear in his eyes. This was hard for him too, something she needed to remember more often.

"Yeah, I think we are."

His only response was to nod. Feeling better about the situation, she finished her lunch as they discussed their plans for tomorrow, plans which included a visit to Henry.

AFTER LUNCH, they took their plates to the kitchen. Tyler stood beside her at the sink, rinsing and drying the dishes as she washed them, her hands plunged into the soapy water. Sunlight filtered through the blinds, laying streaks of gold across her pale blue tank top. The sleeves of Tyler's white shirt were rolled up above his elbows. He held a glass underneath the faucet, turning it, catching distorted images as rivulets of water passed over. Mesmerized, she stared through the glass as the mirage changed, becoming dark and oppressive.

*Something is wrong.*

She turned away from the glass, looking around the kitchen. They were alone, nothing seemed out of place, but the feeling of foreboding would not go away. A single strand of light caught her eye as it pierced the blinds. It bent into an oval stream, causing a golden strand to flow through the air, catching showers of dust. She followed the prism as it reached Tyler's face, passing under his jaw, trailing up his cheeks and briefly touching his brow before disappearing into nothingness. When the light dissipated, Kiara stood paralyzed, staring at Tyler's face. For as many times as she had looked at him, she had never *seen* him before; not like this, not as something other than a friend. Her heart fluttered.

*This is where it begins.*

The floor shook and across the expanse of the kitchen, beige tiles fell away into blackness. Tyler turned to look at her and when he did, the floor opened from beneath her feet and she plunged down into the abyss. She fell through the air, eyes closed, waiting on the impact, but none came.

Kiara opened her eyes. She was in a cavern, the walls and floor emitting an eerie glow. Beside her was Tyler, his body encased in a gummy pink gel-like substance. Through the visceral film, she could see his eyes were shut. In a panic, she fell to her knees, trying to dig him out but her hands only slid across the surface. Tears rolled down her face as she tore at the material, digging with her nails, but it did no good.

The cavern disappeared. She was standing once again

in the kitchen. She pulled her hands out of the sink with a gasp. Pellets of soap ran down her arms.

"Are you okay?" Tyler frowned, drying his hands on his pants before reaching out to her. Without thinking, she backed up a step, and he dropped his arms to the side. "What's wrong?"

She shook her head, afraid to answer. The image of it was too strong, too much for her to handle, the pain and fear of it overwhelming. Spots of amber light flooded her vision as her breathing increased to a dangerous rate. She didn't know what she had seen, what it all meant, but she knew Tyler was in danger because of her.

"I want you to leave."

"What?"

She didn't look at him, but she knew his face well enough to see the hurt and confusion ebbed in his voice. Inside, she felt like she was stabbing herself, twisting the knife. Without him, there was no way she could make it through this.

"I want you to go away. I want you out of my house," Kiara shouted at him.

Tyler, his eyes wide, backed up a few steps but no farther.

"Get out, now."

He shook his head. "I don't know what's going on here or what I've done, but I'm not leaving you like this. It's obvious you're not okay right now."

Sparkles of light twisted the edges of her vision. She picked up a dinner plate and threw it as hard as she could into the sink, shattering it into pieces. Turning back to Tyler, she screamed, "Get the fuck out!"

"Why? Why the hell do you want me to leave? Ki, please just calm down. I love you." He took a step forward and reached out to her.

She shook her head. "I don't want your love."

His face contorted, brows lowered. "You don't want my love?"

"No, I don't."

They stared each other down, his expression changing from one of anger to shock and then back to anger. Kiara felt foolish. She realized what she'd seen couldn't be real. It had to be another hallucination. She wanted to say something to make it better, wanted to explain, but he pushed by her, grabbing his wallet and keys off the counter.

"Tyler . . ."

"Don't bother." He shoved the wallet in his back pocket and headed for the door.

She moved to stop him. "Tyler, please don't go. I'm sorry."

He turned around, his emotions masked behind a clenched jaw. "Don't apologize. That's the smartest thing you've said since we've met."

With a sinking feeling in the pit of her stomach, she realized why he was so upset. Tyler had low self-esteem. He never felt deserving of anyone's love. She couldn't have picked a more effective way to upset him.

"No. It's not what you're thinking." She tried to close the distance between them, but he hurried out. She chased after, reaching the car as he slammed the door and started the engine. As she pounded on the window, he put the vehicle in drive, leaving her standing there.

SHE HEARD the front door open and shut. Footsteps echoed down the hallway and stopped outside her bedroom. She watched his shadow shuffle indecisively before retreating. Across the hall, a door opened. Throwing off her blanket, she tiptoed to his room. Tyler was at the closet, unbuttoning his shirt, his back to her.

She leaned against the door frame. "Hey."

He stopped removing his shirt and pulled it back over his shoulders, turning around. Shoving his hands in his pockets, he met her gaze. "I didn't mean to wake you."

It was past two in the morning and by all rights she should have been asleep, but she couldn't rest, terrified he wasn't coming back.

After he left, she'd tried texting him, only to realize he'd left his cell phone on the counter. She had considered going out and looking for him but, in the end, she decided that would be useless. He wasn't going to come back unless he wanted to. So, she had waited, worried and missing him, but it had given her the time to reflect on her feelings. Right now, she was just relieved he was okay.

"You didn't. I couldn't sleep, anyway." She came into the room and sat on the bed. "Can we talk?"

"Now's not a good time, Ki."

She studied his face. At first glance, he had looked relieved to see her but there was something else. An edge she hadn't seen before.

"Please. I promise, no more fits of insanity. My hands are dish free." She held them out in front of her to prove it and gave him a weak smile. It worried her when he didn't return it. "Tyler, I want to apologize. I don't have a good excuse for the way I acted and I'm sorry. I can tell you why I did what I did, but after I gave it some thought, I realized it made no sense."

"I know that. I'm not mad at you. It's just . . ." His voice broke, and he raised a hand to his eyes, rubbing them. She went to him and pressed her hand against his bare chest. His muscles trembled under her touch and his heartbeat fluttered erratically. He smelled earthy, like minerals and sweat.

"What's wrong?"

"I'm drunk as fuck and high on coke. I don't want you to see me like this."

It shouldn't have surprised her. She kind of assumed he was out doing something like that. She'd just chosen not to think about it. Grabbing his hand, she tugged him to the bed and made him sit. She knelt in front of him. He stared down at her, one hand covering his mouth.

"Tyler, you're my best friend no matter what. You said you wanted to be there for me when you found out I was going through something. I want to be there for you, too. I love you."

"You shouldn't." He scrunched his face. "I don't deserve it."

Kiara crawled up behind him in the bed and wrapped her arms around his waist. "Neither should you love someone who has as many issues as I do. Are you saying you don't love me?"

"Of course not. I just don't deserve your love."

"And yet, you still have it." Kiara laid her chin on his shoulder, breathing deeply. The smell of woman's perfume clogged her nose. Leaning back, she fingered the edge of his collar where a smear of pink lipstick stained it.

Tyler glanced back at the stain, his eyes lifting to meet hers. "I didn't do anything, Ki. I promise."

"It's none of my business," she said, hiding her face in his back, tears pricking the corners of her eyes.

"I think it is," Tyler said. He let out a deep breath. "This is hard. It's like we're stuck in some kind of purgatory. More than friends, less than lovers."

Kiara stilled, her breath catching in her throat. Things

had been changing between them, and she couldn't deny she felt something physical toward him, but *lovers*?

"I shouldn't have said that. You should go to bed, Ki. I've already screwed up enough today."

"I want to stay." She tightened her arms around him, afraid he might make her leave, afraid of what he would do if left alone. He loosened her grasp and stood, holding his hand out. "Come on then, I'll tuck you in."

She followed him, and he pulled down the covers for her. Slipping into the bed, she wasn't sure what to expect. He covered her with the blanket but when he laid down on his side, he stayed on top of them. They faced each other, not talking, until she fell asleep.

20

t's been quite a while since I've seen your face, Tyler. I have to say, you get sexier every time." Henry reached out and shook Tyler's hand.

"I could say the same thing about you."

Henry chuckled, but Kiara saw a look pass between the two.

"Have a seat you two." Henry waved to the couch and took a seat in the chair across from them. Tyler sat close to Kiara but leaned forward on his knees, eyes downcast. For months, she'd feared this moment, but now, she felt sort of relieved to tell the truth. Still, that didn't assuage her guilt for causing both of them so much anxiety.

"Tyler, you said there are some things you two wanted to talk about?"

Tyler met his gaze and nodded toward Kiara. "I think she wants to explain."

Henry looked at Kiara and she became nervous, unsure of how to start. "I guess . . . um, I haven't been well. I've been having these dreams and I wake up with these bruises." She leaned back, lifting her shirt to show

141

him. Henry's eyes narrowed, but he didn't speak. "And I keep having these hallucinations and losing gaps of time. I told Tyler, but then I got depressed and I wouldn't get out of bed or eat or drink."

"When did this start?"

"A few months ago."

"Continue, please."

"I didn't want to tell you because I thought you would send me away, but I don't want to live like this anymore. I know I can't handle this by myself."

Henry leaned forward. "I was told about the depression over the phone, but the bruises were left out. Also, the rest of the story. Why haven't you brought her here sooner, Tyler?"

Tyler put his head in his hands and sighed loudly.

"I'm here now," she spoke quickly, eyes darting between the two men. "And I'm okay. I already feel bad enough putting Tyler through this and I don't need you to put him on a guilt trip. If it wasn't for him being there, forcing me to get up, forcing me in the shower with him, then I would still be in that bed."

Henry stood. His words came out through clenched teeth. "You need to leave, Tyler."

Kiara's mouth popped open. "No, I want him to stay."

She glanced back and forth between the two. Tyler was already getting up to leave and Henry had his fists balled at his sides.

"He needs to leave."

"Why? What the hell is your problem, Henry?" She stood, shaking her head.

"Ki, please don't," Tyler begged.

"No, he has no right." She stared at him, incredulous he seemed so willing to be treated like this.

"No right?" Henry raised his voice. "You come into my

office with bruises, saying you've been hallucinating, that Tyler knew this, and then you tell me he forced you to take a shower with him. I should call the police right now."

"Oh god, no." She breathed. Her head was spinning. "It's not like that at all. He'd never hurt me."

She turned to Tyler. "I'm sorry. I didn't think he would come to that conclusion."

"I did." Tyler seemed resigned to the situation.

"Why didn't you say anything?"

"Because he's right. I should have called him. I should take better care of you and I should have never . . ." He sighed, letting the words trail off.

"Kiara, the only reason I have not picked up that phone is because for some stupid reason I'm giving you two the benefit of a doubt. Tyler needs to step out of this office and you have ten minutes to explain what's going on. Do you understand?"

For once, she didn't argue. She had sense enough to see Henry meant the threat, so she nodded. Tyler stepped through the door.

"And Tyler," Henry spoke over his shoulder, "don't leave the premises."

## 21

Tyler sat, disgusted with himself. He knew Kiara would tell Henry everything. How he threw her in the shower, how he touched her. He felt nauseated, worried he would lose her, unsure if Henry could do anything to take away his guardianship. Even if Henry believed them—and that was a strong *if*— others might not. If he was a suspect for the bruises, they might file a restraining order.

The ten-minute window came and went. Tyler paced up and down the hallway, ignoring the secretary glaring at him, trying to decide what he would do if they wouldn't let him around Kiara anymore. He could run away with her, disappear off the map.

*Would I do something like that?*

He conjured an image of her smiling up at him.

*Yes. I would.*

Thirty-two minutes passed before Henry stepped out into the lobby. He couldn't tell what Henry was thinking.

"Walk with me." The doctor's voice was casual but brisk.

Henry didn't speak to him, but lead the way, opening the back door which led out into a small garden area.

Tyler paused. "Where's Ki?"

"She's in the office filling out paperwork. There are some things I want to talk to you about that I don't want her to hear." Henry tilted his head toward the open door. "May we?"

Tyler decided that he might as well get to the point. "Are you having me arrested?"

The doctor flinched as if struck. "Oh, good lord, no. Is that why you're refusing to step out? No, Tyler. I just want to talk. It appears I owe you an apology."

Tyler couldn't speak momentarily. When he found his voice, the only word that came out was, "Why?"

"Tyler, I'm not going to say I have ever approved of your relationship with Kiara. It seemed too volatile, dangerous for her to trust you so much, and I never could understand your motives. She's a beautiful girl."

Tyler felt small under Henry's gaze, childish.

"It shouldn't have worked, the two of you together, but somehow you've kept your hands off her. Now I see you are someone to be respected. Will you step outside with me please?"

Tyler stepped out into the overcast lawn, scanning the area for police cars. When he detected none, he allowed himself to relax.

The small courtyard was shaded by a large oak tree. A granite bench sat underneath the tree and Tyler headed over to it, making sure he had a good view of the street, just in case. Henry sat beside him.

"What made you change your mind?"

"Kiara told me about what you did," Henry paused, ". . . and about what you *didn't* do."

"I feel horrible for doing that to her, I was so mad. And then . . . I shouldn't have touched her."

Henry leaned his head back, his features pinched. "One reason I didn't want you to be her guardian is because I didn't think you had it in you to deal with something like that, but you did what you had to do." He gave him a glare before continuing. "Calling me before it got to that point would have been a good idea, though. When it came to getting her out of bed, honestly, I would have told you to do exactly what you did. As for touching her, she said she invited you to, and you walked away. I don't know many men who would have the strength to do that."

"I promised myself I would never touch her." Tyler placed his head in his hands.

"Why?"

He looked at Henry in surprise. "Because I don't want to hurt her."

"Well, that's obviously not an issue anymore."

Tyler didn't know how to respond. This was probably one of the most uncomfortable conversations he'd ever had. "Did she tell you she realized it a few months ago?"

Henry chuckled. "I see you came to the same conclusion as me. Is it possible the reason she is going through this now, is that she subconsciously realizes she is attracted to you? I would say it is highly probable."

"Do you think it's me, specifically? Or do you think she's just getting better all around?"

Henry raised his eyebrows. "Well, now you've lost some of that respect you gained. Of course it's you, or, at least, that's the best-case scenario."

"What do you mean?"

Henry stood and paced in front of the bench. His strides were casual, thoughtful even, portraying his natural charisma. Tyler wasn't fooled, though. His eyebrows were deep set and the crinkles around his eyes tightened as if he was trying to keep his worry hidden behind the brown irises.

"Think about it. If what she's going through is happening because she's opening up to you, then that's progress."

"And if that's not the reason?"

"Then we have a big problem."

"There's something else, something she doesn't know about." Tyler told him about what she'd been writing in her fugues. Henry shrugged it off at first. Then Tyler realized he would not understand the significance unless he told him the story about Andrew and the rats. Feeling like he was betraying her, he reluctantly relayed what had happened. When he finished, he asked, "Do you think they are related?"

Henry was silent, his pacing had stopped mid-story and now he took a seat beside Tyler on the bench. There was a gleaming fire in his eyes, one in which Tyler himself understood.

"Are you okay?"

Henry shook his head. "No. Are you?"

Their eyes met. Tyler didn't have to answer.

Henry frowned. "I don't know if all of this is related. She seems to be feeling a lot of guilt over Rebekah, and now this story about Andrew. The two things have got to be connected somehow, but I'll be damned if I can figure it out. The timing is what concerns me. Why now, if it's not because of her feelings for you?"

Tyler nodded. "I'd appreciate it if you didn't let her know I told you that."

"Of course."

"So, what now?"

"I wish I knew, but I can't be sure. As for the hallucinations, I'm inclined to think she is sleep walking, her subconscious trying to sort things out. These creatures, though . . ." Henry bit his lip. "I have no idea why she is conjuring them, and it might take a while to figure that out. In the meantime, she is still a danger to herself. I will start her on a new depression medicine, prescribe a sleeping pill at night, and increase our visits to twice a week. I'm also going to request a series of tests, just to be safe."

A jolt of fear, followed by guilt, ran through Tyler. He hadn't even considered that. "You think something might be *physically* wrong with her?"

"No, I don't, but I can't rule it out until we check." The doctor paused, and Tyler turned to face him. "Also, while we're trying to figure this out, I can't condone her driving or being left alone for any period of time."

It took Tyler a moment, but what Henry was saying finally sunk in. "You're asking me to revoke her privileges?"

"Yes, but she knows. She understands how serious this is. Her only concern is putting you through stress."

Tyler covered his face. "I hate this, Henry. I don't want her to feel like she has no control over her life. It's not fair."

Henry gave him a mild smile. "I understand your concern, but she's fine with it. She trusts you. My question is, are you up to this? Taking care of her around the clock? Or should we get a nurse? How long are you willing to put your life on hold?"

"This is my life. Acting is just a job. Indefinitely, if necessary."

"You're a good man. Are you going to need to leave for a while to wrap things up?"

"Shit. Yeah, I guess I better." The thought made him anxious.

Henry sensed his thoughts. "I have an idea about how to deal with that. Let me check into some things and I'll call you later tonight about it. If you would like my help, that is?"

Tyler no longer held a grudge against Henry. The thorn in his side had been removed. He realized that Henry was offering his friendship, if he was willing to accept it. And he was. He opened his mouth, telling Henry a secret he hadn't been willing to admit to himself. "I'm in love with her."

"I know." Henry acted as if he had just said the most obvious statement in the world. "Have been for quite some time, I believe."

Tyler was still reeling from the truth of it. Thinking it was one thing but admitting it? She was untouchable; a perfect creature that could be destroyed with the smallest of mistakes.

"What am I going to do?"

Henry chuckled. "My suggestion would be to celebrate. She's one hell of a woman, Tyler."

Tyler wasn't in the mood to appreciate Henry's humor. "I mean, she's sick and confused. What if I scare her off? What if she doesn't want me like that?"

This time Henry frowned at him, making him feel petty. "If you keep talking like that, I'm seriously going to request you start using my services. Are you that thick? What do you think she was doing in the shower? Yes, she has issues, but not with you. Trust me, if you think this is a big, scary leap for you to take, it's ten times as huge for her. But she seems willing to try."

"I'm going to screw this up."

"It wouldn't be true love if you didn't screw up now and then."

"There's too much at stake with her, too much to lose."

Henry patted Tyler on the back. "I imagine that thought has been had by every man in history who ever loved a woman. Look, I'm not saying you need to go out there and announce your feelings on a billboard, but maybe you should try to do some little things, see how she reacts to them."

"Like what?"

"A touch here and there; flowers, romance. You're young, you'll think of something."

"And if she doesn't seem to like it?"

"Well, then, I guess you'll be my next patient."

22

"Hey," Tyler said as they got into the car, "I have an idea. Let's have dinner on the balcony tonight. We'll put up lanterns, decorate, the whole thing."

Kiara didn't answer. Earlier, when Henry and Tyler had come back to the office, they both seemed in good spirts. When Henry asked if she had finished her paperwork, she'd nodded and pushed it toward him. After glancing at it, he handed it over to Tyler who signed without hesitation. She had expected something different. Sympathy, maybe? Somber expressions? But no, they just chatted about basketball and food. Of course, their lives weren't affected like hers was. She supposed this was just another day for them.

*He's putting his life, his career, on hold for me and I'm upset because he's trying to act like it's not a big deal. When did I get so selfish?*

"Could we barbecue?"

Tyler gave her a sideways grin. "That sounds perfect. We'll stop at Super Mart and get supplies."

151

She stared out the window as they drove. Shadows of oak and pine cloaked the car as dead leaves berated the windshield, slamming against it with full force before joining an army of fallen comrades on the ground. Tyler had fallen quiet, brooding. This was a lot of strain on him and she knew it was her fault. A part of her, a huge part, worried he was considering leaving. To stay was a huge undertaking and she couldn't figure out why he was willing to do it. She knew they should talk about what happened in the shower, but she was too insecure to bring it up. Things were already unstable enough.

They pulled up into the quaint shopping area and the parking lot was packed. An outdoor event was going on and people moseyed about from booth to booth. There was no way she could go out there.

She looked at Tyler and he smiled. "Do you want to stay in the car? It'll only take me ten minutes to get what I need."

She bit her lip, not wanting to give into the fear, but also too afraid to work her way through that crowd. "I guess I better."

"Sounds good. I'll be out in ten. Make sure you lock the doors, okay? I wouldn't want anybody to take you." He opened his door, but before stepping out, leaned in and brushed his lips against hers. By the time she realized what just happened, he was already facing away and getting out.

*What was that?*

Reaching over she pushed the automatic lock buttons on the door and turned up the heat until the windows fogged with condensation, blocking her view of the crowd. She pulled her knees up to her chest, hugging them close to her body. Something was up with their relationship and she didn't know how to deal with it. There didn't seem to be a single part of her life that wasn't confusing.

Her phone vibrated.

*Filets or sirloin?*

She texted back, *Can't we have both?*

After a moment, he responded, *This is why I love you.*

She smiled.

The warmth of the heat on her skin was making her sleepy. She closed her eyes and drifted off into a void of nothingness. Her phone vibrated again, jarring her awake. She blinked and picked it up. "Hey."

"Where the hell are you?" The concern in Tyler's voice confused her.

"I'm in the car. Did you forget where we parked?"

"No, you're not. Where are you?"

She lifted her head and sunlight assaulted her. The noise of the crowd rushed over her. She glanced around. She was in the parking lot. Two guys brushed against her and she cringed.

Shakily, she said, "I'm in the crowd. I don't know how."

The crowd was too thick for her to tell where they had parked.

"I'm coming." She could barely hear him past the roar of voices. People pushed against her, each touch making her skin feel like it was on fire. She shut her eyes, body stiff, the taste of vomit filling her throat. Someone ran into her and she fell.

"Oh, I'm sorry." A man grabbed her by the shoulders and she screamed.

In the distance, she heard a familiar voice. "Ki?"

Tyler's face broke through the crowd. He gave an apologetic wave to the bystander who had knocked her down. Scooping her into his arms, he carried her out of the mass. She whimpered every time someone brushed past. Tyler opened the passenger door and sat her down on the car seat.

"Are you okay?" His eyes were wide, fearful.

"No," she cried. "I don't know how I got there. I fell asleep, and I thought I was still in the car. I'm losing it completely."

"No, you're not. We'll swing by the pharmacy and get your new meds. Between those and Henry working with us, we'll get through this."

She bit her lip. Tyler buckled her in before going around to his side. He seemed to calm, but she noticed he gripped the steering wheel so hard his knuckles had turned white.

"Do you really believe we will get through this?" she asked, not because she wanted to be reassured, but because she wanted him to tell her the truth.

"I think we will. It might take time, but eventually this will all pass."

"Okay."

"Until then, though, I'm putting a fucking tracker device on you."

She laughed, even though she wasn't sure if he was joking.

"Are you scared?" he asked.

"Yes." After a few seconds she added, "Are you?"

"Yeah."

"TYLER, WHEN ARE YOU GOING BACK?" Kiara asked over her shoulder as she hung up a Chinese lantern. He gave her a dirty look and ignored the question. "You're just not going to answer me, huh?"

"You know better."

The lumps of coal, soaked in a lethal amount of lighter fluid, refused to catch, no matter how many times Tyler tried. The long, red-handled lighter kept blowing out, caught in the brisk wind. Stepping down off the ladder, Kiara came and stood on the opposite side of the grill to block the wind. As he clicked the lighter on again, she inspected her decorating skills. The balcony was large enough to accommodate a love seat, three chairs, a hot tub, a patio table, and a fire pit with plenty of space left over. A triage of lights and lanterns accentuated the area, separating the space from the incoming darkness and giving off an air of seclusion.

The coal caught fire and Kiara took a few cautious steps back, having seen how much accelerant he'd used. When the flames burned down and fire light was replaced by billows of grey smoke, they took a seat together at the patio table.

Tyler led the conversation. "Actually, that's something I wanted to talk to you about."

Kiara's heart rate picked up. "You mean about leaving?"

"No. I mean, yes, but not in the way you are thinking." The glow of lamplight flickered, shifting in the breeze and casting an ominous shadow over the table. "I'm guessing you've figured out by now that I will be staying with you for as long as needed."

"Actually, I wasn't sure."

"I'm insulted you would think otherwise. Anyway, there are a few things I need to take care of back home— two to three days max— and we need to decide how we want to do this."

"You're wanting me to come with you?"

"That would be preferable, but only because I don't like leaving you for that long. Henry has another idea that he called me about this evening." Tyler fidgeted. She knew he was going to say something unpleasant. "You remember that waitress friend of yours? Jennifer?"

"Yes." Kiara wasn't sure where he was going with this.

"Well, Henry talked to her to see if she might be willing to take a part-time job helping out around here. She said yes."

"Babysitting me, you mean?"

"Yeah, I kind of thought you might take that badly. Look, before you shrug it off, just hear me out. Henry thinks it would make our lives much easier, and she would be a good backup in case I had to leave to run errands around town. He says she's an honest person and would keep quiet about us, plus, you like her, Ki. Would it hurt to make friends with someone? Also, she is working her way through college and could use the money."

"Ugh, I hate it when you do that. Now I'll feel guilty if I say no."

"Good, because they are coming over tomorrow so we can all talk about it together."

Kiara's mouth popped open. "You're fricking kidding, right? Oh, my god, how embarrassing. Why? What is there to talk about?"

"She already knows about you Kiara, but she doesn't know everything. Henry thinks it'll give you both a feel for each other. That way, if you feel okay with it, you can tell her yourself. Also," Tyler hesitated, slumping in his seat as if defeated, "I hate to say this, Ki, but with your sleep walking and hallucinations . . . well, it's not just you that needs to decide whether they want to do this."

She understood his meaning. Jennifer needed to decide whether she would be willing to take care of someone so crazy. She was already dreading the meeting.

"Hey, it's going to be fine." Tyler shifted his chair close

and put his arm around her shoulder. "We will see how it goes, okay?"

"Okay."

"Oh," Tyler said, reaching into his pants pocket. "I have something for you."

Maybe it was his tone of voice or maybe it was just the dim lighting, but she sensed he was suddenly nervous. He pulled something out of his pocket and looked around. "Hold on just a sec. It's too dark out here."

Tyler stood and stepped inside the house. After a moment, a few of the lights blinked on, illuminating the space where they sat. He came back out and pulled his chair in front of hers.

"I got you a gift." He twirled what looked like a small, grey square around in his hands. "Had it for a while and was saving it for . . . you know, a holiday or something, but I figured now's as good a time as any."

Kiara, curious to see what was causing him so much anxiety, held out her hand but he continued to hold on to the gift.

"Okay, what is it?"

Tyler looked down at the box and slowly handed it over. "Here."

It was a jewelry box, small, covered in a dark velvet. Flipping it around in her hand, she used her nail to feel where the front was and snapped it open. At first it confused her. Why was she was staring at what looked to be a very expensive ring? As her eyes took in the detail, she realized what he had done. She pulled the ring out of its sheath and let the box fall to the ground. Several years back, Tyler had taken her on a trip to the falls and they had visited a flea market there. It was one of the best times of her life. While walking by a booth, *this* ring caught her eye. They designed the entire concept of the ring after a tree. One side was a strong trunk with clear jewels but as it wrapped around, the limbs died and blackened, the jewels turning red and black. The design was significant; she saw her life reflected in a fake, cheap piece of jewelry. This, though . . . this was not cheap, nor fake.

"Oh my god. How? Where did you find this?"

"I went back and bought it. I had some modifications made though. Do you like it?"

Kiara was breathless. "It's beautiful. How much did this cost you, Tyler?"

"A bit."

"More or less than my house?" she teased.

"About as much, honestly."

Kiara laughed, but he didn't join her. The smile dropped off her face. "Please tell me you're kidding?"

Tyler opened his mouth but shut it again, looking uncomfortable. The light caught the inside band on the ring and she saw the inscription in it.

*I'll Always Be There.*

The wheels began to turn in her head.

*There's something more here that I'm not seeing.*

"Please don't be upset about the money, Ki. I have plenty."

"Why are you nervous?" Kiara asked.

"Because it's an expensive gift, and I wasn't sure how you would take it."

Not believing him, she continued to stare until he became uncomfortable. "Fine, I originally decided to have it made as sort of a joke, just in case you said yes one of these times I asked you to marry me. I thought it would be funny, but then I felt it would be cheap and disrespectful to give you something like that. I don't know, it's just that one thing led to another, and it ended up being the ring you have now. It seemed inappropriate to give it to you as a joke."

"So, what you're saying is this is an engagement ring?"

"It's just a gift, Ki."

Kiara ran her fingers over the delicate jewels, thinking. She wasn't an idiot, she knew things were changing between them. She'd be a fool to deny it after their shower, after what he said the other night, but it had never occurred to her that he might want more.

Without taking her eyes off the ring she whispered, "You said it was hard, that we weren't quite lovers, weren't quite friends. What did you mean by that?"

Tyler slouched in the chair. "I was messed up the other night. If you don't want the ring, I understand."

"That's not what I asked. You're avoiding the question. I'm asking you if you *want* us to be more than friends."

He exhaled sharply and shut his eyes. Seconds passed, maybe minutes. Finally, he opened them and whispered, "Yes."

She looked down at the ring, heart galloping in her chest. A new world was opened to her, one that was terrifying and amazing at the same time. A large part of her wanted to run, to get away from him as fast as she could, away from what she was feeling. Tyler must have sensed it because he leaned back, giving her room. She glanced up, saw his face, and another thought, a stronger one, entered her mind.

*He's mine.*

Those two little words changed everything.

"Do you think it will fit?"

"What?"

"The ring?" Kiara handed it to him and held her hand out, waiting. "Let's see if it fits."

Tyler paused, but then leaned down and shakily slid

the ring on her finger. She flexed her hands, allowing it to catch the light, admiring it.

"It fits perfect. Thank you." Kiara stood up and stretched. Tyler was gaping at her. "So, are we going to get the steaks started or are you going to let me starve?"

"I, um . . . yeah. I'll grab them now."

The rest of the night went on as planned. They ate and drank, talked and laughed. On occasion, Tyler would touch her arm or place a hand on her leg, doing little things to remind her they could be something more when she was ready.

23

yler stretched over the back of the chair and shut his eyes, working his neck side to side to remove the stiffness. After sitting at the computer for several hours going through emails and accounts, he felt sore from the middle of his back up.

*How the hell does Kiara do this all day?*

Thinking of her made him smile. Last night, she'd given him a glimmer of hope when she kept the ring. This morning, though, she'd surprised him. He was standing at the stove, cooking omelets, when she came up behind him and placed her arms around his waist. She commented on how good the food smelled, keeping her arms around him the whole time they were talking. Later, when he told her he needed to plan his trip, she'd kissed him on the cheek before leaving the room. Henry's words came back to him, *"Do the little things, see how she reacts."*

Right now, he was damn near giddy with the way she was reacting.

Tyler pushed his heels against the floor and rolled the

161

chair backward toward the library door. He glanced down the hallway in both directions but didn't see or hear Kiara.

He stood and kicked the chair back toward the desk, cringing when it went too far and hit the wall on the opposite side of the room. *Shit.* He stared at the chair for a minute, feeling taunted by it. Giving the offending chair one last glance, he turned down the hall in search of Kiara. Her laptop was sitting on the edge of the coffee table, close to the fireplace, but she was nowhere in sight. Tyler walked around the couch and picked up the laptop, moving it away from the heat. Given the fact he'd set the alarms before checking his emails, he wasn't *too* worried about where she was. He was considering installing a camera system, but worried it would offend her. It would give him peace of mind to see what she was doing, though. Hearing her voice gave him some relief and he worked on his speech to convince her it was a good idea as he made his way to the kitchen.

Kiara was sitting Indian style on the floor. It was odd seeing her there, but he wasn't concerned, not yet at least. As a matter of fact, she seemed serene, calm. She reached out and cupped her hands in front of her as if holding something he couldn't see. Her lips curled in to a smile.

"What are you doing, Ki?"

"Hush." She swept one hand around in a caressing motion, as if she was petting something. It was so realistic, he shivered.

He tried questioning her again. "What are you holding?"

"Hush," she ordered. "You need to leave. I can't listen well with you here."

The brush off was final and abrupt. He took a few breaths and walked toward her. She didn't acknowledge his presence, but he noticed she let out a frustrated breath when he sat down. Her eyes were closed. Maybe she really was asleep. If so, this would be the first time she'd interacted with him during one of her fugues. He was curious about what she might say. "So, what are we listening to?"

"Them." She nodded to the space in front of her.

*Creepy.*

Her nostrils flared and she frowned.

"What are they?"

"Takers."

Tyler shivered. "And what do they take?"

"Us."

"What do you mean?"

She removed her hands and opened her eyes. The way she looked at him reminded him of the first time he saw her.

*"Are you real?"*

"I've told you already. Many times. You refuse to listen."

As confusing as the conversation was, Tyler knew he needed to stay. "I'm listening now. Can you tell me one more time?"

She opened her mouth to speak. The overhead light appeared to glow with a greater intensity and he had to shut his eyes against the glare. By the time he opened them again, her mouth was shut again and she was facing away.

"Ki, are you going to tell me?"

"I just did. No more questions."

Her hands moved in the air, following the same terrifying motion as before. Even knowing it wasn't real, a nagging doubt hung in the back of his mind. Chill bumps raised on his arms.

"I don't like this at all, Ki. I want you to move away from it."

She ignored him. He reached out to shake her.

"Don't touch me."

"Ki, you're sleep walking again. I need to wake you."

"If you touch me, I can't promise I won't hurt you."

"Go ahead then, maybe that will wake you up."

Another sigh, more impatient. "Leave, now. I don't have much time."

"Okay, that's it." He tried to grab her by the shoulders, intent on shaking her awake but she was quicker. Lashing out, she grasped him by the wrists and opened her eyes, piercing him with a hateful glare. She twisted and pain shot up both of his arms. Tyler yelled, his vision going dark around the edges. Finally, she released him. "Go. I don't have time for this."

He scrambled backward while Kiara turned back to whatever she thought she had been talking to, ignoring his existence. For a split second, she seemed like a stranger to him. It wasn't because of what she did or even the way she was acting, it was the *sense* of her that was different. There was an acute awareness, a subconscious knowing he always had whenever she was near. In that second, he felt empty, drained of her.

He stood, cautiously approaching. She turned. Their eyes met, and the floor shook, causing him to lose his footing and fall forward. Two of the cabinet drawers slammed open and knives of all sizes flew out, piercing the floor between them. She raised her eyebrows.

His throat tightened, making it hard to breath. He backed toward the entryway and stood. No matter how many excuses he made to himself—earthquake, coincidence— he knew she had caused this.

Too afraid to be with her, and too afraid to leave her alone, he stayed in the doorway, watching. Kiara glanced at him one last time before turning away. For the next ten minutes, he neither moved nor spoke as she continued to pay attention to a creature that did not exist.

Then, she stood and came toward him. When she passed by, she didn't stop. He heard the door to her bedroom shut.

## 24

Kiara barely registered crossing from her room into the quiet hallway, partially because she was lost in thought, but also because she wasn't sure what she was doing there in the first place. She had come up with a solution for the next part of her story and was working it out in her head as she made her way through the house. Excited, she searched out Tyler to discuss her idea but a quick glance in the library let her know he wasn't there.

A noise from the direction of the den caught her attention and she smiled. The sound of Tyler anywhere near the vicinity of the kitchen always cheered her up. She turned the corner and saw him kneeling, picking something up. He didn't seem aware of her presence as she approached.

"So when did we decide to rearrange my utensils?"

His head snapped up and he stumbled backward, losing his balance. She thrust her arm out to steady him, but he flinched away from it and fell, his left elbow colliding with the tile floor. The term 'deer in headlights' did not adequately describe his expression but it was the first thing that popped into her head.

She held out her hand to help him up. "Sorry, I didn't mean to startle you." He stared at it, apprehensive. "Tyler, what's going on?"

He didn't answer her question but took her hand instead. She tugged him up, eyes on his face. Something was wrong, *bad* wrong. The whole event in the kitchen lasted less than a minute but every second of it was engrained in her mind; his fear, his apprehension, and the way he was looking at her like she was something out of a nightmare. Pulling his hand away, he crossed his arms over his chest and his eyes flickered toward the door. It didn't take a psychologist to pick up on the body language he was sending.

*He wants to leave. Why? What did I do?*

His lips were in a tight line and he was clinching his jaw. Her bottom lip trembled, and she bit it, holding it still between her teeth while fighting an alarming fear. His eyes softened and he gave her a small smile, but she could tell he was struggling to even do that much. Tyler leaned over and began picking up the remaining knives as if nothing happened. "Thanks."

Feeling awkward, Kiara joined him and gathered as many as she could to help. "So, what happened?"

"I, uh, pulled the drawer out too far." He turned and looked at her. "You don't have to do that. I'll get them."

"I don't mind." She walked over and brushed against him as she placed the last of the knives in the drawer. She could have sworn he shivered. He took a step back and leaned against the sink.

"So, how's the story going?" He crossed over his chest and seemed to study her shoes.

"It's, um, going well. Tyler, what is—"

"I'm going to go into town to get some things we're running low on." He stepped around her, grabbing a set of keys off of the counter. "I'll take the rental in case you need the SUV for something."

*He doesn't want me to go with him?*

Her anxiety began to rise. He had barely left her side since he got here, and now, he couldn't get away from her fast enough.

She bit her lip. "Do you want me to go?"

"No, you can stay here, get some more writing done. I'll be back in a couple of hours." He gave her another tight smile before brushing past her on his way to the garage door.

"Will you?" she called after him, unable to help herself, trying not to cry.

"Will I what?"

"Will you be back?" She heard fear in the high-pitched tone of her voice and she wiped at her eyes, embarrassed.

Tyler stopped and turned around, the keys dangling from his right hand. His eyes met hers and confirmed her fears. He wanted to leave. And although she knew he was trying to hide it, he could no longer pretend she hadn't picked up on what he was thinking. Kiara couldn't stand to look at his face, to see the knowledge there, so she dropped her eyes down to the keys which became a silver blur as tears gathered.

He raked his hands through his hair and sighed. "I'll be back, okay? I'm just going to go get a few things."

He walked away quickly before she could say anything else, and she heard the door slam shut behind him. For a short while, she just stood there, shocked. He had seen her tears, her fear, but had walked out anyway.

She waited for five minutes, thinking he might still be sitting in the garage and would come back in, but the minutes ticked by and she was still alone. Kiara walked to the garage door and opened it. The rental was gone. Panicking, she ran back in the house and went to his room, pulling drawers open. His clothes were still there, so was his bag and his laptop.

*Am I just being crazy?*

She had been sure he was leaving her, wasn't coming back, but why? Yesterday and this morning they had been closer than ever before. She thought he was as excited about it as she was. Just now in the kitchen, though, he looked like he couldn't stand being around her.

*Am I being oversensitive?* She shook her head. *No, he all but admitted to it.*

Frustrated and still scared, she went to the living room and stared out the front window at the driveway, hoping to see his car. Wishing she could do something, *anything* to make sure he stayed, she picked up her phone and stared at it, not knowing what she could say to fix this.

An idea began to form in her head, one that she had been tossing back and forth for a while, undecided. On impulse, she decided and go with it. She typed what she wanted into her phone's search bar and found what she needed. There was a location twenty miles away in Louisville. She dialed the number and a sweet lady answered the phone. As she spoke, her eyes wandered to the laptop sitting on the coffee table.

She thanked the woman and hung up, staring at the computer. Peeking at the wall clock, she saw that it was now one fifteen in the afternoon. She started writing at eleven this morning, except she had no recollection of doing it.

Two hours scoured from her memory, two hours in which she had planned on working on the new idea she had for her story, the same one she was having when she walked out of her room and found Tyler. The last thing she remembered was pacing around thinking about it.

*For two hours? If I wasn't writing, what was I doing?*

*The knives . . .*

*Did I try to hurt myself? Worse, did I try to hurt him?*

Her phone buzzed in her hand and she shakily held it up to her face. There was a text from Tyler. *Please text me occasionally, so I know you're okay. I'll be back in a bit.*

He wouldn't text if he didn't care. She calmed down a bit. Grabbing her keys, she started toward the garage, glancing at the blank computer screen on the way by.

*Maybe he should leave me.*

25

*re you okay?* Tyler pressed send on the phone.

He hated himself for leaving, for thinking about not coming back, and even worse, for the fact that she knew all of it. He shut his eyes and saw her standing there, tears running down her cheeks while all he could think about was getting away.

*I'm a complete piece of shit.*

He was three miles out from her house when he had pulled over to the side of the road, breaking down, shaking and crying. He was scared, worried that he couldn't take care of her, worried that she was getting worse and he might lose her for good, and he couldn't lie— he was a little scared of *her*, too. Scared of a five-foot-four, hundred pound girl.

He glanced down at his wrist. She shouldn't have been strong enough to do that. He suspected a small fracture, but a doctor was out of the question because he was worried they might have some difficult questions about it.

*What about the knives, Tyler? You didn't forget about those, did you?*

"It's not possible," he mumbled under his breath. "She couldn't . . . it was a freak accident, that's all."

After ten minutes, he turned the ignition and veered onto the blacktop.

*I just needed to get away for a bit, get my emotions under control.*

He hoped it was enough to last him for a while because he couldn't afford to leave her alone again.

By the time he pulled up to the electronics store he was beginning to panic. She hadn't responded to his text. She might be hurt, either physically or emotionally. He put the car in reverse and started to back out to go back when she responded.

*"I'm okay."*

A noise escaped his chest and caught him off guard. Apparently, he wasn't as in control of his emotions as he thought. He typed in *thanks*, but hesitated before sending it, adding *I love you* at the last second. She responded immediately, *"I love you too."*

*I will never, ever think about leaving her again.* He stepped out of the car.

Since he was going to stay, he needed to be prepared.

He decided to not park in the garage, but at the front instead so he could sneak in his purchases later without having to carry them across the whole house. He grabbed the few bags of groceries he bought and unlocked the door. "Ki?"

He walked over to the dining room table and set the bags down. "Hey, where are you?"

No answer.

*What if something happened? Because I wasn't here?*

He walked quickly, taking a glance in the kitchen and

into the storage room, finding them both empty. Panic coursed through him and he ran outside and glanced off the patio. He was so convinced he would see her broken body down below that, for a brief second, he did. His heart stopped and his legs shook, starting to collapse under him before he realized it was just an oddly shaped bush.

He raced back into the house and checked room by room. Standing in her room, he pulled out his phone, his hands shaking so bad he could barely type. *"Where are you?"*

He waited two minutes. She didn't text back. He hit the call button, listened as the phone rang five times and then rolled over to voice mail. Would she have left? He started toward the garage but heard a noise.

A minute passed, maybe two, and he decided the noise had been a figment of his imagination. Then he heard it again. It was muffled sounding, airy almost, like a gasp, and it seemed to be coming from somewhere in the room.

The bottoms of his blue jeans chafed against the wood, but the rest of the house was silent. It came again, this time a little louder. From behind him.

He turned and stopped when he was halfway between the closet and the bed, straining to listen. The noise was louder there, more rhythmic. Like heavy breathing. He walked a few steps closer to the bed and knelt, laid his ear against the wood. His arms were shaking; he could barely hold himself up. The blanket was draped over the bottom of the mattress leaving only half an inch of area for him to look under, just enough to block his view.

The conversation from this morning replayed in his head.

*"What are they?"*

*"Takers."*

He knelt again and lifted the edge of the cover. He froze.

Kiara's black hair lay across her face in a wet tangled mess, her eyes bloodshot.

"Ki," he whispered.

Turned on her side, facing him, she lifted a trembling finger to her lips. Her face was wet with some sort of pinkish gel.

From quivering lips, she uttered, "Must . . . ascend."

A chime blared. An electronic voice announced, "Garage door open."

Heart pounding, he reached for her. There was someone else in the house.

His fingers were mere centimeters from hers when he heard Kiara yell from the living room, "Tyler? I'm sorry I missed your call."

He jerked, turning his head in that direction. When he looked back under the bed, he was alone in the room.

Kiara set her purse down and glanced nervously toward the garage. She knew Tyler was back because she saw the rental, but she was still a little unsure whether she would find him packing his bags. She didn't have to wonder long because he burst into the dining room before she got the chance to look for him.

"Where the hell have you been?" Tyler asked. His eyes were wide and beads of sweat covered his forehead.

"I just . . . I went out for a bit."

"Why didn't you tell me? At least call and let me know? Do you know what it felt like to come home and not be able to find you? I've been running around in a panic. You couldn't even answer your phone when I called?"

"I thought I would be back before you."

"You thought wrong. You're not even supposed to be driving."

"You left the keys. In case I needed them, remember?"

"I meant in an emergency. Fuck, Ki, you could have fallen asleep behind the wheel. You know better, or else you wouldn't have snuck out thinking you would be back before me."

"You know what? You're right. I didn't think you would be back before me because I wasn't even sure you were coming back." He opened his mouth to argue, but she cut him off. "I wouldn't even blame you if you did. I know I was sleep walking again. I figured it out after you left and whatever I did I'm sorry, but you could at least have the decency to tell me why you're leaving."

Her comment must have hit the mark because his angry glare became an apologetic frown and he reached out to her. She held her hand up.

"Please, let me finish. Look, I didn't mean to scare you. You've never asked me to check in before and tell you what I was doing so how was I supposed to know? I didn't want to tell you what I was doing because it was a surprise, okay? And I couldn't answer my phone because I had my hands full."

Tyler let out a deep breath, his anger fully diminished. She felt stupid for losing her temper especially since the whole point of her leaving was to do something special for him. "Tyler—"

"No, don't. I shouldn't have flipped out on you." He shook his head. "I felt guilty for leaving you alone, so when I came home, I panicked instead of dealing with it calmly. I didn't even think to check the garage until just a second ago." He closed the space between them and wrapped his arms around her. "I'm just glad you're here."

"Me too." She leaned back and looked up at him. "Can we talk this out? Be honest with each other?"

"I'd like to." He let her go but didn't step away. "How about I make some drinks and snacks and we sit down and really talk?"

"Um . . . actually, there's something I need to show you first." She smiled, excited and nervous at the same time.

"Okay. What is it?"

"It's a surprise. Can you sit? Here on the floor and I'll be right back."

"On the floor?" A look of concern swept across his face but it was gone so quickly she wasn't sure if it was ever there in the first place.

She nodded.

"Okay, on the floor it is." He sat down and crossed his legs.

She waited until he looked completely settled before she ran out to the garage and grabbed her surprise. Kiara ran back in carrying the bundle in a blanket. Tyler raised his eyebrows. She leaned down and let the wiggling, excited puppy loose. Immediately, he jumped up on Tyler and licked him.

"You got a puppy." The childlike expression on his face made her giggle.

"Yeah, I know you wanted one, and you said you wouldn't be able to have one because you travel so much but I thought you could just keep it here if you leave." She was rambling and knew it.

"Ki, you hate dogs." He laughed, scratching its exposed belly. She sat down in front of him and the black and grey puppy twitched excitedly.

"But I like this one. He's cute."

"You have told me time and time again how messy they are. I'm not going to ask you to take care of a puppy for me."

"There's a no return policy on this pup, so you're just going to have to get over that."

Tyler smiled. "Is he a blue heeler?"

"Yeah, the lady gave me some paperwork on him. Said

he's pure bred. There were others, but I liked that he has one blue eye and one green eye because it matches us." She furrowed her brow. "Now that I think about it, that's kind of creepy of me."

Tyler laughed. "No, I love it. Does he have a name?"

"Pigmy."

"Pigmy? Did you name him that?"

"No, he came that way. She said he was young enough that we could change it if we wanted, but I don't know. It grew on me on the way home."

Tyler smiled at her. "Pigmy it is then. Thank you. This is the best, Ki."

Without warning, he leaned forward to kiss her on the lips. She wasn't prepared for it, nor was she prepared when Pigmy decided to join into the fun by running in between them and licking her on the mouth.

"Oh, god, no." She pushed the offensive puppy away and wiped her mouth. "Fricking nasty!"

Tyler was still laughing as she raced to the bathroom to wash her face.

27

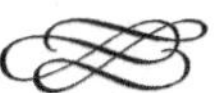

The doorbell chimed and Tyler left to answer it. Kiara braced her hands on the counter to keep them from trembling. Dinner with guests was the last thing she wanted. She'd argued with Tyler. Told him they couldn't drag Jennifer and Henry into this mess. By this *mess*, she meant herself.

Tyler told her about the knives and the creatures.

*Takers.*

The name still gave her chills.

Tyler argued that Jennifer needed the money and it wouldn't hurt to let her do *some* things around the house. He'd left the words *"as long as she's not alone with you"* out, but they still hung in the air.

Voices drifted out of the dining room. It was time. Pigmy danced under her feet and she smiled at the puppy. "I know, I'm nervous too. Better get this over with though."

She smiled and greeted their guests as she entered the dining room. Pigmy decided he needed to introduce himself to Jennifer by bouncing underneath her feet and wagging his tail. With a squeal of delight, Jennifer picked

179

him up. Kiara studied her; tall and slender, tan, with chocolate hair pulled back into a ponytail. Cat-shaped eyes that widened with surprise when Pigmy licked her nose. Once upon a time, these were the kind of friends Kiara had. Perfect. Carefree. Now they were the type she avoided.

Henry must have sensed her hesitation because he patted her arm. "She's a good person, Ki. Smart and humble. Give her a chance."

Kiara straightened her shoulders and took a deep breath as she approached Jennifer.

"Oh my gosh, he's just adorable, Kiara." She spun the over-excited puppy around in her arms. "How old is he? When did you get him? What's his name?"

"His name is Pigmy, and we got him today. He's three months old."

Jennifer put the puppy down and he rolled over for a belly scratch. "He may be the cutest, chubbiest puppy I have ever seen. I'm going to be in so much trouble when Timmy smells him on me. Totally worth it, though."

"Timmy?" Kiara furrowed her brow. "Oh, that's right. Your cat. I'm so used to you calling him Little Demon that I forgot he had a real name."

Tyler gave her an encouraging smile.

"How is he doing? I'm surprised you didn't bring him with you."

Jennifer laughed. "He's real grumpy about car rides. Makes him super gassy too and I didn't think Henry would appreciate him smelling up the car."

"Ha! You should have brought him. I'd love to hear Henry explain the psychological reasons for a gassy cat."

Henry rolled his eyes. "Speaking of smells, what smells so delicious? Is this Tyler's famous cooking I've heard so much about?"

"It's chicken parmesan, one of Ki's favorites. Thought I'd use it as a tactic to lure Jennifer in to working for us." Tyler winked at Jennifer and left to check on dinner. Jennifer's olive complexion took on a shade of scarlet. There wasn't a single woman in the world immune to Tyler's trademark wink.

Jennifer fanned her heated face with her hands. "Oh my god, I'm so embarrassed. I've never had a movie star wink and me before or cook for me. Please don't be offended."

"No offense taken. Tyler has that effect on all women," Kiara laughed. "It's taken me years to train him not to hump anyone's leg, pee on the floor, or bite."

"Who says I don't bite?" Tyler came out of the kitchen carrying several platters and nipped Kiara on the ear. She yelped and smacked him on the arm.

"Jerk."

"You mean sexy jerk, right?"

"You're sexy until you open that vulgar mouth of yours."

Tyler's gaze dipped to the waistband of her pants before meeting hers, a cocky smile dangling on the corner of his lips. "If you had any idea what this vulgar mouth of mine was capable of, you wouldn't be saying that."

It was Kiara's turn to blush. "Tyler Devin Reed, behave yourself!"

"Yes, ma'am." With a chuckle, he nodded to the patio door. "We thought we could have dinner on the balcony since the weather is so nice. Also, because we decorated it the other day, and it seems like a waste to not use it every chance we get."

Kiara grabbed the salad and bread bowls as everyone filed out. Once the table was set and everyone's plates were made, they began to dig in. The first few bites were so delicious Kiara moaned out loud. A quick glance around the table let her know she wasn't the only one in food heaven. Everyone had equal expressions of ecstasy, everyone but Jennifer. She hadn't touched her food and was staring off into the mountains.

"Do you not like Italian?"

"Oh no, it's great." Jennifer turned away from the mountain view and directed her attention to Kiara. "It's just—I'm sorry, I know it's rude to say, but you're like really rich and this place, the mountains . . . everything is so beautiful. You and Tyler are super nice and not snobby at all." She shook her head. "That's not what I meant. I mean, I knew you weren't, but I just didn't expect it to be so *normal.*"

Kiara and Tyler glanced at each other and burst out laughing.

"I'll take that as a compliment, although you'll find that we're anything but normal lately," Kiara said.

Jennifer nodded. "I feel like such a child, that's all. I grew up very poor, but I never thought I would act like such a fool the first time I got invited to a famous person's house."

"If you didn't feel a little weirded out, we wouldn't trust you and you wouldn't be here. Please don't hesitate to act like yourself, and you can ask us anything you want," Tyler said.

Jennifer nodded and picked up her fork. For the next fifteen minutes, the conversation revolved about how wonderful the food was. Henry suggested Tyler open a restaurant in town and give up the acting business altogether. Kiara didn't think that was such a bad idea. When Tyler walked around and refilled everyone's wine glasses, Henry chided her about drinking on her medication.

Kiara stuck her tongue out but pushed the glass away. "So, Jennifer, what are you going to school for?"

"I'm finishing up my associates right now. I plan on attending Veterinary School, but I should save up enough money first. I'd like to do it without having to pay back student loans."

"Wow, that's awesome. I honestly had you pegged as a dancer or something like that."

Jennifer smiled, but it didn't reach her eyes. "I probably would have been. When my mom and I lived in New York we didn't have much, but she scraped up enough to send me to ballet class. I loved it and was the top student."

"What made you change your mind?"

"When I was eleven, my mom and I were in a car wreck. A hit and run. It crushed my leg and they had to reconstruct the bones. My mom died instantly, and I will have a limp for the rest of my life."

"I'm so sorry." Kiara wished she could take away the pain she saw on Jennifer's face.

"Don't be. It was a long time ago." Jennifer took a drink of her wine. "Anyway, I was shipped off to live with my dad out here. He was a mean and abusive drunk, so I spent a lot of time outdoors with the animals and I found a new passion there. Since no one would allow their kids over to my house, I had very few friends and a lot of spare time. I started reading up on veterinary care. By the time I was sixteen, I'd had enough of my dad, so I lied about my age, got a job, and moved out. He didn't miss me at all. A year later he had a heart attack and died."

Kiara shook her head. "I owe you an apology, Jennifer. I had no idea your life was so hard. Sometimes I get so wrapped up in myself that I forget other people have difficult lives, too. Because you're so pretty and happy all the time, I just assumed your life was perfect, and that was judgmental of me."

"Oh no, please don't apologize. I find it's best to not let the past eat at you and ruin your future. My mom was always a positive person. I guess it just rubbed off on me."

"Maybe I could learn something from you then." Kiara smiled weakly. "With what's been happening lately, I need a little of your attitude."

"I'd be happy to help, and not for the money either. It's ingrained in me to take care of people and animals. It makes me happy. Please say you'll let me help out?"

Kiara met Tyler's eyes over the table. Letting her help would give them an excuse to help her pay her way through college. She needed to know why she wouldn't be able to do more though. "Henry told you about my illness and about what has been going on lately, right?"

Jennifer nodded.

"Good. There are things you could do to help, such as run errands for us and keep me company here and there. And we will pay you well, but I'm not going to get you involved in something you don't fully understand without telling you the rest."

Henry spoke, "Kiara, I already told her everything."

"No, you haven't. There's been some, um, new developments." She nodded to Tyler. "Can you tell them what happened today?"

"Are you sure?"

"Yes."

For the next several minutes, Tyler explained the events of the day while Kiara drank her wine.

When Tyler finished, Henry shook his head. "You don't really believe she caused the knives to fly out, do you?"

"I don't know what I believe right now."

Henry asked Kiara, "What about you?"

"I don't know either. I mean, I don't believe in stuff like that, but I believe Tyler when he says it happened."

"Tyler, I know you believe what you saw, with the knives and her under the bed, but you're under a lot of stress and that does strange things to the human mind. I can understand why the two of you would be hesitant to have Jennifer alone without both of you present, but you need her now more than ever. This situation can take a lot out of a person and to be brutally honest, you need a break, Tyler."

Kiara blinked. Why hadn't that occurred to her? After the incident earlier today, she could tell he wanted to leave, that he'd needed some space. "He's right."

"What?" Tyler faced her, his mouth hanging open.

"I need you, but I need you to be strong, too, and to do that, you're going to need a break now and then. We need to work something out."

"No, I want to do this. I'm not incapable. I didn't live with an abusive father and not learn to take care of myself. Plus, I like you," Jennifer pleaded, her eyes on Kiara. "We could be really good friends and it's going to be hard to have a girl's night if Tyler follows us around the whole time."

Tyler raked his hand through his hair. "Jennifer, you need to realize what you are asking. Kiara will still be afraid of you touching her, she may sleepwalk and become violent, and hell, she may have a form of telekinesis. This is what you're asking to take on?"

"I can handle this. Please give me a chance."

Tyler met Kiara's gaze.

"Is this what you want, Ki?"

She nodded. "Yes, Henry's right. You'll only be gone for a few days and we'll be fine."

"I'm only twenty minutes away, Tyler. I'll drop everything and come if they need me, I promise," Henry added.

"Okay, if this is what you want." Tyler sighed.

"Alright then, that's settled." Henry clapped Tyler on the back. "I'm going to hit up the restroom."

Jennifer watched Henry leave, her bottom lip tugged between her teeth. When he shut the patio door behind him, she leaned in. "Okay, so I have a quick question. I mentioned it in the car to Henry and he told me not to bring it up, but I can't help but wonder if either of you have considered that these things Kiara's seeing are real?"

Kiara opened her mouth to deny it, but the look on Tyler's face stopped her. "Tyler? You don't? Right?"

"I didn't, but after this morning . . ."

Tyler didn't finish his sentence. He focused on straightening a pile of napkins.

Jennifer broke through the silence. "It's just that sometimes after people have bad things happen to them, they see the world differently. After my mom died, I started seeing things, little visions. I would get a picture in my head of my friends calling and suddenly the phone would ring. I knew things about complete strangers I couldn't have known, stuff like that. It didn't last for long, three months maybe, but it was super freaky. The doctor said I had post-traumatic stress syndrome, but I wonder if what happened caused a part of my brain to wake up, a part we don't usually use. I know I sound stupid, but maybe you can just see something the rest of us can't."

"You don't sound stupid. Pretty rational actually." Kiara shook her head. "But I don't think that's what's going on here."

Tyler and Jennifer shared a quick glance, but Henry came back out and the conversation was dropped.

As it became late, everyone said their goodbyes.

Jennifer practically bounced out the door after agreeing to the amount they wanted to pay her.

Later that night, Kiara took Pigmy to bed and Tyler stayed up. He kissed her on the forehead and left the room.

As she drifted off, Kiara smiled. The last few weeks had been hell, but now things were looking up. She and Tyler didn't have to handle it alone. Maybe everything would be alright after all.

Later, she would look back and realize those were the best weeks of their lives together.

That night, after Tyler was sure Kiara was asleep, he went out to the car and brought in the packages. He set the cameras around the house, except for the one he would put in her bedroom tomorrow, and connected the wi-fi transmission to his laptop. He set up a passcode, making sure Ki couldn't accidently access it. With the computer on the nightstand in his room, he managed the first restful night of sleep in weeks.

As had been habit for the last few nights, Tyler opened his eyes to check the computer screen. So far nothing strange had happened, and he was feeling a little silly. He started to close his eyes again but sat up quickly, scrambling for the headphones. Kiara was standing in the library on screen three. He clicked the feed and zoomed in.

She turned and looked at the camera. The night vision setting made her eyes shine white. Tyler wiped his sweaty palms on his pants.

She couldn't know about the cameras, could she? No, he'd hidden them too well.

A shadow moved across the far wall.

"What the fuck?" he mumbled.

Whatever it was must have been a trick of the light because it was gone. Another movement, something small crawled behind her. Pigmy. Kiara picked up the puppy. She held him in front of her face before cradling him in her arms. She turned and exited the library.

He watched her walk down the hallway and into her room where she set the puppy on the bed. She turned and stared at the camera again and he shivered. There was something odd about the way she was acting. Kiara tugged off her shirt.

*Oh, shit.*

She threw it on the floor and then hooked her thumbs under her shorts and slid them off. Tyler moved to shut down the camera feed. While his hand hovered over the button, Kiara slipped the bra straps off her shoulders and smirked at the camera.

Tyler shut the laptop, his heart racing.

*She can't know.*

After twenty minutes, he opened the laptop again. She was sleeping with Pigmy curled up at her feet. He pressed rewind, scrolling to when he'd seen the shadow. Even zoomed in, he couldn't make out anything.

Tyler shut his eyes and prayed for sleep.

He left the lamp on.

TYLER GRABBED breakfast and went in search of Kiara.

"What are you doing?" Tyler asked, bowl of cereal in hand.

"Googling pictures of you and Photoshopping them holding cuddly teddy bears."

"No, you're not." He glanced at the computer. "Holy crap, you really are. Hey, that one is pretty good. You must have been bored this morning."

Tyler pulled up a chair and sat down beside her.

"Nah, I'm just trying to make a little extra money on the side with my Teddy Bear Tyler website." She grinned at him.

"Too bad somebody already beat you to it. Scoot over for a second." He set his bowl down and typed something in the search bar.

"Oh my god." Kiara turned away from the screen. "Seriously Tyler, you're naked. Close that!"

"I'm not naked, I have a teddy bear. See?" He pointed at the screen.

"That teddy bear is exactly where I'm trying to avoid looking. Now close it." Her face was bright red, making him laugh even harder. He closed the image.

"You are such an ass. How do you even pose for pictures like that?"

"You get used to it after a bit." He picked up his cereal and continued eating.

"You don't get insecurity issues or anything?"

"Nah, they Photoshop out all the bad stuff."

"Oh. Can they Photoshop muscles and stuff in too?"

He dropped his spoon into the bowl. "What are you trying to say, Ki?"

"Nothing." She held her hands in front of her face. "I mean, you have muscles and everything. Just not like that. You're more of the medium to small frame kind of guy."

Tyler gaped at her. "You are evil and hateful, you know that right?"

"I didn't really upset you, did I?"

"No, of course not." He slipped his shoes on and opened the back door.

"Where are you going?"

"To chop some firewood with my small muscles."

THIS TIME he was still awake when she got up. He turned off the lamp so she wouldn't see the light and put on his headphones. At first, she simply paced from room to room with a concerned look on her face, but then she sat down on the couch. Pigmy jumped up beside her and she patted him on the head.

Tyler was nervous about watching her after what happened the other night. The message she was sending was clear. *"I know you're watching."*

So far tonight though, she hadn't shown any signs she noticed the cameras at all. He knew his Kiara didn't know about the cameras. Kiara in a fugue state was different. Maybe it was crazy to think she had some sort of telepathy, but it was the only answer he could come up with.

Kiara sat on the couch for a long time before she stood. She walked to the back of the couch and stopped. A dark mass appeared out of nowhere in front of her.

"Leave." Although her voice sounded firm, her shoulders were tense. The shadow came closer, and she backed into the couch. Pigmy scattered out of sight. "You can't do anything. It's too soon. He's not ready to see."

*Oh, shit.*

Tyler reached up to rip off the headphones, heart thudding in his chest.

"Tyler!"

He looked at the screen. She was shaking her head.

"Don't move." She pointed her finger at the camera. "Stay there."

"No way," he muttered.

Throwing the headphones off, he headed to the door. It wouldn't budge. He checked the lock and pulled again. The bolt was unlocked but the door still wouldn't move.

"Ki!" He screamed her name. No answer. Tyler slammed his body against the door. It still didn't budge. On his third try she spoke from the hallway.

"Go to bed, Tyler."

"Ki? Are you okay? Let me out, please."

"Go to bed." Her footsteps got further away but stopped suddenly. "Tyler?"

"Yes, Ki?"

"Don't leave your room tonight. It's not safe for you."

He ran back to the computer and watched her lay down. After a minute, he got back up to check to door. It was unlocked and opened easily. He wanted to go to her, to demand to know what was going on. Instead, he heeded her warning and stayed in his room for the rest of the night, terrified of every shadow.

Kiara watched from the window as Tyler paced around the edge of the trees, talking on the phone to Jennifer. She didn't want to admit to a pang of jealousy when he took the call outside, but it was there, nonetheless. There was also a part of her that knew Tyler was keeping a secret from her. It had something to do with his *plan*. This secret was probably the reason he was outside on the phone.

Her breath fogged up the window, and she wiped it clean with her hands. Winter was settling in the mountains and Tyler was leaving tomorrow night so he could get back before the weather got bad. Jennifer would stay with her during that time which was a mixed blessing. The offer for Kiara to go with Tyler was still on the table, but the trip by car would take days, and there were too many variables. Being away from him would be hard, though, and she already ached inside at the thought.

It didn't help that things between them seemed stagnate the last few days. He was keeping his distance, physically at least, and she wasn't sure why. Sighing, she turned away from the window. Maybe it was for the best. If things moved too fast, she wasn't sure she could handle it. She enjoyed his touch, enjoyed the way he made her feel, but there was still an underlying fear at the thought of taking it much further.

*This constant push and pull of emotions will be the death of me.*

Kiara rubbed her arms, trying to warm them. It was too early in the season to turn on the heat, leaving the house chilly. Earlier that morning, Tyler turned the electric fireplace on low and she turned away from the window, planning on wrapping herself in a blanket in front of it. She lost her balance, and nearly fell when the room shifted, spinning around her. Her vision blinked in and out. Light and dark, light and dark. With every flash of light, she saw things moving at the edge of darkness. A ripping noise, loud enough to make her head vibrate, came from the floor. The wood appeared to be shedding, like a slick skin. Beneath it, red tissue pulsated.

The door slammed shut behind her and she blinked. The room became normal again. Still shaky, she took a few deep breaths and continued walking, pretending she had not heard Tyler come in. Telling him what she saw would only worry him more.

Tyler spoke from behind her. "Well, that's settled. Jennifer will be here tomorrow afternoon before I leave and she's bringing her cat. I might warn you though, she also mentioned bringing tons of girly slumber party stuff."

"Oh no." Kiara gave a shaky laugh and turned to face him.

"Jesus, Ki. What happened?" She followed his gaze. Her shirt was covered with blood. Tyler stepped over and lifted her chin. "It looks like a nosebleed. Did you fall?"

"No," Kiara said. "I didn't even know I had one."

"Okay, well let's get some pressure on it and get you cleaned up."

She followed him to the bathroom and used tissue to hold her nostrils together while Tyler wiped her off with a rag. When the bleeding stopped, she took the rag and finished cleaning up. Without looking at her, he very calmly stated, "I'm cancelling my trip."

"Tyler, no. It's just a nosebleed."

He pulled the towel off the rack, drying his hands. "Yeah, just a nosebleed."

"You're being ridiculous. People get nose bleeds all the time. It's normal."

Tyler threw the towel in the sink. "Nothing about this is normal. Not the nose bleeds, not the sleep walking, not the hallucinations. How the fuck can you sit there and tell me it's okay? I watched knives fly out of the cabinets by themselves! It's not fucking okay. There is nothing normal about what is happening."

He covered his mouth as if trying to stop the words.

Kiara was too startled to react to his outburst. He let his hands drop to the side. "I'm sorry, Ki. I didn't mean to yell. I'm just so scared of losing you."

"You're not going to. Please, don't do this to yourself. You're under so much stress you're seeing everything as a sign of the apocalypse. You not only have to go on this trip, you *need* to. I will miss you, hell, I already do, but I'll be fine."

He let out a deep breath. "You're right. Of course, it's going to be fine."

"Good, cause for our last night together, we're going to lie in bed all night and have a Tyler Reed movie marathon." She grinned at him.

"The hell we are. I don't love you that much."

"Where are you going?" Tyler blinked, and sat up in bed. They'd stayed up half the night and watched movies, none which he starred in. Before falling asleep, she'd curled up to his side. For the first time in a long while, she slept peacefully.

"Out to do some yard work." Kiara stepped out of from behind the closet door, still pulling down the cotton dress she'd just slipped on.

"In a dress?"

"Yep."

"Do you own a sunhat and some lacy gloves to go with that?"

"Of course." She smiled, reached in the closet, and pulled out a hat.

"Why in the world would you go do lawn work dressed like that?"

"I always liked the idea of it. Like in the movies where they're gardening in dresses and wearing hats. Something about it is feminine. It makes me feel sexy." She twirled around and winked.

"So, wearing a dress and playing in the dirt makes you feel sexy? Wow, I never thought you were messed up until now."

She refrained from commenting until she was nearly to the door. "Maybe so. All I know is that it makes me feel good. I'm sure it doesn't hurt that I'm not wearing panties, though."

"Jesus, Ki."

She laughed as she headed out the door.

About an hour later, Tyler joined her outside and sat on the bench. "I brought you a coke."

She dropped the hose on the ground and sat beside him, taking a sip of the cool soda. The sun was heavy in the sky, blanketed by a wasp of sonorous purple clouds. She watched as they obscured the sun again, leaving the white-capped mountains in the distance partially veiled by shadows.

"You might want to turn the water off. You're creating a lake over there."

Kiara glanced at the shiny green hose whose mouth was now completely under a large pool of water and shrugged. "Nah, I would just have to turn it back on in a minute when I watered the other side."

"Hey, it's your yard. What do you want to do today?"

Kiara twisted around to face him. The circles under his eyes were so perfectly outlined she could trace asem with her fingertips. His normally spiked hair was lying across his forehead and his well-maintained five o'clock shadow was scraggly.

"You're gawking again. This is becoming a problem, Ki."

She knew why he looked that way. He was trying to hide it, but the stress was getting to him. An apology sat on her lips, but she decided against it. What good would it do either of them? He would just brush it off.

"Like I said before, you're nice to look at."

"Is that so?" He asked, his voice silky and suggestive. "I could say the same thing about you."

*Ah, he's playing the game.*

Her mood improved a bit. Maybe they could forget about all the stress for a while and just have fun today.

"Do you see anything you like?" She let her voice drop until it became sultry.

She knew the game was stupid and weird. She'd be mortified if anyone found out they played it. In retrospect, she wasn't even sure why they'd started playing it. He would always embarrass her by making sexual innuendos, which she knew was his way of teasing her, until one day, she made one back. Somehow, that lead to them playing *the game*. They would do this back and forth until one of them got embarrassed and quit. Kiara always lost.

His face broadened into a grin. The circles around his eyes seemed smaller, compressed by smile lines as he chuckled.

"I thought we were playing the game. Did you give up already?" She teased.

"Oh, no. I'm all game." He bit his lip and smiled coyly, the kind of smile that brought out dimples and crinkled the corner of his eyes. "I see lots of things I like. How about we find out if you're honest about not wearing panties?"

"Do you really want to know?" She let her thighs open a bit for the soft material of the skirt to slide between them. A small look of surprise covered his face, but he reined it in quickly. The game was mostly words. Occasionally, he might pose or make a lewd gesture, but it never went this far. Today, she was going to break that perfectly composed mask he'd spent years of acting to prefect.

"Actually, it's not the panties I'm interested in."

"Then what is it you're interested in?"

"What's underneath." His gaze slid up the length of her legs, lingering on the thin material folded between her thighs, before it lazily crept up until it reached her chest.

Tyler licked his lips. Kiara swallowed. Her nipples grew taught. Tyler's eyes might as well have been his hands from the reaction they had on her. The old Kiara would have quit and admitted loss by now. The new Kiara wasn't going to back down.

She set her glass of coke down so he couldn't see how bad she was shaking. "Hmmm . . . and what would you do once you saw what's underneath?"

He inhaled a sharp breath, his eyes briefly flashing to her face. Her heart galloped and she cowered beneath his stare. The temperature outside seemed to rise several degrees. His eyes were dark, hungry. It was as if he wanted to devour her. In all their years together, he'd never once looked at her like that. Had he, she would have been terrified. Now she never wanted him to stop.

"What would you want me to do?" Tyler cocked his head to the side.

Kiara struggled to find her voice. She was hyperaware of the ache spreading from the center of her stomach to her toes. Her mind was blank. She couldn't think of an answer.

Tyler leaned forward. "I mean, of course, if I wasn't such a gentleman, as you put it the other night."

He'd managed a deadpan expression. There was no longer any evidence of the desire she'd seen. There was no way he could have missed how it affected her. Hell, she was practically panting. Now he wanted to pretend he was just paying the game? Like he didn't look at her like she was his last meal?

"Just fold, Ki."

*Just fold?* Just pretend her best friend didn't want her? That he didn't know he could arouse her so easily? She knew he wanted more but up until the moment he'd looked at her that way, she'd never truly been able to decide if she could take it to a physical level.

Tyler raked his hands through his hair, frustration crinkling the corners of his eyes. "Hey, I didn't mean to upset you. Let's just cool it a bit."

"Do you remember when we were in the shower?"

Tyler nodded slowly. "It's not something easily forgotten."

She took a deep breath, the words stumbling out of her mouth. "When we were in the shower, I wanted you to touch me. I wanted you to slide your hands all over me, press yourself against me. I wanted to feel your mouth against mine, to have you kiss away all the memories of what he did to me. I wanted——"

"Stop. Please, just stop." Tyler let out a shaky breath and cupped his face between his hands.

She sat quietly on the bench and blinked back tears. A line had been crossed, one which would be impossible to forget. Worse, she'd been the one to cross it. The game was a part of their friendship. It was fun. It wasn't going to be that way anymore. Fear and sadness gripped her chest. There was stability in their friendship. This, whatever it was, was not stable. Quite the opposite. She stared into the bloated sky. When they were in the shower, she had wanted those things. At the time, though, she wasn't sure if it was because she was unstable when it came to physical contact. Now, she knew the truth. So did he.

"Hey." Tyler reached out and took her hands in his.

"I'm sorry. I shouldn't have reacted like that. Remember our promise to take things as they come? Let's do that instead of over thinking. Things have been hard and stressful enough, and we don't need to let that get between us, okay?"

She let out a deep breath. He was right. It was time to stop analyzing everything.

"I guess I won the game."

"I didn't even know you knew phrases like that."

Needing some space, she stood and picked up the water hose. It had created a miniature lake in her absence. "I own the *Dictionary of Lewd Phrases*. It's a must have for any writer."

"That's cheating," he complained.

"We never set any rules that I can recall," she countered.

"They were unspoken."

"You're just a sore loser."

He smiled at her, and her body responded in an inappropriate manner. Needing to do something, anything, to get her mind off her hormones, Kiara sprayed him with the hose.

He gasped and stood quickly; his shirt drenched. "You did not just do that."

"The hell I didn't," she laughed.

His smile hardened, and she saw the intent in his eyes before he stepped toward her.

"Uh-uh, stay back." Pointing the hose at him, she backed up a few steps. A wet pool of dirt coated her sandals.

"And why would I do that?" He approached with calculated confidence. "You see, I'm already wet, so your threat doesn't bother me."

Tyler was three feet away, but she knew he could grab

the hose when he was within an arm's length. She called his bluff and stuck her thumb across the end of the opening, spraying him with water again. A backlash of wet droplets hit her in the face, and she wiped at her eyes with her other arm. Backing up blindly, she tried to give herself enough space before he attacked.

He was too quick. He grasped the hose and pulled.

"You are so going to get it now." Having the height advantage, Tyler twisted the hose in her direction. Water poured down the front of her chest, the sudden cold shocking her.

"No," she giggled, "stop. That's freezing."

"Yeah, I know." He pushed the hose forward. She grabbed it underneath his hands and tried to pinch it shut, slowing the flow of water.

"Oh, no you don't." He reached for her hand and she pushed the hose backward, spraying him directly in the face. He sputtered and moved it off to the side. Trickles of water ran down his face. His light brown hair was plastered to his forehead, but his lips were curved into a smug smile. She tackled him. Grabbing the hose, she slipped back down to the ground. Her foot landed in the mud; the hose tangled around it. Before she could try to get untangled, Tyler pulled it away. There was a rush of air before she hit the ground.

Everything seemed to vibrate, and a shrill ringing filled her ears. Pain shot from the center of her spine through her arms and legs. She was vaguely aware of Tyler's voice, but when she tried to speak, the words seemed stuck behind a vacuum. As quickly as it had happened, the world rushed back in. The sound of running water and birds became painfully loud for a split second. She became aware of the cold, sticky mud, underneath her backside. Tyler's face was above hers.

"Ki, where are you hurt? Don't move, okay?" Holding the side of her face with one hand, mud from his thumb rubbing against her cheek, he reached into his pocket and pulled out his phone.

She forced herself to speak, surprised by how rough and weak she sounded. "No, no, don't call anyone. I'm fine."

"Are you sure? Where all do you hurt? Oh god, Ki, I think you got knocked out." His hands were trembling.

"It's okay." She laid her hand over his, trying to calm him. "I just got the air knocked out of me for a second. My ass took most of the impact and it might hurt to sit for a while, but I'm fine."

He took a deep breath and covered his face with his free hand. She took the opportunity to try to move, hoping she wasn't lying to him. Her shoulders ached, and her lower back and rear would certainly be bruised, but they moved without any difficulty.

He opened his eyes.

"Okay, let's make sure first. Can you move your head side to side?" She rotated her neck to the left and right to show him she was okay. Halfway through, she got the giggles.

"What's wrong?"

The panic in his voice made her laugh even harder. Tears ran down her face. She knew her reaction was irrational, but she couldn't control it. "It's my ass."

She squeezed the words out through giggles. Her voice was high pitched, girly, and that made her laugh even harder. If Tyler looked unsure earlier, he looked positively afraid now.

"I really didn't," she squeezed her eyes shut, trying to stop, "wear panties and now my ass . . . is . . . stuck . . . in . . . the . . . mud."

"Jesus, Ki," he mumbled.

It took a few more seconds, but she was able to reign in the giggles. "I'm sorry. I don't know what came over me."

He let out a long breath. "I imagine it was the shock. Do you think you can get up?"

"I think so, if I can get my ass unstuck." She lifted her hips and winced at the suction noise caused by the mud. She leaned her head back, a mixture of embarrassment and amusement. He chuckled.

"Oh my gosh, do not laugh at me right now."

"Sorry. You're right though, it is kind of funny."

"Very, in a 'we never talk about this again' sort of way."

He smiled at her, their faces mere inches away. Water slid down his brow and he blinked the droplets off his dark lashes. An overwhelming need scorched through her. She opened her lips slightly and tasted his warm breath. The cold water running down her back did nothing to put out the building heat inside. She could see her desire reflected in his swollen pupils. He leaned in closer and a few droplets of water dripped on her face, wet trails running down, reminding her she was real. Gently, his thumb caressed her cheek and just that slight movement provoked such a strong ache it threatened to overwhelm her.

He leaned in, his nose pressed into her cheek as he brushed his lips against the side of her mouth. The roughness of his five o'clock shadow scratched against her chin. She turned her head, met his lips with her own. The kiss was tender, sweet, but she wanted more. She pushed his lips open with her own and slid her tongue across them. His breath quickened, and his body tensed. He broke off the kiss and stared into her eyes. Emotions flickered across his face—fear, worry, desire. The desire seemed to be winning out. All he needed was a little nudge.

"Don't stop," she whispered. "I want this. I want you, all of you."

He inhaled a sharp breath. Kiara didn't hesitate. She pressed her lips against his again. The dam broke, and he responded greedily.

Tyler tangled his fingers in her hair and slid his tongue in her mouth, fervently tasting every inch of hers. She pulled him on top of her, seeking his warmth as the ground underneath them seemed to dissipate. He met her need with his own.

Tyler lifted her off the ground and knelt, placing her legs so that she was straddling him. She wouldn't have stopped, she would have taken him right then and there in the mud, but he pulled away. It wasn't until then she realized she was shaking. Her chest heaved and she could barely breathe.

Tyler tenderly caressed her face. She broke down and he pulled her in, rocking her while she let go of the past.

Sighing, Tyler opened his computer and pulled up the email Henry forwarded this morning.

TYLER,

*Maybe this is something her captor, Anthony, believed in and her subconscious is trying to recall it. He had a history of dabbling in the dark arts. It's my thinking he mentioned something about these "creatures" and that's why she's seeing them.*

*I asked a colleague of mine who has a degree in mythology. He was able to shed a bit more light on the subject.*

HENRY

*--forwarded message--*

HENRY,

.   .   .

GOOD MORNING, my friend! I was happily surprised to see your email. It's been too long since I've had someone as enjoyable as yourself to debate philosophy with. These young colleagues of mine tend to just nod and agree with everything I say. We must get together sometime soon!

I SUPPOSE THOUGH, that I should get to point of this email. I'll be honest, I'm curious as hell about what drove your interest in this, but I will respect your insistence for patient confidentially. Although, one day, I will expect an explanation. Such a fascinating topic!

I'VE RUN across these creatures in my research, but I dare say my knowledge of them isn't very strong. Your girl is definitely not the first person to see them though —they date back to mythological times. Some call them Shadow Creatures, others call them demons, although I don't see any demonic references. There are literally thousands of recorded sightings that describe things similar to what you have, but none of them are as precise. (Which is why I would love to talk to your patient.) The response to these creatures is typically fear, although there are no incidences in which they have caused harm.

MANY REPORTS STATE they saw these creatures before something terrible happened. In most cases, they claim death occurs to someone close to them. The psychic world claims they foreshadow tragic events, such as bombings, terror attacks, etc.

IN MYTHOLOGY, these creatures were given a different distinction. It's hard to explain correctly, but in most references, they seem to portray them as part of the cycle of life, beings that have their place in *our world. The Greek called them* οι οπαδοί των νεκρών *– which loosely translates as "followers of the dead".*

Jennifer showed up at four in the afternoon with a large bag and oversized carrier in which resided a very irritable, squished-faced tabby cat. Pigmy, in his excitement, terrorized the already distressed feline until Kiara locked him in the bedroom. His barks echoed down the hall and Timmy, once released from the cage, ran and hid somewhere out of sight.

Jennifer didn't seem concerned. "He hides all the time. He'll come out when he's ready."

After both girls assured Tyler several times they would check in with him often, and he made sure Kiara understood how to use Skype, he grabbed his bags and made his way to the door. Jennifer hung back while Kiara walked with him.

"With one hand on the knob and the other on the side of her face, he whispered, "I can stay." She nearly agreed without thinking.

Her chest tightened, and she struggled not to cry and embarrass herself in front of Jennifer. "I love you."

Tyler removed his thumb and placed his lips against

hers for the second time that day. Warmth spread through her. She clung to him, not willing to let go of the warmth. The kiss deepened until she was lost in it. Jennifer cleared her throat, and they separated, but Tyler didn't remove his hand from her face. "That's it. I'm not going."

Kiara grinned at him as Jennifer stomped over.

"Go. Shoo." She opened the door and tried to push him out. "It's girl time now."

Tyler laughed. "Okay, okay."

"I love you." He kissed Kiara one last time and addressed Jennifer before walking out. "I froze some meals for the next few days. Whatever you do, don't let her cook."

"Is he being serious?" she asked Kiara.

"Yes, and out of all the rules he's given you to keep me safe, that's probably the only one that really matters."

She heard Tyler chuckle and then he was gone.

Already missing him and dreading the time apart, she shut the door and tried to put on a tough face for Jennifer.

FOUR HOURS LATER, the two women were sitting in the middle of the living room floor with the fireplace blazing. A half-empty bottle of tequila, two shot glasses, and a pile of quarters set between them. One of Tyler's movies played in the background. Kiara bounced the quarter on the floor, and it shot across the room where a hyper puppy tried to chase it down. "I'm going to be finding quarters all over the house for the next year."

Jennifer laughed. "Not unless Pigmy finds them first. So, okay, I've waited all night to ask and I'm drunk enough to do it now—what gives between you and Tyler? I mean, is he like your boyfriend?" She nodded to the ring on Kiara's hand. "Are you two engaged?"

"Oh no." Kiara twisted the ring around. "I mean, I don't think so. I don't know what we are. I've never thought about giving it a title."

"Like he's never called you his girlfriend or anything?"

"No, but honestly, until recently, we were just friends." Kiara blushed. "Today was really the first time we even kissed."

"Wow, I thought you two had been together longer than that. Do you think he's always felt that way about you or is this new?"

*That's a good question.*

"I don't know. With my condition, he couldn't touch me before this. Well, he could a little, but it took time for me to build up the trust and be comfortable with him. If he did, he didn't give any hint of it."

"I'm sorry, I don't mean to pry. It's just, wow, he's like super-hot and you're gorgeous and you two have this crazy past together. I couldn't help but be curious."

"No, it's fine. I haven't had a girl to talk to in so long that I forgot how. Tyler's like my world. He's the only person I've been around since, well, you know, and I'm used to being able to say we are best friends. Now things are hard to explain. He's still my best friend, but it's more. When he touches me, I feel alive and scared all at the same time. We have this saying, 'just take it as it comes' and that's what I'm trying to do, but sometimes I can't help but wonder where it's going."

"You could ask."

"Nah, he wouldn't answer. I know him well enough to know he's trying to hold back and let me make all the decisions."

"That's respectful."

"Irritating is more like it."

Jennifer laughed. "I can see that. Okay, so what do you want to happen? Sex? Marriage? Just friends?"

Kiara giggled and poured herself another shot. "I think I just figured out why Henry was so insistent on hiring you. I imagine he did it because he knew you would make me talk about things I wouldn't mention to him."

"Is it working?"

"Remarkably so. I've thought about sex but it still scares me, so I don't know if I can go through with it. It worries me because I don't know if I can keep him. To be honest, I'm a little jealous thinking about him being away and all the exes he has there, but he's not mine so it's not fair to, you know, to say anything."

"Oh, I wouldn't worry about that. Hold on." Jennifer grabbed her purse and dug until she found her phone. "Here you go."

She handed the phone to Kiara. "He made a statement for the press a few days ago concerning the two of you. Guess he never mentioned it."

Kiara read the article Jennifer had pulled up on the screen.

*"Kiara Moore is my best friend, inspiration, and the love of my life; we both value our privacy and would appreciate the support of our fans and media in that regards."*

"Holy crap!" Kiara gasped. "I had no idea."

"Well, announcing he's in love to the whole world should convince you he's not sleazing around with other women."

"Guess so." The girls fell into silence. Oddly enough, it didn't bother her. Even when she had girlfriends, she hadn't felt that connection—where it was okay *not* to talk. Tyler was the first one she'd experienced that with. "So, what about you? Boyfriend?"

Jennifer stretched her legs out in front of her. "Not really. There's this guy at school but it's nothing serious, not yet at least. He's got a nice ass though. It just doesn't feel meant to be, you know? Did you ever wonder about you and Tyler? If you two would end up together if what happened didn't happen?"

Kiara opened her mouth to speak but then shut it. For a moment, the room wavered. Walls flickered in and out. Behind them, darkness. An overwhelming sense of being watched filled her with dread. The world solidified again, but the sense of being watched didn't go away.

Jennifer leaned forward. "Hey, are you okay?"

"Yeah, um, I'm just a little woozy from all the tequila." She rubbed her arms, suddenly cold.

"I'm sorry if the question upset you. I swear I have no filter." Jennifer shook her head. "Let's skip that question and go scrounge the kitchen for some of that food Tyler left us."

*Tell her.*

Kiara furrowed her brow. Where had that thought come from? Tell her what?

*Tell her NOW!*

Pain lanced through her head. She pinched the bridge of her nose and groaned.

"What's wrong?" Jennifer placed her hand on Kiara's shoulder and she cringed. "Do I need to call Tyler?"

"No. Don't call him." Kiara slowly stood, the pain disappearing. "I fell earlier today and hit my head. Probably just moved it wrong. Come on, I want to show you something."

Jennifer hesitated, eyed her suspiciously. Kiara gave her a fake smile. After a moment, Jennifer took it and she led the way to her bedroom. Kneeling in front of her closet, she dug through piles of shoes, fallen clothes, and hangers.

Just when she began to doubt she'd find what she was looking for, her finger tips landed on a small hat box.

She walked to the bed and set the box beside Jennifer. "This is where I keep the stuff from the hospital and articles about what happened to me and Tyler."

Kiara reached in and pulled out several thick files. A picture slipped out, landing on the blanket. Jennifer picked it up. "Oh wow, is this you and Tyler?"

"Yeah. I'd forgotten how bad we looked." Her bruised face was unrecognizable. Tyler looked haunted and thin, but they were both smiling. "A nurse took this of us while we were sitting in the rec room together. I think it amazed them how good we were for each other."

She stuffed the picture back in the box. "Anyway, that's not what I wanted to show you. Ah, found it." She pulled out a dark blue folder and scattered newspaper articles across the bed. Kiara searched through the pile, pulled out two different clippings, and handed them to Jennifer.

Jennifer skimmed over the articles. "Okay, I've got to be honest. I'm not really sure what you're trying to show me."

Kiara nodded to one paper. "That first article, the one about my abduction, do you see the name of the town?"

"Yeah, it's Richmond. You were taken after a book signing, when you left the mall, right?"

Kiara nodded. "Yes. I was taken at 11:45 on the morning of August 15th, 2014. Now, look at the other article again."

"Actor, Tyler Moore was spotted today at the Richmond mall. This picture was taken as he signed autographs for several excited fans." Jennifer's eyes widened. "Oh my god, you were there at the same time. Holy shit! What if you two had met then instead? That's insane. Did you see him?"

"I don't think so. Not that I remember, at least." Kiara blushed.

"You're not sure?"

"No, it's not that. It's just sometimes I have this weird dream."

"Do tell," Jennifer said, leaning in.

"It starts in the mall, right after the signing. He runs up to me, book in hand, asking me to sign it. He says he's a fan of mine. When I go to sign it, I see the receipt. The time of purchase was only a few minutes before. I figure he's hitting on me, so I write my number on the receipt. I mean, who wouldn't? Before I leave, he asks me out and I let him know I already gave him my number. That's where the dream ends. It's probably just wishful thinking. It sounds crazy, I know, but sometimes I wonder if maybe that happened, and I just don't remember. After Andrew took me, I had a hard time recalling that day since he kept me so drugged."

"What did Tyler say?"

Kiara bit her lip. "I never asked him. I don't know . . . it just feels wrong, like if I do, then something bad will happen."

"Wow. Well, I won't tell him then." Jennifer's gaze trailed over the shelves in the room and she swallowed. "Still, it makes you wonder."

"Anyway, it doesn't matter. We're together now." She shoved the box back in her closet. "That reminds me, though. Could you do me a favor sometime? I packed all these boxes a few weeks ago to take to the Care Center for their charity auction this summer. If you don't mind dropping them off for me that would be great. My closet could use the room and some of this stuff is worth a lot. Plus, it saves me from having to be around all those people."

Jennifer narrowed her eyes. "You're just trying to make me feel like I'm not being paid to do nothing."

"Is it working?" Kiara smiled back.

~

IT WAS TOBY who woke Jennifer up, not the repetitive ringing of the cell phone. The noise startled the cat and he bolted across her chest, nails piercing the blanket. Jennifer cursed at him, pried his claws out of the material, and sat him on the floor. The phone, which had stopped ringing during her wrestling match with Toby, began another shrill sequence of rings.

*Who the hell would be calling this late?* She picked up the phone. Tyler's name was on the caller ID. "Hey, what's going on?"

"Stay in your room."

"What?"

Tyler whispered as if he was afraid someone would hear him. "I want you to very quietly walk over and lock your door. Do it now."

Without hesitation, she did what he asked, although a million thoughts ran through her mind. What was out there that he was afraid would get her? What about Kiara? Was someone else in the house? She could hear Tyler's unsteady breathing. "What's going on?"

"Give me a sec, okay. I'm going to put you on hold and call Henry. Don't hang up."

The line went quiet and each minute that passed became more and more terrifying. Jennifer grabbed Toby and cuddled him to her chest. She had just about decided to take matters into her own hands when Tyler picked up the line again. "Okay, listen, Henry's on his way right now. It shouldn't take him long."

"What the hell is going on, Tyler?"

Letting out an audible breath, he said, "I'm not sure. She got up about an hour ago and started pacing the living room, muttering something I couldn't make out, but I think she was saying, *I need more time.* All of a sudden, she raced to your room but before she got to the door . . ." Tyler paused.

"Tyler?"

"Hold on. She's coming back." His voice was so low she could barely hear it. Jennifer let her eyes shift to the door where a flicker of movement could be seen in the shadows. She jumped when Tyler spoke, his voice full of fear. "They're blocking her again."

"They who? Tyler, you're really scaring me."

"Those creatures. I can't see them like she does. It's more of a black mist. I don't know how to explain it. I've seen it before but every time I play the videos back, it's gone. I don't know if they can hurt her or if she's causing them. I don't know what to do. She looks scared."

"What should I do?"

"Nothing. Just wait for Henry, okay?"

"Are you okay?"

"No, not at all. I should never have left." There was a tremor in his voice. She couldn't imagine how frightening this must be for him to watch from so far away. She was terrified, but there was a part of her that knew she needed to be the strong one, for all of them. Breathing deeply, she held her breath and counted to ten. *Okay, I can do this.* "Tyler, I'm going to go get her."

"No."

"Listen, you can't stop me and more importantly, if they are real, they don't seem to be able to hurt anyone. You said they are just blocking her right?"

"They may not be able to hurt you, but she can. You

are in more danger than she is right now. Stay where you are."

"Fine."

Tyler was silent. Seconds seemed like minutes. Jennifer couldn't stand the silence. "What is she doing now?"

"I can't tell. It looks like . . ." There was a long pause. Jennifer waited.

"No!" He screamed in her ear. "She's going to the balcony. Go! Go now!"

Jennifer jumped off the bed and raced into the hallway, her bare feet smacking across the floor. The balcony door stood wide open and she burst through it, scanning the entire area. It was empty.

"Oh god, no."

"What?"

Jennifer didn't realize she was still holding the phone to her ear until she heard his panicked voice. Ignoring him, she ran to the edge and looked over. It was dark but the light from the full moon was enough for her to make out everything below. She didn't see Kiara anywhere.

"I can't find her? Do you see her?"

"No, I don't have any cameras outside."

"I'm going to grab my shoes and check the yard."

"Please hurry." Whatever strength he had to want to protect her must have gone out the door when Kiara did. Jennifer ran back in and searched quickly for her shoes, which she spotted under the dining room table. "Okay, I've got them."

"Jennifer . . . the door . . ."

"What door?"

"The balcony door. There's something moving behind it," he whispered. "I think it might be her."

She turned, slowly facing the balcony door. Behind the blinds was a dark silhouette, a moving shadow. Jennifer approached; her hand shook as she reached for the knob. She took a few steps back and swung the door closed.

The first thing that struck her was how still Kiara was. It was unnatural. Her eyes were closed, and she had her chin pressed against her chest, black hair fell across her face. "Kiara?"

Tyler's voice cracked. "Is she okay? Is she breathing?"

"I don't know." Jennifer reached out and touched her arm. "She's so cold."

"Check her pulse."

As she moved to wrap her hand around and check, Kiara lashed out, and grabbed her by the wrist. She didn't have time to scream before her phone flew from her hand and slammed against a wall on the other side of the room. Kiara lifted her head. Her eyes were milky white. *Inhuman.* Jennifer fell to her knees. There was another loud crash as the camera Tyler had hidden flew out from behind a stack of books and smashed to the floor where her cell phone now lay, destroyed.

"Please don't hurt me." Tears fell down Jennifer's cheeks. Kiara remained emotionless. Out of the corner of her eye, something moved. Jennifer swiveled her head to look and immediately wished she hadn't; dark creatures swarmed, closing in on them.

Kiara opened her mouth and spoke, her flat voice echoing throughout the house. "I'm sorry for this but there is no other way. I need him to see."

The creatures screamed, an unearthly noise. They closed in on the two as a bright light emanated from Kiara and closed around her and Jennifer, pulsating, growing stronger and stronger.

The last thing she remembered before passing out was Kiara whispering, "He has to ascend."

~

THE DOORS WHOOSHED SHUT behind Tyler, but he didn't notice them nor the nurse who yelled at him to stop running. Corridors with black and gold signs flew by. He stopped at the elevator to press the up arrow. The large green numbers announced it was on the sixth floor and descending slowly. He turned to the stairwell and hit the steps, taking two and three at a time. As he rushed through the entryway on the fourth floor, people stopped to stare. He pushed open the door to room four twenty-three and stepped inside.

A dark room with a single light over the sink and a strong smell of astringent held a sterile looking bed in which Kiara lay. He came to her side, gently moved the IV line so he could touch her sleeping face. "I'm here, Ki."

A monitor beeped in the background, a steady but slow thrumming. Her eyes twitched slightly, but she did not wake. Tyler ran his finger over the plastic mask on her face which hissed quietly while supplying her with oxygen.

"Her blood pressure dropped so they gave her some oxygen to stabilize it." Henry startled Tyler. He had not noticed anyone else in the room.

"Doctor?" Tyler didn't take his eyes off her as he asked the question.

"Not yet. Should be soon, though, and he is supposed to review the tests first thing."

Tyler focused his attention back on Kiara. When the camera feed went out and he was blind to what was going on, the fear was so great it was paralyzing. The time it took him to pull up Henry's phone number seemed like an eternity. He had no idea how Henry got in, maybe the door was unlocked or maybe he knew where the spare was, but Tyler would never think to ask. The last thing he remembered before panic took over was Henry saying she was having a seizure and hanging up to call an ambulance. Everything after that was a blur; the plane trip, the car ride, all of it spent terrified thinking he was going to be too late. Even as he had her in his sight, he still couldn't believe it.

Henry had texted and called as much as he could until Tyler's cell phone battery ran out about two hours ago. He had never felt so in the dark in his life. He moved to hold her hand but stopped short. "They restrained her?"

"They had to, Tyler." Henry stood and came to the other side of the bed, his face burdened. "She woke up during the tests. She was confused and scared, which only heightened her fear. They had to do something. They gave her Valium so the restraints wouldn't frighten her too much. They think that's why her blood pressure dropped."

"Has she woken up other than that yet?"

"No."

Pulling at the fabric, he worked to release her from the straps. "I'm not going to have her wake up to find she's tied down."

Henry frowned but instead of arguing, he began to undo the restraints on the other side.

"And Jennifer?"

Henry pointed behind Tyler. He saw a small form curled up in a blanket in an uncomfortable looking vinyl chair. "I offered to get her a ride home, but she refused to go. I think she wanted to stay to make sure she was okay," Henry hesitated, "and I think she wanted to talk to you."

"Did Jennifer tell you what happened?"

"She did."

"And?"

Henry's frown deepened. "You need to understand she

was unconscious when I got there. The doctors checked her over and said she fainted."

"I know. Why are you reminding me of this?" Tyler's agitation with Henry was growing.

"Because she had some very odd things to say. Things I believe she dreamed while unconscious and I don't want you to take them to heart. This is hard enough without believing in demons and ghosts and telekinesis."

"I saw them too, Henry." Tyler had raised his voice but immediately dropped it back down to a whisper when she stirred. "Look, I have it on camera. I can prove at least part of it to you."

As he said that, Tyler realized he couldn't. For beginners, he'd left the computer at his house when he ran out earlier that night, and second, he knew the shadows would be gone from the video when he did get to check it.

"Please don't take this personally, Tyler. If I were to believe any of this was possible, the three of you would be the people I believe. It's just, well, to put it frankly, it's not possible."

Tyler started to argue but stopped when Kiara's eyes flickered, opened slightly. "Tyler?"

"Hey." He leaned down and kissed her on the forehead. "I'm here, Ki."

When he touched her shoulder to further console her, she flinched.

"She's had a hard night, Tyler. She's still pretty groggy."

Tyler appreciated Henry's effort to console him, but he still feared a relapse from her. Kiara seemed to gain full consciousness because she looked around the room and tried to sit up. "Jennifer?"

"She's fine. She's right over there, sleeping."

"I don't know what's going on," Kiara whispered.

"It's okay," Tyler took a chance now that her eyes were fully open to touch her on the cheek. "You had a seizure and Jennifer fainted. We're just waiting on the test results and then we can go home."

She shut her eyes. "I love you, Tyler, but you're a bad liar."

He chuckled and she opened them again, met his gaze. "Will you stay with me?"

"Of course."

She scooted over and patted the bed. Lowering the railing, he slid in beside her but hesitated to draw in close. Almost immediately, she curled into him and fell asleep.

Not taking his eyes off her, he merely nodded to Henry when he said he was going to give them some privacy. Tyler must have fallen asleep because it was several hours later when a nurse came in and announced the doctor would be by in a few minutes.

Tyler shifted out from under her and stood, taking the cold cup of coffee Jennifer was offering him.

"Are you okay?" he asked.

She looked like hell, with swollen eyes and hair sticking in every direction. Worst of all was the look she had on her face. Something about that look chilled him to the bone.

"I'm fine. I'm sorry, Tyler. I tried, but . . ."

"This isn't your fault at all. Jennifer, you did the best you could."

"They say I passed out, but I didn't. Something happened. I can still feel it." She ran her hands over her face as if she was trying to brush something away.

"Feel what?"

Jennifer didn't get the chance to answer. There was a knock on the door and a man in the blue scrubs introduced himself as Doctor Kevin Michael. After speaking shortly to all of them, he waited as Tyler woke Kiara. Tyler was impatient to find out about the test results, but the doctor didn't seem to be in a hurry to approach the subject.

Once a short exam was done, Dr. Michael turned toward Tyler and asked, "And you're her guardian, is that correct?"

"Yes."

He then nodded to Jennifer. "I would like to speak to these two in private, if that's okay?"

"Sure," Jennifer nodded. She gathered a few things and stepped out, leaving them alone with the doctor.

TYLER HEARD the knock on the door but didn't bother to say anything. It's not as if the doctors and nurses would listen if he told them to go away. Condensation collected on the window. Outside, the barren streets melted into a blur through the watery glass.

Henry spoke from the doorway. "Where's Kiara?"

"She's in surgery."

"*Surgery?*"

"They're doing a biopsy."

Tyler faced Henry, tears sliding down his cheeks. "She has a mass in her brain."

Henry took an unsteady step forward. The door in room four twenty-three shut quietly behind him.

## 33

## THREE MONTHS LATER

Kiara wiped vomit off her chin and looked at her reflection in the mirror. Her hair was brittle, lifeless; there was no sign of the former lustrous black locks. Her face was hollow, thin, her eyes dull and waxy. Her lips seemed to stay chapped, perhaps from dehydration or from rubbing them with a rag like she was doing now. Some days she wished she could take back the fugues and hallucinations over cancer. Most days, in truth, and today was one of those days. Surgery was coming up soon, a topic she and Tyler avoided talking about it.

Her chances were good. Her body had responded well to the chemotherapy and other than being sick around the clock, it had done what they hoped it would. Not to mention, it explained everything that had been happening to her. The doctor said the hallucinations were caused by the pressure, and not once since that fateful night had she seen the creatures nor lost any sense of time.

Tyler knocked on the door. "Doing okay, Ki?"

"Yeah, I'll be out in a minute." She turned the water on and brushed her teeth. Although she appreciated the space he gave her, lately it had been too much. The diagnosis made her realize that compared to possible death, her fears were trivial. She was ready to take the next step with Tyler but whenever she thought about broaching the subject, he seemed to know what was coming and would find something he suddenly had to do. A couple of times while they were kissing, she had even made a move to take it further, but he pulled away every time. Kiara wiped her face on the towel and glanced in the mirror one last time.

*Maybe it's because you look like crap.*

She found Tyler in her room, looking through the closet.

"Hey." He smiled at her; his eyes tight. "Are you feeling better?"

"Yeah, I'm fine."

"Good." He took his shirt off and grabbed another out of the laundry basket.

"Tyler?" she asked as he stood with his back to her.

"Yeah?"

"Don't put that on please." He stopped, shirt in hand, but did not turn around. She walked in front of him and he looked down at her with so much love her heart ached. Needing to touch him, she put her palm on his cheek and stood up on her toes, kissed him gently. He kissed her back. When he tried to pull her close, she placed a hand on his chest.

He frowned. "What's wrong?"

"Do you still think I'm pretty?"

"Are you serious?" He sighed. "Ki, that is the stupidest thing I think you have ever asked me. You're gorgeous, breathtaking. Is this because of the chemo?"

She nodded and looked down at her hands. "That, and because you don't want me."

"Have you lost your fricking mind?"

She didn't say anything.

"You don't think I want you?"

"I don't know. I've tried to . . . you know, give you hints and stuff, but you don't seem interested."

"I don't seem interested?" Tyler shook his head and breathed deeply through his nostrils.

"You don't have to repeat everything I say. I'm embarrassed enough."

"Ki." He reached under her chin and tilted her head up until their eyes met "I want you so much that I feel like I'm dying every time we touch, but I'm not a mind reader. Between you feeling sick all the time and not knowing how far I can take it, there's no way I'm going to try to sleep with you. If that's something you want, you're going to have to tell me."

"If you want me so bad, why do you look so scared?"

"I feel everything when I'm around you. There's no filter, no way to shut things out. I'm so vulnerable. Every time you look at me, I feel you all the way down to the core of who I am. You're this angel who magically erases all my faults, leaving me naked and bare. I'm afraid to touch something so perfect and beautiful but compelled to give you everything I am. Of course, I'm scared."

Leaning down, he placed his lips against hers. Her stomach clenched in anticipation and she deepened the kiss, letting her hands trail down, touching areas she hadn't touched before. When he pulled away, silence stretched between them.

They both needed something. The question was hers to answer.

"Take me to bed."

Her breath hitched when they locked eyes. His were smoldering, dark. Tyler cupped his hand under her jaw and leaned down. His lips brushed hers, soft and gentle. He pulled back slightly.

"Are you sure?" he whispered.

Her heart was beating so hard her whole body trembled with it. She couldn't find the strength to tell him, so she pleaded with her eyes, hoped he could see what she wanted.

He leaned down again. This time the kiss was deeper. She ran her tongue across his lips. He exhaled and he pressed into her, all control lost. His tongue slid into her mouth and everything else became a blur.

He pulled away and whispered, "Don't let me hurt you."

34

Tyler reached for her. His hand landed on an empty pillow and he opened his eyes, blinked against the bright light pouring into the room. Kiara was standing at the window, hands pressed against the pane. Facing away from him, silhouetted against the overcast sky, he could see her naked body underneath the thin t-shirt she was wearing.

*She's mine.*

He smiled at the thought and stretched. Tyler let his eyes trail over her, enjoying how the light highlighted the area between her slightly spread legs. "Good morning."

She turned and smiled, her eyes lit up like a child's. "It's snowing."

"Is it now?" he asked, swinging his legs over the side of the bed and slipping on his boxers.

Coming up from behind, he pressed his hand on the pane above hers and looked out. Huge flakes fell from the sky, covering the ground in an array of white. The trees were already bowing down under the weight of the snow.

His breath fogged the glass. "Wow, you weren't joking. There has got to be at least a foot out there already."

She raised her eyebrows. "Can we go play?"

Nuzzling her cheek, he ran kisses along her jawline. "Yes, but not right now."

"Why not?" She pulled away; bottom lip stuck out.

He tugged the t-shirt over her head and threw it on the floor. With his hand cupped around her breast, he trailed kisses along her collar bones.

"Are you ever going to let me wear clothes again?" she asked.

"Probably not." He slid his hand between her thighs, fingers coaxing her open.

Kiara moaned. "Mmmm . . . you may be right. Clothes are the pits. Why haven't we been doing this the last five years?"

"Because you're a prude."

"Asshole," she mumbled.

"I love you, Ki."

"I love you, too."

They didn't speak again for several hours.

He dodged the first snowball but the second one hit him in the chest. Cold seeped through his jacket. He gathered a handful of snow and rolled it into a ball.

"You took too long," she yelled from behind a tree. "Now I have enough ammo to last me all day."

She peeked around the side of the tree and he threw his snowball, missed her by inches.

"Guess I'll just have to come and take your ammo then." He raced to her, dodging several snowballs along the way. When he was close, he grabbed her and wrestled her into the snow.

"No fair," she cried out, laughing.

"It's perfectly fair." He grabbed a handful of snow and shoved it down her shirt. She screamed.

"That's freezing! Let me up!" He chuckled and pulled her to her feet, helping her remove the lodged snow.

"You're mean, you know," Kiara said.

"Yes, but I'm sexy as hell."

"That's true."

The snow swirled around them, flakes landing on their cheeks and eyelashes. It felt solitary, like the world only existed for the two of them, suspended in time.

"Marry me?" he asked.

"Okay."

"Really?" The word slipped out of his mouth.

She bit her lip and nodded. Grabbing her around the waist, he lifted her in his arms and spun around.

The surgery went well.

The doctor was positive most of the tumor was gone, but they wouldn't be sure until the next few scans.

Kiara and Tyler spent their first Christmas together as a couple and Pigmy joined in on the fun. Henry and Jennifer came by for Christmas dinner and they sat around the table enjoying their time together like a family.

The Holidays were spent eating, making love, laughing and crying. They lived the best life they could with hand they were dealt.

Good afternoon, Kiara, Tyler." Dr. Johnson shook both of their hands. "It's a pleasure to see you again."

Tyler shook the doctor's hand. "No offense, Dr. Johnson, but I can't say the same about you."

The doctor chuckled and took a seat behind his desk. "No offense taken. You're not the first person to tell me that."

Kiara glanced over at Tyler. Although he was smiling, he was gripping the hand rest, his knuckles white.

"I'm not going to keep you guys waiting, I know how stressful this must be. I have good news, though."

The doctor pulled out some files from the folder and laid them side by side in front of them. "This," he said, pointing at a murky spot on the scan, "was the tumor before we started treatment. This is the tumor now."

Kiara stared at a tiny dot on the picture.

"Okay, so what does that mean?" Tyler asked, eyes locked on the doctor.

"That means the tumor is nearly gone. With a few

more chemo treatments, I expect I won't be seeing you two for anything other than checkups."

Tyler bit back a smile.

She squeezed his hand, trying not to let herself get hopeful. "What are the chances it will continue decreasing? What percentage are we looking at?"

"One hundred percent."

SHE WAS STILL TRYING to wrap her mind around what the doctor said as they made their way to the parking lot. Kiara made it to the car before she realized Tyler wasn't behind her. He was a few meters away, staring at the sky. "Tyler? Are you okay?"

He looked at her, a smile dangling from the corner of his lips. "Marry me."

"I already said yes!"

"No, I mean, now. Today." As he strolled over to her, Kiara realized why he seemed so strange. Tyler wasn't just happy; he was euphoric. "We'll go to the courthouse, Henry and Jennifer can come too, and then we'll take a vacation—Hawaii, Europe, anywhere you want to go."

She gave him a weary smile. "Tyler, I want to but I still have chemo—"

"We'll get a referral from Doctor Johnson, do the chemo while we are on our Honeymoon."

She bit her lip. More than anything, she didn't want to ruin his happiness. She didn't want him to live in denial either. "I know you're happy about the news, I am too, but that doesn't mean I will be okay, and. . . I don't want to put you through that."

He reached up and touched the side of her face. "Listen

to me, I have been counting the seconds on the clock the last few months, worried about not having the next minute with you. I'm through with that. You have a good chance and I'm going to hold on to that. I'm not going to walk away because you're sick, Ki. I'll be here regardless of the outcome and I would rather be here as your husband. Please say yes."

She reached into her purse, pulled out her phone, and handed it to Tyler. "I say you better call Henry and let him know he's your best man."

THEY STAYED in a small resort cabin in Hawaii for two weeks, visiting the local hospital for her treatments as requested by Dr. Johnson. Most days they explored the island, hiked and swam. Some days they stayed in bed, talking or watching movies. They laughed, smiled, made love, and ignored the rest of the world around them.

Toward the end of the two weeks, she was lounging in one of the chairs staring out into the ocean when Tyler joined her. "What are you thinking about?"

She reached out and touched his hand. "About how happy I am, about how much I love you."

He leaned over and kissed her. "I love you, too. So, what's next?"

"Well, I haven't ever seen your house and then there's your premier in a few weeks, and yes, I overhead you on the phone. I had to let it slide when we were best friends but now that you're my husband I don't expect you to keep things from me. Plus, there's your career. Then I started thinking, whose house do we live in? Or do we keep them both?"

"I guess I hadn't thought about that. Do you want to

see my house? Actually, I should probably call it *our* other house?"

"Yeah, that would be nice. Also, you might want to call about the premier and let them know we are coming."

He raised his eyebrows. "Ki, are you sure you're ready? Lots of people in close quarters."

"Yeah, I think I can. If you're with me, at least."

He stood and put his hand out for her.

"Where are we going?"

"I'm taking my wife to bed to make love to her."

"Wow, you look gorgeous."

"I feel weird, though." She came down the last of the steps reaching for his hand so she didn't stumble. "I don't think I've worn heels in over five years."

Tyler looked down at her shoes and followed the slit up the front of the dress to her upper thigh. She waited for his comment.

"Okay, we're not going."

"Oh no, it's too much isn't it? I don't want to embarrass you."

"No, you're absolutely gorgeous, stunning. And when I think of anybody else looking at you, I suddenly get the urge to get into a bar fight."

She laughed. "You'll just get another lecture."

"Please, god no." He leaned in and kissed her. "We could stay here. There are still a few rooms we haven't made love in."

"Oh my god, you're tempting." She pushed him against the wall and untucked his shirt. "I'm sure we have time for one quick—"

His phone vibrated. He glanced at it and frowned. "That's the limo, dammit. They're here."

She pouted when he tucked in his shirt.

"If you don't put that lip back in, I'm going to bite it." She pushed it out further, and he nipped at it, causing her to yelp. "Are you sure you're ready for this? We don't have to go."

"Yeah." She nodded. "I've got to get used to it sometime. It's a part of being with you."

"Okay, let's go."

CAMERAS AND LIGHTS flashed all around them the moment they opened the car door. He held her close and tried to keep her from the crowd. People were screaming his name, making her nervous. She squeezed closer to him.

"Miss Moore!" She heard her name being called too and tried to ignore it, but the reporters were persistent. "Miss. Moore, can we have a word with you? What's your relationship with Tyler? Kiara Moore?"

She could sense Tyler's irritation growing. He wouldn't be upset if they weren't calling out to her specifically. Another reporter, this one closer, screamed her name, "Kiara Moore!"

Tyler stopped and faced the reporter, stared him down. "It's *Reed*."

"I'm sorry? What was that?" The reporter leaned in with his microphone.

"It's Kiara Reed. Now excuse us."

She couldn't hear anything over the roar of the crowd after that.

## 37

"*I* missed this place so much." Tyler threw their bags on the floor and slumped onto the couch. Their first flight back was delayed and then they had a two-hour layover in Dallas, not to mention the numerous times they were stopped by people who wanted to take pictures of them. He closed his eyes and rested while she fluttered around, turning on the lights and opening windows to clear out the stuffiness.

Pigmy jumped in his lap for some attention. Jennifer and Henry had taken turns watching over him, but the puppy never seemed to get enough affection.

Kiara slid in beside him on the couch just as he was drifting off.

"I can definitely see why this place appealed to you so much after these past few weeks."

He chuckled. "Are you regretting marrying a movie star?"

"Most definitely." She nuzzled his neck. "I don't regret marrying you, though. Although, all this romance stuff is getting old already."

"Jerk." He wrapped an arm around her and sighed. "I'm hungry, are you?"

"Starving." She stood and stretched. He noticed her stop mid-stretch, staring at the wall.

"What is it?" He stood and placed his hands on her shoulder.

She shook her head. "It's nothing. I thought I saw something, but I think I'm just being paranoid since we haven't been here in a while."

"You're probably just tired. Come on to the kitchen and let's get some food."

Tyler trailed behind as she led the way to the kitchen. After a few seconds of digging, she threw him a bag of frozen pizza rolls. He decided not to argue about her low-brow choice of food and started the oven.

"Oh my gosh."

"What?"

Kiara pulled a bottle out from under the cabinet and held it up to him. "I forgot Henry gave us this champagne before we left. Are you up for a night of champagne, junk food, and bad movies?"

"Champagne and pizza rolls, huh? Good thing you're so high class or I might be embarrassed by you."

"Oh, hush." Kiara wrinkled her nose at him. "So, are you in or not?"

He stared at her, his heart skipping a beat. The way she smiled, how she looked at him—a lifetime did not seem like long enough to have each other.

"What? You do like champagne, right?"

"Of course. Except you have to save the last part of the bottle so I can drink it off of you later."

She raised her eyebrows. "How exactly does that work?"

"I wouldn't know. I've never done it before."

He gave her an innocent look and she narrowed her eyes. "I'm going with your pitiful cover up but only because I want to."

He laughed and turned back to the stove.

"Do you want to use the champagne glasses or the—"

Kiara didn't finish her sentence.

"Champagne glasses or what?" Tyler asked.

She didn't answer.

He turned to face her. Kiara was frozen in place, staring off into space, her eyes glazed over.

"Ki?" he whispered.

She looked up at him. His heart dropped to the floor. There was so much misery and suffering in her eyes. Tears trailed down her cheeks.

"I'm so sorry," she whispered. "It's too late."

A trickle of blood ran from her nose, dropping to the floor. Another one joined it. She collapsed to the floor, champagne bottle shattering beside her. He charged across the kitchen, sliding down beside her, shards of glass embedding in his knees.

"Ki!"

She began to seize, body flailing, eyes open but unaware.

"No, no, no, no, no . . ." He rolled her onto her side, reached into his pocket for his phone, and dialed 911.

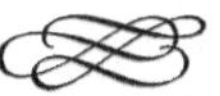

*He cannot see.* The phrase was not said in words, only images. Tyler blinded by flesh.

"Then she will help."

*Perhaps. It's never been done before. We don't know what will come now. Things are . . .*

Another image, blackness descending upon the earth. The creature slithered backwards over the balcony, its piercing eyes holding hers, hackles rising.

*He has made you weak. You cannot stay.*

"Being stuck here wouldn't be so bad." Kiara knew she was taunting it, but the words rang true. The creature hissed.

They stared at each other until she finally broke. "Fine. I know I can't stay, but I will keep fighting."

*If you must.*

The wind broke and she turned, taking in Tyler's profile from the window, memorizing it before she let go, her mind following the creature out into the darkness.

Kiara blinked. She'd fallen asleep again. It happened more often as the days passed by. Tyler slid open the balcony door and stepped out. She smiled at him and he smiled back.

*He's getting so thin.*

His eyes were sunken and dark, clothes hung loosely on his body.

*When was the last time I saw him eat?* She couldn't recall. The last few weeks were a blur.

"Hey, I wanted to see if you were ready to go in?" He knelt and fixed the blanket across her lap. Taking her hands, he pretended to hold them, but she knew he was only checking to see if she was cold. She stared at him, memorized every line, amazed by how beautiful he was, how she still fell more and more in love with him every day. As much as he tried to hide it, she knew he didn't see her the same way. Fear of losing her had consumed him to the point of obsession, trying to cheat time, pushing his feelings in a corner. There was no reason to blame him. She would do the same if the tables were turned.

"It's getting cold so we should probably get you in soon." Sweetly, he reached up and felt her face, but she knew inwardly he was screaming at how tiny and fragile she had become.

"Can I have a few more minutes?"

He bit his lip and worked on tucking the blanket around her legs. A tuft of wind caught his long hair, brushing it off his forehead. He kept his eyes downcast and asked very casually, "Who were you out here talking to?"

"When?"

"Just now, right before I came out."

"I thought I had fallen asleep."

There was no sense in arguing with him. Since the aneurism and the discovery of a new tumor, the fugues had returned. Considering the diagnoses—months if they were lucky—the lapses in time no longer seemed important. She had handled the news well, or at least as well as could be expected. After the discovery of the first tumor, a part of her always knew something like this was going to happen. At first, she tried to blame it on being pessimistic and pushed the thought away, but it only lay there and festered. When the doctor gave the diagnosis, in a way, it was sort of a relief. There was no more reason to pretend everything would be okay and that there was a happy ending for her.

Tyler had not taken the news well at all. While the doctor described the diagnosis and their plan (which basically was to make her more comfortable during the little time she had left) he had simply stood there, holding her hand, the pressure steadily increasing. Dr. Johnson finished by giving his deepest regrets, but Tyler remained motionless.

The doctor approached him and placed his hands on his shoulder, asking if they had any questions or would like him to send in a grief counselor.

She hadn't been looking at Tyler. She had been staring at the clouds out the window when she heard his voice, low and dismayed. "You said she was going to be okay."

"Tyler, these things happen."

"I wouldn't have taken her away if I had known." This time, she took her eyes away from the window and tried to focus on what he was saying, a feeling of foreboding coming over her.

The doctor must have sensed it too because he took a few steps back before saying, "There's no way to predict these sorts of things. It wouldn't have made a difference."

Her husband, her best friend, had then let go of her hand. He took several steps across the room before grabbing a rolling stand and slinging it into the wall, making a noise that carried so much misery she would forever hear it every time she looked into his eyes. Dr. Michaels pushed the red button behind her and ran over to restrain him, which was a mistake because Tyler turned and attacked him. Security burst into the room and Tyler was pulled away, escorted from the premises. After calmly blotting his bloody nose on a paper towel, Dr. Michaels had left, leaving her alone and dying, with only the rhythmic beeping of machines to keep her company.

Tyler eventually calmed down, and it took a lot of convincing from Henry to have him allowed back in. That was the day she lost him. The light went out in his eyes and he walked around, a shadow of himself, a broken man. There was nothing worse than watching him die inside and not being able to do anything about it.

"It's okay. Don't worry about it. I was just curious."

Out of the corner of her eye, she saw Mrs. Marty, the full-time nurse, pass by the window, only glancing out before walking off. She went out of her way to make sure she never interrupted them. Not like Tyler left her much to do other than check her vitals, and he had started to learn how to do that also.

*God, I love him.*

He reached up and touched the ring she now wore on a necklace since she'd lost too much weight for it to stay on her finger. Another deep look of sadness crossed his face and she yearned to be able to tell him it was going to be okay, but she could not let the lie escape her lips.

"Tyler, I can't take this anymore, watching you suffer. I feel like it's my fault and I miss us. We have so little time left together and I want you to be happy."

Angry tears fell down her cheeks and she brushed them off.

He pressed his forehead against hers, breathing heavily.

"I'm doing the best I can, Ki." There was a long pause and his next words were those of a tormented man. "I don't want you to die."

Kiara tried to breathe, but her throat was too tight to allow air. She fought against the misery that threatened to break her apart. "I don't want to leave you."

"It's okay. We're going to be okay." His hand pressed against the back of her head, pulling them closer together. "We're just going to take it as it comes, right?"

"Okay." She nodded, pulled away to wipe her runny nose. "You look like hell by the way."

He chuckled lightly through tears. "You should see yourself."

"Fair enough," she smiled. "Are we still doing dinner with Jennifer tonight?"

"If you're up to it."

She nodded and was about to tell him to take her in when his face changed, his eyes became covered in skin, the sockets hollow.

*He can't see.*

The moment was so brief that it was gone before she had a chance to blink.

Toward the end of the meal, Kiara began to doze off, the pain killers making her drowsy. Tyler took her to bed and Jennifer offered to clear the table and see herself out. When he came in the room thirty minutes later, he was surprised to see her sitting on the couch, wringing her hands.

"Hey, I'm sorry. I thought you would have left by now. I hope you weren't waiting on me."

"No . . . it's just, um . . ." Her eyes darted between him and the floor. "I wanted to talk to you. Is Kiara asleep?"

"Yeah, pretty much instantly. I didn't want to leave her until I was sure though." He sat on the couch, wishing her away so he could go back to Kiara. "What do you want to talk to me about?"

She shifted in her seat. Tyler looked closely at her. With everything that was going on, he hadn't noticed how tired and unkempt Jennifer looked. She met his eyes and whatever pain was etched in them seemed to have her backtracking.

"Nothing." She stood up. "It's nothing important. I

just, uh, wanted to chat, but I didn't realize how late it was."

The last thing he needed was to deal with anyone else's emotions, but he couldn't shut everyone out, at least not yet.

"Jennifer, I know this is hard on you and I see how much you and Henry work to keep your pain hidden. I appreciate it but I would rather be treated like a person instead of a glass jar. You're not going to break me." He glanced toward their bedroom. "At least not until she's gone. So please, talk."

Jennifer sat back down. "I don't really know where to start. Henry made me promise to never tell you and I wasn't going to, but, I don't know, maybe it will help somehow."

Tyler cringed at the words but tried not to let it show. There was nothing that could help him now. *Not unless . . .*

That was the one thought that kept him going. Somehow, he held onto the hope that the visions meant something, that her telekinesis could somehow save her. As the weeks passed that hope had lessened greatly, along with her withering health. Once she was gone, he had no reason to keep moving on. Henry had asked him bluntly what he was going to do after she was gone and he had responded with 'I don't know,' but that was a lie. One way or another, he had no intention of living a life without her. He hadn't given up yet. The doctors had, Jennifer and Henry had, but not him.

"Maybe what will help?" He tried to keep the sarcasm out of his voice.

"It's about what happened the night I stayed, after the cameras went out. It's also about what's been happening since then."

He sat up straighter. Without waiting for him to

encourage her, she told him the whole story, word for word about what happened that night after they lost contact.

"He needs to ascend," Tyler muttered the words. "What do you think that means?"

"I don't know. I am sure she was talking about you, though." She seemed to gather courage before looking him straight in the face. "Henry and I have been talking. We're both hurting here too, Tyler. It's hard enough to lose her, and it's going to be worse if we lose you, too. Do you not think we know what you're thinking? You can't be selfish and try to take your own life. Can you imagine what that would do to us? Do to *her* if she found out?"

Her words cut through him and he hated her for it, for making him doubt. She had no right. They didn't understand how much pain he was in. He hurt so much he worried he would die before her, his heart giving up before she did.

"You wouldn't tell her that," he said through clenched teeth.

"No, I wouldn't do that to her. But if you don't get the idea out of your head soon, she's bound to figure it out, if she hasn't already."

"Is that all you came here to say?"

"I won't be goaded into getting angry at you, Tyler. For someone who says they aren't made of glass, you sure are acting like it. I wanted to talk to you because you're my friend."

Tyler sighed. She was right, he was acting an ass. Expecting him to be emotionally stable right now would be cruel and stupid though. Still, he could try. "I'm sorry."

"Me too." She reached across the couch and patted him on the hand. "I'll leave you alone on the first issue for now, but only because I don't think you'll do anything soon and because there is something else I wanted to tell you."

Jennifer glanced around the room again, eyes darting to the corners. "I've been seeing things and having these dreams. I think she did something to me."

"What do you mean?"

"Ever since that night, I've been seeing shadows out of the corner of my eye and hearing voices. The dreams are the worst, though. I keep dreaming of these things and places. I think I know what they are."

"The creatures? You think they are real?"

For over a month he'd held on to the hope that Kiara's visions meant something, meant that she had a chance. Supernatural or not, he was willing to believe in anything if it could save her.

"I know they are real. I saw them, she saw them, you saw them Tyler."

"What do you think they are?" he asked in a rush.

"I think they take souls. In my dreams, they show us, all of us. They show us as being good and then over time, being bad and selfish, trapped here in this world unable to move on. I think those things take us on. But there is no one to take anymore. They seem . . . hungry. It's hard to explain, it's all in images. Sometimes I hear her voice in my head. She keeps saying, 'he has to see.' Honestly Tyler, I'm scared to death."

"You think they are angels?" This was not what Tyler wanted to hear, but it was better than no chances.

"No." Jennifer shook her head and shivered. "Not at all. I think they are something different entirely."

Tyler hovered over her. "What else have you seen? Tell me exactly."

Jennifer stood and backed away from him, only stopping when she ran into the coffee table. "You need to understand. I'm not telling you this so you will think there's anything you can do to change things. I just thought . . ."

She hesitated, running her hands through her hair. "Fuck, I don't know what I thought. I shouldn't have said anything. Henry was right."

"Tell me," he demanded. "What do you think? It must be something or you wouldn't have bothered."

Wide eyes held his before she found her voice. "I think they are here to take her on. I think she believes you're going to kill yourself and you won't be with her. I think when she kept writing 'I watched him die'. She didn't mean Andrew, she meant you and I think that's what she meant by, 'he has to ascend'. I think she wants me to stop you somehow."

"You don't know anything." Anger swept through him, betrayal. She was making this up and he knew it, could practically imagine her and Henry sitting around and coming up with this tale. He wanted to push her, shove her against the wall and force the truth out but he was afraid the noise would wake Ki. Instead, he backed away and pointed toward the door. "Go home, Jennifer."

"Tyler—"

"Let me explain something to you," he said, his fists clenched. "She brings out the best in me but without her there is nothing holding me back from anything. Do I make myself clear?"

"Fuck you, Tyler," she spat back. "I'm not afraid of you, nor am I going to tuck my tail and run like some terrified child. Do you think you can just call me a liar, threaten me, and get away with it?"

"If you're right and she wanted me to know all of that, why didn't she just tell me herself? Did you ever think about that?"

The volume of their argument had risen to a dangerous level, and he started to get nervous about waking Kiara. Jennifer must have thought the same thing because she came over to him, close enough to touch his chest. "Yeah, I did, but now that I told you and see how you're reacting, I think I understand why she didn't. I think I know why I keep hearing her say, 'he can't see.'"

The fight was lost as the reasoning behind her words rung true. There was no hope, nothing supernatural could save her. If she was trying to do anything, it would be to save him. It resonated in everything she was.

*Oh god, no Ki. I can't live without you.*

To himself, to Jennifer, to the world, he whispered the words he'd refused to accept since hearing the news. "She's going to die, isn't she?"

Wet eyes met his and her chin quivered before she nodded, causing the tears to cascade down her face. "I'm so sorry, Tyler."

He walked away, through the room and out the door. A few yards from the house, his feet gave out from under him. A scream choked off by a grief-stricken sob tore from his chest and echoed in the dark. He lay on the ground, wallowed. Grasping handfuls of dirt and grass, he screamed into the earth while Jennifer sat close by, joining him in anguish but knowing there was no comfort she could give.

40

She had fought so hard, so damn hard. That was worth something, wasn't it? Tyler tried to pretend it would all be okay. Couldn't she just do the same? For him, she'd try. He'd bought candles, hundreds of them because she told him the light hurt her eyes.

One lie. One lie wouldn't hurt. In truth, she wanted it dim. Dim because sometimes things looked whole in the dark. You could see the outline of a picture in the dark, but you couldn't make out the cracked glass the picture hides behind. She wanted it dim so he couldn't see her cracks, couldn't see how fragile the vessel that held her was. But, when the candlelight flickered, her shadow would too. A reminder that soon, the candle would go out and the shadow would fade into the darkness.

At some point, Kiara stopped passing by the mirror. It wasn't the distance that bothered her. It was what she saw in it. The woman who stared back still had her hair, still had the same eyes; eyes as green as sea foam, eyes which had seen pain, which had shed tears for loss, had shed more for love. But how frail had the rest of her become?

Her hair had grown thin, her body even thinner. The mirror didn't show her. No, it showed a lie. It showed only the surface, contained no depth. It didn't show her secrets. Didn't show her memories. Didn't show the sad child who'd grown into a strong woman. Most of all, it didn't show a woman who loved a man. That woman was strong, she was full of life, glowing. The mirror was nothing but a shallow pool of silver glass.

Not that she'd had a chance to look at herself lately. She fell on the way to the bathroom one night and within two days she could no longer walk. Staying conscious became difficult. Tyler never left her side.

When she was awake, they would talk and hold each other. She begged him to stop worrying, that her last wish was for them to enjoy their time together. Sometimes when they talked, he would close his eyes so he wouldn't see her dying body, but instead remember her as she was. During rare moments, they could forget the pain and laugh and joke of the past. Most were colored with an ache so deep they could only hold each other as they were torn apart.

Still, she held on. Three days passed, then four, all in a haze. On the fifth day, she felt death coming and knew she couldn't hold it at bay any longer. Doctors and nurses stopped by, their voices fading in and out. She sought out Tyler's face as they spoke to him and there was nothing more painful than watching him suffer.

Henry stopped by, tears streaming down his face as he tried to say goodbye. Tyler excused himself to give them privacy.

"I'll take care of him," he said, seeing her agony while watching him leave. "I'll do the best I can."

She took a few shallow breaths, trying to speak without using the little strength she needed to keep.

"Tell him I tried. Love him."

He squeezed her hand. "I will."

"Tell Jennifer . . . forgive me."

"There's nothing to forgive. You tried your hardest."

"I know what . . . what I would destroy . . . even her . . ." She shut her eyes.

"Don't worry about that right now. You've been like a daughter to me. I love you so much."

"Tyler . . . need him . . . out of time. . ."

"Okay." He leaned down and kissed her forehead.

She opened her eyes and fought against the darkness. Henry stepped into the hall and placed a hand on the side of her husband's face, whispering something she couldn't hear. Tyler looked past him, and a sob escaped his throat. Their eyes met and she forgot about the pain, needing only to hold him during her last few moments on earth.

Tyler hurried to her.

"I love you so much." His breath warmed her cheeks as he held her face, his tears falling on her lips.

"I love you . . ." His lips touched hers, their tears mixing. "Try . . ." Kiara stopped speaking. Blinked. There, at the end of the bed, she saw herself standing, healthy and radiant, between two dark creatures.

HE HELD on to her nearly lifeless body as the warmth left her. She was staring at the end of the bed. For a second, he thought she'd already slipped away, but then she smiled.

She looked at him, her eyes wide and clear. *Beautiful.* Kiara touched his face. "Not . . . the end. Story . . . a part of you. Carry it . . . on. You'll . . . remember?"

"Of course, baby." Tyler had no idea what she meant but he didn't care, he only wanted her to stay.

"Don't forget . . . promise me."

"I won't ever forget you." He kissed her lips, memorized them as the last of the warmth seeped out.

"I love you." Tyler clung to her, repeating the words until they were no longer a separate phase but a lullaby of the heart.

Her chest sputtered, the breathing shallow. Tyler stared into her eyes, watched the light fade. Touching his lips to hers, he shared her last breaths.

Her chest rose one last time and then stopped.

. . . o know she is looking down upon us, from Heaven, and that she no longer feels pain. It is we who suffer, that are yet to be called upon . . ."

Tyler stared at the coffin. He stared at it until he could make out every grain of wood underneath the coat of polish. Beneath it, between the rails of the silver lowering device, were wide green straps holding up the coffin. Beneath that, a grave; a dark chasm surrounded by synthetic grass. That's where they were going to bury her. In the ground. Alone.

Somewhere in the deep recess of his mind he was mildly aware of what was going on. Henry took care of the arrangements, but he didn't know what they were. The roads were blocked off and security put in place, so the media was not allowed in. He knew that somewhere outside this cemetery there was a world which was still functioning as if nothing had happened.

For him, the world had stopped.

" . . .Let us pray."

Someone put their hand on his shoulder, but he didn't

bother to look or care. Four days. Four days in which he had been clinging to life. A life he no longer wanted. But what if Jennifer had been right? What if Kiara didn't want him to kill himself?

Because of that lingering doubt, he held on to living. Although, the pain was so unbearable he didn't know how much more he could take.

Henry tugged on his arm. His voice sounded miles away. "It's time."

Glancing up, he realized the funeral was over. They were lowering the coffin, waiting for him to do something. Jennifer handed him a rose and propelled him forward until he stood in front of the heavy wooden box which held his wife's body. She tossed her rose in and it thudded on the coffin. The sound made him queasy. He squeezed the stem of his rose tighter, felt the pinch of the thorns. People came by, talked to him, hugged him, but he neither spoke nor touched them back, only stared as the casket holding her body disappeared into the ground.

Another hand tried to pull him away.

He shoved it off.

"Tyler, come on, let's get you home," Henry said softly.

Tyler shook his head and wiped his eyes, the back of his hand scraped against the beard he hadn't bothered to shave in longer than he could remember.

"We'll just sit then." Henry led him back to his chair and sat beside him.

As they sat in silence, the crowd left one by one. Some time must have passed because the workers, looking hesitant and unsure, picked up their shovels. He imagined her tiny body stuck under the ground, entombed in darkness, and fear gripped his heart.

"They can't cover her," he whispered. "What if she can't get out?"

"She's not here, Tyler. That's just her body under there."

Tyler noticed Henry's face for the first time in days. His hair had greyed considerably and the tears that stained his cheeks seemed to be permanent. Agony twisted his features as he spoke. "I'm sorry, but she is not coming back. I wish with all my heart that she was."

"I dream of her, every time I sleep. She keeps trying to tell me something but I'm not listening because I'm just so happy to have her. Then I wake up and for a moment I forget that she's gone." Swallowing past the lump in his throat, he continued, "It's like she dies again every time. What if she was trying to tell me not to bury her?"

"She would never do something like that, and you know it." Henry grasped his hand. "In all my life, I have never seen two people who loved each other so completely. Hold on to her memory Tyler, but don't do this to yourself. She wouldn't want that."

A throbbing pressure squeezed his temples. Everyone seemed to know what she would want, how she's 'happier now' or 'in a better place' and he hated every one of them. How dare they assume they know anything about her? He wanted to scream at all of them, scream at Henry. He was sick of their lies. Instead, he let the anger simmer inside, so he had something to focus on other than the pain. "I want to stay here for a while. Alone."

"Tyler, she wanted me to take care of you."

"It doesn't matter what she wanted anymore!" His voice echoed across the empty cemetery. He stood; his fists clenched. "It doesn't matter."

"I can't make you leave, Tyler, and I won't, but I would like it if you would come stay with me for a while. You could use the company. Hell, I could use the company." When he didn't respond, Henry sighed and stood. "I'm always here when you need me. Please call me later and let me know you're okay?"

Unable to stand the look of pity on his face, Tyler focused on the laces of his shoes and nodded.

Henry squeezed his shoulder and walked off. The workers filled the grave and took down the canopy as the sun set behind the trees. When they needed to take the chairs, he sat down on the ground beside the grave and traced her name on the headstone. Henry had asked him if he wanted an inscription. He thought about it, but in the end, he decided there were no words to describe how beautiful she was, and they left it blank.

For hours he sat there, reliving every moment he could remember with her, drilling it in so he would never forget. Eventually the workers left, and the day turned into night. He wrapped his arms around his head to shut the world out. Tyler yearned for her scent, the taste of her, but he felt nothing but empty ground. He pressed a kiss onto the cold stone. "I love you, Ki."

## 42

For weeks, he searched the house, looking for her, praying for her. He could sense her, sometimes he even saw her out of the corner of his eye or heard her voice. But when he turned around, there was nothing.

Henry came by often and begged him to come stay with him for a while, but Tyler didn't want to leave, afraid he would miss her if she came back. Of course, he didn't tell Henry that. Lately he had been getting a look in his eyes that made Tyler think he was considering having him committed. So, he lied and said he needed to travel soon, asking him to take care of Pigmy while he was gone.

The puppy was the only comfort he had, but he too seemed to be suffering from their loss. It was during one of these moments when they were both curled up on the couch in misery that Pigmy popped his head up, his tail wagging. Tyler nearly ignored his change in attitude but then he heard her voice. It had come from one of their rooms. He'd rushed down the hallway to find her.

*"Tyler."*

His name floated out from the closet and he pulled the

doors open. For ten minutes, he searched every inch of it while Pigmy watched, only to find it empty of her presence. He collapsed on the floor. Out of the corner of his eye he saw her white dress, the one he teased her for wearing when she gardened. He pulled it out and held it to his face, covered it in tears.

EIGHT WEEKS PASSED, each one ticking by. He'd started to think of ways to die without committing suicide. Each time he did though, he heard her voice begging him not to.

Jennifer called, asking him if he could keep her company, but he declined. She and Henry were taking turns keeping watch, and although he appreciated the gesture, he wanted to be alone.

"Tyler, please. I miss her, too. It worries me that you keep brushing us off."

*Us. Well, at least she's not trying to pretend she called me on her own.*

"I'm really not in the mood for company. Please don't take it personally. I'm doing okay though. I've been reading, taking walks, things like that."

"You're lying through your teeth. I'm guessing you've been moping around watching videos of her."

He paused the video and sighed. *The woman is damn near psychic.* "Look, I'm not trying to commit suicide, but you can't expect me to be happy. This is the best I can do."

"I won't pressure you, Tyler. I just want you to know that I'm here."

IT HAD BEEN three days since their last conversation. Tyler didn't know if he should be grateful or worried. He got the answer to his question around mid-day when the doorbell chimed, and he glanced out. Jennifer was standing on the porch. He sighed and opened the door just wide enough that his body filled the entryway.

"Hey."

The way her eyes roamed over him, pausing at his stained shirt and wrinkled pants, made him self-conscious. He tried to recall the last time he showered and couldn't.

"You look like hell, Tyler." Her ponytail whipped around as she finished her statement and gestured toward the silver vehicle sitting in the driveway. "Henry loaned me his van so I could come pick up those boxes Kiara packed for the Care Center charity."

Tyler frowned. He vaguely remembered her mentioning something but that had been eons ago. Also, they were playing him. Both Henry and Jennifer knew he wouldn't go against Kiara's wishes by not allowing Jennifer to get the boxes.

"Um . . . yeah, I'd forgotten about that. I'll drop them off later today."

"That's ridiculous." She walked around him and ducked under his arm. "I've already borrowed the car and everything."

Tyler rolled his eyes before closing the door behind her. Jennifer looked around the room. The house wasn't a complete mess, since Tyler didn't do much but lie around, but it wasn't as clean as Kiara would have kept it. Still, there was a twinge of guilt.

"Jennifer—"

"Well, I'm going to start on those boxes."

*No 'how have you been?' No questions? What's going on here?*

The last couple times they had talked, he'd been short

with her, but as far as he could remember, it wasn't anything explicit enough to warrant her cool attitude. Before he could ask though, she walked away.

He followed her and leaned against the door frame as she opened the closet door. "Hey, I was just about to take a shower and—"

"Go ahead. You certainly need one." She didn't turn around when she spoke.

*What the hell? Well, whatever. Good riddance anyway. It'll just make it easier when I . . .*

He let the thought trail off.

*When I what?* "Okay then. Just lock up behind yourself when you go."

Tyler took one of the longest showers in his life, partially because he needed it, but also because he worried Jennifer might linger. Although, with her mood, he thought the likelihood of that was slim. Therefore, he was surprised when he came out and found her cleaning up the house. "What are you doing?"

"Picking up." She stopped washing off the table. "This place is a mess."

"You don't have to do that. It's not your job to take care of me."

"Really?" Jennifer raised her eyebrows. "Because I got a check in the mail the other day, accompanied by a letter that says it is."

*Dammit, Ki.*

She had insisted they keep paying Jennifer when she was gone, but he'd never asked how she planned on doing it. He sighed and sat on the couch.

"Don't be mad. I didn't know she planned it either." Jennifer plopped down beside him. "I would do it anyway and I think she knew that."

"I know." He scooted over, putting room in between

them. "I don't suppose you'll just cash the checks and not worry about taking care of me?"

"Nope." She glared at him.

"You want to tell me why you're so pissed off at me then?"

"I'm not mad at you at all. I'm sorry if I came off that way." She stared into the distance. "I haven't had much rest lately. Honestly, I came because I'm worried about you. I miss you . . . I miss her."

Tyler grabbed her hand and squeezed. "I know. I'm sorry I've been making this so hard on you."

"Don't worry about it. I like a challenge." She squeezed his hand back. "I'm guessing you've already figured out today was a ruse to check on you?"

He nodded.

"It would be a hell of a lot easier on me and Henry if we didn't have to make an excuse to stop by."

"I'll work on that."

Jennifer stood. "Good. How about we come over for dinner this Friday? Henry hasn't been able to stop talking about your cooking. I've even caught him scouting out some commercial property in town."

Tyler tried to smile but the pain ran too deep for him to accomplish more than a smirk. He followed her over to the table as she picked up the last of the boxes. Her visit had made him feel a little better.

"Hey, thanks for—"

One of the books slid off the top of a box and landed on the floor. A slip of paper drifted out of it. He picked up the book while she gathered the paper.

Jennifer stopped, mid-rise. "Oh shit."

Her hands trembled around the sheet of paper.

"What is it?"

Face pale, eyes wide, she met his gaze. "Nothing."

She shoved the paper in her pocket and reached for the book. Tyler frowned and read the title. It was one of Kiara's novels. Did Jennifer think he was going to freak out over seeing one of her novels? Hell, the house was full of them. Maybe the paper then?

"Can I have the book, please?" She looked at him, then her eyes darted to the floor.

"Is something wrong?"

She shook her head. "I just realized that I'm running late."

The tremor in her voice was the last straw. "No, you didn't. What was on that paper?"

"It's just trash. I really need to go. I'm going to be late returning Henry's car."

She cut her eyes to the floor again and tugged on the book. He pulled it out of her hands. There was no doubt about it, she was hiding something from him.

"Show me that paper." He held out his hand. Jennifer bit her lip. Taking a deep breath, she reached into her pocket and pulled out an old receipt. On the back were the words, '*Call me,*' and a number he didn't recognize. They meant nothing to him. "What's is this about?"

"I told you. It was just trash."

"Stop the bullshit lies. Something has you spooked. I deserve the right to know what it is."

Jennifer shut her eyes and mumbled something under her breath. When she opened them again, her cheeks were red.

"It's nothing. It's stupid of me to even mention this." She shook her head. "I guess the best way to start is to ask you. Did you ever meet Kiara before the hospital?"

"No." He furrowed his brow. "Why do you ask?"

"I'm probably being paranoid, but can I see that?" Jennifer nodded to the book. He handed it over. She flipped to the front, eyes scanning the page. Her face paled and she handed the book to him with the front cover open. "Read this."

He took the novel. Scribbled in Kiara's handwriting was the sentence, "*To Tyler Reed, my biggest fan, at least for the past five minutes since he bought this novel.*"

"What the hell is this?"

Jennifer waved to the chair. "Have a seat and I'll explain."

Tyler did as she asked, listening intently as she told her story.

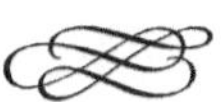

# 43

An empty bottle of scotch smashed against the wall, shattered into pieces. Pigmy yelped. Tyler stumbled over to the startled puppy, pushed his hand along the wall to keep from falling. He nuzzled the trembling puppy against his chest as he whispered consoling words. Pigmy must have sensed his mood because he brushed his rough tongue along Tyler's cheek and wiggled to be let down. With a clicking of nails and two gentle barks, the furry beast disappeared down the hallway. Tyler resumed his place at the kitchen table, reading and re-reading the words Kiara had dreamed she wrote to him over five years ago.

With thoughts born from intoxication, he pulled his phone out of his pocket and found Henry's number. Squinting, he typed *Take care of Pigmy*, and sent the message before scrolling through the images on his phone until he found one of Kiara.

*Damn you. Why the book? What were you trying to tell me?*

Hours after finding the novel he'd received confirmation from his agent. Yes, he had been close to the area at the time and on the day in question.

"I would have remembered meeting her," he spoke to an empty room but heard nothing more significant than the sound of his own voice. "I would have remembered you!"

It made no sense. *If* she had signed an autograph for him and *if* that had really happened, why'd *she* have possession of the book?

No, he shook his head. It couldn't have occurred. Then why make it up? Why leave the book where he would find it? The receipt had no legible date or time. He had no idea if it had faded from the years passed or if she'd tampered with it. If she was trying to leave him a message, he was clueless.

He ran his thumb over her image and tried to recall the feel of her skin, how she smelled, how it felt to hold her. The phone rang in his hand, interrupting the memory. He merely glanced at Henry's name on the caller ID before turning it off. In the silence, he heard her voice drift through the house.

*"Tyler."*

"Ki, please, why? What were you trying to tell me? You wouldn't want me to live like this. I know you wouldn't."

The answer never came, but he didn't expect it to. He heard her all the time, spoke to her, looked for her. Henry said it was to be expected, that sometimes the mind hears and sees things it was used to hearing and seeing. At first, he hadn't believed him, but after nothing came of his searches and begging for her to show herself, he decided the doctor was right. Now he rarely got up to go look.

Talking to her, though, he would probably never stop doing that. "I would have remembered you."

Looking through the window, the Chinese lanterns

swung in the evening breeze. Somehow, when he wasn't aware, winter had turned into spring and then summer. Kiara's garden was in full bloom, flowers swaying in the wind. Outside, the world had changed but he would be forever stuck in winter. Their house sat alone in a world that no longer felt alive.

*"Tyler."*

*I love you Ki, always.*

*"Tyler."*

Shadows floated across the balcony and he saw her reflection, transparent through the window. He walked over to the glass, pressed his hand against hers. It disappeared as she faded away.

Tyler stepped outside. The warm breeze brushed his skin. "I can't do this, Ki. I'm not strong enough."

Wiping the snot off on his sleeve, he got down on his knees. "Please forgive me."

His soul, tortured, torn apart, could take no more. Ki didn't necessarily believe in an afterlife or at least none that she spoke of. She never once asked him what he was going to do after she passed. She had to know, had to see the truth in his eyes, and she never once asked. Why not?

*Because she understood, because she wouldn't have gone on without me, because she knew there were things worse than death.*

He stood and walked to the edge of the railing. Tyler watched sunlight fade into dusk. As the last of the rays disappeared, he stepped over the edge of the balcony. In the tree line below him, darkness gathered, but it was not darkness caused by night. Two shadows, thick and omniscient, slithered out of the trees. The creatures which had tormented them for months, the ones he'd never seen clearly enough to understand their essence, now waited for his death. He should have been afraid but for some reason he was expecting them.

Tyler looked down at them and laughed, took one hand off the railing to flip them off. "Fuck you."

They remained still.

"Bring her back to me!" Tears streamed down his face, and he wiped them away. "It's not fair! Bring her back!"

"*Tyler.*" Her voice, like silk, caressed his ears as she stepped out from beneath the trees.

*It can't be.*

"Are you real?"

She shook her head.

"I miss you so much. I loved you so much. It's not fair that they took you away!" he screamed.

Her bottom lip trembled.

"You're never coming back, are you?"

She shook her head again. He wasn't surprised by the answer. Inside, he already knew.

He spent a moment staring at her, remembering. He could taste her lips, smell the soap she used in the shower, remember the way her hair tangled around his fingers.

"Then I'll come to you." He let go of the balcony.

# 44

The shrill alarm woke him. He felt around the side of the bed until he found his cell phone. Squinting, he saw the time was 5:30 am. Tyler shut off the alarm and tried to remember why he'd set it in the first place. The spinning room made his stomach churn. He sat up and a blonde-haired girl moaned and rolled over.

*Chloe? Her name's Chloe, I think.*

Breathing in and out through his nose, he waited for his stomach to settle as he took in the surroundings. A mattress, dirty, with a threadbare blanket was the only piece of furniture in the room other than a thin pair of sun-bleached curtains covering the window. A gold, burnished ashtray sat in the corner, full of cigarette butts. Beside him, on brown and yellow carpet sticky with age, were two empty needles and a small bag of white powder. He picked it up, gathered a large amount in his nail, and snorted it. Pain flared through his sensitive nostrils, followed by immediate alertness and excitement. The woman stirred, and he finished quickly, not wanting to be there when she woke up. Tyler found his pants lying on the floor. He slipped them on and found his shirt and shoes on the way to the door.

Leaving the bedroom, the hallway opened into a living room. A young boy, maybe three, was sitting on the couch eating chips and watching TV. Tyler didn't see anyone else in the house.

"Hello," the child said.

"Hi."

The kid smiled. The t-shirt he wore was made for a child twice his age and his diaper sagged, fully absorbed to its max.

*Is nobody watching this kid?*

He vaguely remembered something about a babysitter last night, but no one was present now. He couldn't help but feel disdain for the mother who got drunk and let her child walk around by himself in the morning.

"Hungry."

"Why don't you go and wake your momma up?"

"Momma get mad."

*I guess this isn't a one-time thing.*

Tyler walked to the small kitchen and looked in the cabinets, most of which were empty. He checked the fridge and found some butter, milk, half a coke, and some slices of cheese. There was nothing else edible, so he brought the kid the cheese, which he gratefully accepted.

"Okay, then. Well, I have to go."

*Why am I explaining myself to a toddler?*

The boy waived and turned back to his show. Tyler stood there for another moment, unsure of whether to wake his mother. In the end, he decided it wasn't his problem to deal with.

He turned and walked out the door.

～

HE MADE it less than two blocks when he saw a bakery and went inside. Twenty minutes later, he returned to the house. Tyler waved at the boy when he walked in and went straight to the bedroom, shook the woman on the bed. She moaned and blinked a few times but didn't wake up. He shook her a second time. She responded by sitting up.

"Hey. I brought breakfast and coffee and your kid's awake. I'll go set the stuff out in the kitchen."

The woman, girl really, looked confused but nodded. Tyler set the doughnuts, bagels, and coffee out on the table. He glanced in the other room and saw her changing the boy's diaper. She lifted him up and headed his way.

"Thanks for breakfast."

"Yeah, no problem." He looked down uncomfortably, wondering if he should offer to leave her money. Then again, she might think he was paying for the sex. "Well, I have to get to work."

"Okay, sure."

He smiled at the boy and stepped out the door, wanting to get a little further away before he called a cab. This wouldn't be his first one-night stand, but it damn sure was the first one that left him feeling like a complete ass.

*What the hell is wrong with me?*

"HEY MAN. YOU COMING OUT TONIGHT?"

Tyler turned at the sound of his co-worker's voice. Damon wasn't his friend, but he was closer than many, mostly because he could always rely on him to supply drugs.

"Nah, not tonight man. I'm fucking beat."

"Okay. I'll catch you later."

Tyler left for his trailer. As he walked into the empty

space, he seriously reconsidered Damon's offer. He wasn't fond of keeping up the pretense of friendship, but it was better than being left to his own company. Then again, he wasn't lying when he said he was beat. He ached from being up most of the night.

He threw his keys on the dresser and went to the bathroom. The mirror reflected a stranger. Lately, his skin had begun to sag a bit, looking pasty and pale, and although he tried to ignore it, the yellowing in the whites of his eyes had spread rapidly over the last year. He knew the reality of his drug addiction, could see the effects on his body and it caused him great anxiety. That was the part about addiction that made it so hard to overcome—the drugs got rid of the anxiety.

Frustrated, he took off his clothes and jumped into the shower. Hot water billowed out of the shower, laying a curtain of condensation on the glass.

He shut his eyes.

Behind him someone whispered, "You're getting wet."

He turned around quickly, but there was no one there.

3:00 AM

HE WOKE UP, screaming, crying from something awful, something he couldn't remember. All he knew was that when he came to, he was screaming the name Kiara.

12:00 PM

He left the set for lunch and found a deli close by. Sitting around and talking to the people he worked with didn't appeal to him. Although he was usually able to put on a friendly demeanor, today he didn't feel like he could pretend to care about their mundane conversations.

A couple stood in front of him in line. Young, maybe late teens. They boy laughed and intertwined his fingers in hers, saying something about it being his turn. As far as Tyler could tell, they seemed to be playing some type of word game.

A gentleman behind him chuckled. "They look like they're having fun."

Tyler smiled politely, uninterested in acknowledging the man, but he felt like he had no choice since the statement was directed his way. "Yeah, they do. Guess you have to be privy to the rules, though, because it doesn't make any sense to me."

"Those are the best games," the man smiled. "The secret ones that you only share between the two of you. It makes them special."

*Do you want to play the game?*

"You alright there, son?" The man's face blurred.

"She's a writer."

"Who is? The girl? Do you know them?" The elderly man nodded to the couple.

*I don't know. I don't know why I said that.*

"No. Sorry, I was thinking about someone else."

"Perhaps your own soulmate?" Although he smiled when he said this, the look of concern had not left his face. Tyler couldn't blame him. He was worried about his own sanity.

"Perhaps so." He turned around, glad it was his turn at the counter so he wouldn't have to continue the conversation and possibly make a bigger fool of himself. Having lost his appetite, he ordered the first thing he saw on the menu without regard of whether it appealed to him or not. The lady behind the counter took his order, and he sought out a spot off to the side while waiting for them to call his name.

*What the hell is going on with me?*

Tyler glanced around the café. He saw couples laughing together, singles with laptops open, businessmen with files spread out between them. Not a single person there felt real. There was no one he could connect with, no one with whom to share his secrets. Alone, afloat in this world with no connections, no purpose, he ached for something more—even though he didn't know what that might be.

He heard his name called. Tyler approached the counter, thanked the young boy with a frown and bad acne for his food, and took the slender brown bag from him. As he made his way out, sunlight glinted off the silver door handle, blinding him. Someone grabbed his shoulder.

He expected to see a fan, and that would have been unfortunate, but instead he found himself looking back into the elderly gentleman's face.

"I'm sorry, son. I know it's none of my business, but you seem sad. Sometimes old farts like me get real senti-mental. I just couldn't let you walk out of here without letting you know that I'll keep you in my prayers."

*Jesus.* "Um . . . thanks . . . I appreciate it."

"As silly as it seems, sometimes it helps to know someone else cares enough to add you to their prayers."

Uncomfortable and mildly embarrassed, but slightly moved, he thanked the man and started to walk off.

"One more thing, son."

Tyler looked back over his shoulder, but the man was staring at the door, not him.

"You need to ascend."

"What?" The words meant nothing to him but at the same time, he felt like they meant everything. "What did you say?"

The man lifted his head and met Tyler's eyes, brows peaked above his bumpy nose. "Sorry son, my mind was wandering off on me. Guess you're not the only one who's a little thoughtful today."

"Guess not." His voice was steady, but his heart was beating hard in his chest. He turned and stepped out into the sunlight.


12:45 P.M.


HE PASSED by a pet store and stopped to stare at a spotted brown and grey puppy. It wagged its tail and jumped up, paws pressed against the clear surface. Tyler smiled and leaned down, tapped on the glass. The puppy pawed at it, peed himself in excitement. He chuckled and started to tap the glass one more time but stopped short when he noticed the puppy's eyes. One blue and one green. Before he knew what he was doing, he walked into the pet store.


1:38 P.M.


HE FINISHED SETTING out the dog bed, food, water, and puppy pad in the bedroom of his trailer while the excited puppy—which he named Pigmy—followed him around sniffing everything. He scratched him behind the ears and

277

lectured him to not chew up his stuff while he was gone, then went back on set.

10:00 P.M.

*WHAT IS WRONG WITH ME?*

He collapsed on the bed and asked himself the question for the hundredth time.

He'd felt out of place all day, had been annoyed by the tiniest things, irritated by how everyone seemed to be so focused on trivial details.

*Like you have anything better to focus on.*

Absently, he reached over and petted the snoring puppy who had merely scoffed at his own bed, finding Tyler's more appealing. He hadn't bothered to fight him on the issue though, because for the first time in a long time, he didn't feel completely alone.

*A puppy. I connect better with a dog than I do people.*

Frustrated, he got off the bed and reached under the mattress, felt around until he found a plastic bag. He unrolled the bag and shook it until the powder fell to the bottom. He stared at the residue for a few minutes.

*What are you waiting for?*

He started to unzip the baggie.

*"Tyler. Please don't."*

He curled up into a fetal position, feeling weak and nauseated. The voice, so familiar but not, kept echoing through his head. Even though it caused him pain, he tried to hold on to it, aching to hear it one last time.

After a few minutes, he got up and flushed the entire bag down the toilet.

3:23 AM

HE WOKE UP SCREAMING, crying from a dream that was quickly fading from his mind.

4:00 AM

HE OPENED HIS EYES AGAIN. A loud keening filled the room. In the darkness, large, black things slithered across the walls. He shook with fear. One of the creatures turned its head, milky white eyes met his.

"Go away," he whispered.

The creatures disappeared.

5:00 AM

HE ROLLED out of bed and stumbled to the bathroom to relieve himself. When he was finished, he turned toward the gleaming porcelain sink and stopped. On the mirror written repeatedly with marker were the words, *I watched her die.*

5:10 AM

*I'M sick and won't be on set today.* He pressed send on his phone.

7:45 AM

A VOICE SPOKE from behind him.

"Are you real?" This time he didn't bother to turn around.

"I don't know."

He sat down to breakfast in a small, nearly empty diner, tried to eat, but couldn't stomach more than a couple bites. A guy with blond hair stared at him over a paperback book. After a moment, the man stood and approached his table. Tyler stared down at his plate, hoping he would take the hint and leave him alone.

"Excuse me."

*No such luck.*

"Yes?" The indiscrete features of the man made it hard to place an age, mid-twenties maybe? *Jesus, Tyler, get it together.*

"You're Tyler Reed, right?" The young man gave a nervous smile.

"Yes." The sound of the man's voice reminded Tyler of nails scraped across a chalkboard.

"I was wondering . . . well, I know it's rude . . ."

*Too bad that's not going to stop you.*

". . . and all, but I loved your work in *The Breaking*, and

I wanted to see, if you don't mind, I mean, if I could get your autograph?"

The guy was holding a piece of paper and pen on the top of his book.

"Yeah, sure."

Tyler held his hand out, watched as the man shuffled his paper and pen around, his hands shaking. He finally just handed Tyler everything.

Wanting to be done with this entire situation, Tyler grabbed it and hurriedly began to scribble. "What's your name?"

"It's Andrew Gibbens."

*To Andrew, a great fan. Tyler Reed.*

"Man, this must be my lucky day. I not only got an autograph from one of my favorite actors, but I was just leaving to go to the mall because my favorite author is doing a book signing today."

"Is that so?" He finished scrawling the message, wishing Andrew would stop talking and leave.

"Yeah, man. That's her book under the paper. She's brilliant. Have you read her work?"

Tyler moved the paper off of the book and read the title, *The Awakening.* Curiously, he picked up the book and flipped to the picture description on the back. Andrew spoke again and his voice held a note of awe. "That's her, Kiara Moore. She's beautiful, isn't she?"

"Yeah, she is." Tyler stared at the picture mesmerized, although something about her made him sad. He closed the book and handed Andrew his stuff back.

"Thanks a lot, man."

Tyler didn't respond. Something was wrong here. Absently, he picked up his set of keys and began to rotate them around while thinking. He wanted to take the book and rip it out of the guy's hands.

"Oh, wow man, is that a prop from the movie?" Andrew was gaping at the decorative mace on his key set. "Wow, it is, isn't it? Does it work?"

Hoping to persuade him to leave, he unclipped the mace from his keys and handed it over. "Yes, it works. Here, you can have it. I have several."

"Awesome." Andrew ran his fingers down the miniature spray can. "Are you sure?"

Tyler nodded and directed his attention back to the keys, but the guy just stood there, staring.

*Jesus, leave already.*

Out loud he said, "You might want to hurry to meet that author. I heard the traffic on the interstate is really bad today."

"Crap, I better. I don't want to miss meeting Kiara Moore."

At the sound of her name, his vision blurred again, the same as it did the day before.

Andrew must have picked up on his sudden change in demeanor because he asked, "You okay, man?"

"She's afraid of rats." The words escaped his lips before he knew he was going to say them.

"Oh, do you know her?"

Tyler shook his head, disoriented. "No, I've just heard."

"Okay, cool. Thanks for the insight. Anyway, I've got to head out so I can catch her." Andrew gave him a strange look. "Thanks for the autograph and the prop."

He turned and walked away.

*Stop him!*

Tyler found himself standing to do just that but stopped before he took his first step.

*I'm losing it.*

He turned and ran to his truck.

10:30 AM

HE FINISHED DRESSING after his shower and turned the TV on for some background noise.

*It's a nervous breakdown. I just need to relax, maybe take a break from acting for a while. Go somewhere far away, maybe close to the mountains.*

He laid on his bed, covered his face with his arm. In the background, he heard the news going on.

"The local citizens are prepared to take their petition against the new toll road to the City Council during the next meeting. In other news, today, Kiara Moore, a well-known horror author, is doing a book signing at the Richmond mall from nine to eleven AM. We were able to catch her before the signing to discuss her latest book, *The Awakening*."

Tyler uncovered his eyes and stared at the screen. A blonde headed reporter was sitting in a chair across from a girl with long black hair and large green eyes. *She's beautiful.*

The reporter started the conversation. "Good Morning, Miss Moore. Well, I think I can speak for everyone when I say we are excited to have you here today."

"Thank you, Jeannette. I'm excited to be here."

*It's her voice.*

He climbed off the bed and sat in front of the TV.

He ran his fingertips across her face on the screen.

"So, this is your third book, and it's rumored there is going to be a series. I guess the big question is, is this *the end?*"

Kiara smiled. "It's hard to say. As I writer I would have to say that, no, this is not the end, that when you read a story, it becomes a part of you, and you carry it on."

Tyler gasped.

*Not the end. Story . . . a part of you. Carry it . . . on.*

*Don't forget . . .*

*I'll never forget you . . .*

"Ki?" The memories rushed in, every smile, every touch, the love, the loss.

Tyler fell to his knees.

10:50 AM

THE CARS in front of him stopped. He slammed his brakes, cursing loudly. The mall was on his right; he could see the top of the building in the distance. He pulled his truck over to the side of the road, got out, and started running.

11:06 AM

THEY WERE TAKING down the signs. His body shook, sweat drenched his shirt. The lady at the front desk asked, "Can I help you?"

"Kiara Moore?" He forced the name out between large huffs of breath.

"I'm sorry. The book signing ended at eleven."

"How long ago did she leave?"

"Maybe two minutes."

He started to run again but stopped as he passed by a stand showcasing her novel. Grabbing the book, he brought it to the checkout and threw a wad of cash on the counter. The lady counted it and made out change. "Are you a fan?"

"Yeah." He looked out the window, searched for her.

"I put the receipt in the book."

"Sure." He grabbed it and ran.

THE MALL WAS PACKED, people streamed in every direction. It was small with only a single floor and it took him less than five minutes to sprint from one end to the other, scanning every face he saw, but none held his interest. His heart pounded and his chest hurt from breathing too hard, but he didn't stop.

*They gave me a second chance.*

That thought had become a mantra since he remembered who she was. Unfortunately, it was followed by the fear that he would lose her—again—that his chance would only last so long.

*What if Andrew finds her first?*

A thousand thoughts, hundreds of conversations, and yet he could not recall them ever discussing the exact moment or time of her abduction. For some reason, he felt that if he didn't get to her before Andrew, then his chance would be over.

So, he ran, his eyes bulged, and sweat drenched his clothes. The crowd parted as he neared, something about him sending them as far away as they could get. Eventually, his legs gave out from under him and he fell, landing hard. Black spots swirled in his vision and he struggled to remain conscious.

He had run miles on end and his body refused to go any further. Trying to stand, his legs buckled again. Tears of frustration streamed down his face, and he ducked his head into his hands, letting them stream through his fingers.

*I've lost.*

"You take care, too. Thanks for the advice." Her voice drifted to him, drowned out all the others. He lifted his head. Kiara was standing in front of a darkly lit store with band t-shirts covering the walls. In her hand was a black and red bag. Another girl, young, with several facial piercings, waved as she stepped away.

*Ki!*

She was younger, fuller, with a carefree smile on her face. He'd never seen her before she'd been changed by her abduction. She had a confidence about her, an *assuredness* that had never been a part of *them*. She started walking toward the door and he wiped his face, cleaning off the tears and sweat.

*Will she remember me? Will we have to start all over? How do I hide it from her if she doesn't remember? What if she doesn't like me?* His insecurities and fears drained away as she got closer the entrance of the mall.

*No!* He chased after her. "Ki?"

She didn't turn or acknowledge him, so he yelled louder. "Ki!"

Tyler was closing the space, unsure of what to do when he realized he was still holding her book in his hands.

*I asked her out. She said I pretended to be a fan and asked her out.*

"Miss Moore!"

The bag hanging on her arm stopped mid-motion as she turned toward him. Her face, alive and healthy, showed mild recognition but did not hold the love it once had. A stranger for which his heart burned, and his entire soul belonged to, did not know him from anyone else, and yet he held hope; knew he loved her enough for them both. He would never give up until she loved him back.

"Hi, I'm sorry to bother you. I was hoping to catch you before you left but I got held up." He smiled, calling upon all his acting skills, and held the book out to her, hoping she wouldn't notice how bad he was shaking. "I know it's a little late, but I was wondering if you would mind signing this?"

"Of course," she said. Her beautiful smile beamed at him. "You're that actor, right?"

"Yeah, I guess so." He ran his hands through his hair. "Tyler Reed. It's nice to meet you, Miss Moore."

"It's Kiara. Nice to meet you, too." She reached out to shake his hand.

Wanting more than anything in the world to touch her again, he stepped forward to take her hand, but something stopped him. A feeling, a knowledge so strong he knew it to the essence of his soul.

*This isn't right. This isn't right at all.*

Beautiful green eyes met his and there was a light behind them, a look of hope.

"This never happened." Tyler took a few steps back. "I would have remembered you."

At his words, her lips curved into a smile. Before he could determine what that smile meant, the floor began to shake. He was knocked to his knees. Cracks appeared, tearing the walls and ceilings apart, as concrete dust rained down on them. His eyes darted around. There should be screaming, running, but they were the only two in the entire mall. The cracks grew, and shards, large pieces of decorated rooftop, cracked like glass and fell to the floor, leaving only blackness behind them.

As the pieces fell, Kiara stared down at him, an inde-terminable expression on her face. The world was falling apart, his world, and he knew he had not been given a second chance, that he had never met her before the hospital. That left only one thing.

"Ki," he whispered. "I'm dead, aren't I?"

She nodded.

He wept, placed his head on his knees as the world turned black.

Time is different in darkness. It spins no web, leaves no mark, only passes internally to those who are left within.

Tyler had no concept of how long he had been in the dark, the only company was his own tortured mind. He remembered jumping off the balcony, remembered the sound of the air whooshing by as he fell, but did not remember the pain of impact, nor anything afterward.

She had died. He had killed himself. Could he find her in death, or would he spend eternity alone with his thoughts?

The darkness was thick, sticky, *warm*. Sleep was taking over. He didn't fight the lure of slumber, instead he grasped it with all he had, a chance to escape this pain.

"Tyler." The sweet sound of her voice caressed him, but he couldn't fight the exhaustion, couldn't respond. All he wanted to do was dream of her.

"Open your eyes, Tyler."

His eyes were open. Could she not see in the darkness? Was she as blind as he was?

"They're open, baby. Just need to sleep for a while."

"No. They are not. Open them, for god's sake. Please, if you love me, open them."

*I love you so much.*

He tried to do as she asked but couldn't. The darkness was too thick, it pressed down on him. His lids were heavy, numb, and he could not remember how to lift them. "I can't."

"You have to. Think about how it felt to blink, to open them in the morning."

Her words were confusing, but he did as she requested. He brought an image forth, lying beside her in the bed, opening his eyes to her beautiful face. Everything became brighter, pinkish in tint. His vision was distorted, as if he were looking through a sheet of filmy, textured glass. Inhaling deeply, he choked on thick, gelatinous material. Tyler struggled for air, clawed at his throat, his vision darkening around the edges. Kiara's voice seemed to come from miles away as her hands frantically forced their way into his mouth, clearing his airways, cleaning the stickiness out of his eyes.

Gasping, he tasted dank, cool, wet air and fought for more. He was pulled into a sitting position, his back pounded on until the sweet, viscous liquid rose from his chest and he vomited. Gagging on his own stomach acid, his throat burned with the intensity of purging itself. When the violent episode ended, he blinked the last remnants of the substance from his eyes and saw Kiara fearfully watching him.

"Ki?" His voice was raspy, unfamiliar, as if he hadn't used it for a long time. At the sound of it, Kiara grabbed him by the face and kissed him, tears streamed down her cheeks. Her mouth, wet and sweet, destroyed the last remaining sleepiness. Tyler kissed her back, not caring about anything else in that moment except for the feel of her skin, the taste of her breath. She pulled back and smiled.

"Are you real?" he asked.

"Yes."

"But you died. I saw you die." With dismay, he realized she might be nothing more than a dream, a demented vision brought from his broken mind. It didn't feel like a dream though. The scorching rawness of his throat and painful spasms which rocked his stomach were testimony to that. There was a similarity between this moment and the one in which he awoke in the hospital after overdosing.

*What if none of this has been real? What if I jumped and lived? What if I'm hooked to some sort of machine, keeping me alive?*

"I'm scared, Ki."

"I know." She touched the side of his face. "We're together, though. That's all that matters."

"What if this is all in my head?" For the first time, he noticed his surroundings. They seemed to be in a dimly lit cave. A reddish, yellow light radiated around them, but he could find no source of the illumination. The walls appeared spongy and flesh-like. A clear pink gel substance covered everything; the same substance that filled his lungs and covered his body. The domed cavern, suspended beyond the eerie glow, seemed endless. The ground beneath him was slick and ridged. Underneath his fingertips, warmth radiated from the surface and he detected a slight pulsing, as if the ground itself was alive. His stomach lurched, and he quickly removed his hand.

Kiara appeared clean, untouched by the residue surrounding them. No longer sick or unhealthy, her beauty shone. "It's hard to explain. I will tell you, but they are coming, and we don't have much time before they get here."

"They who?"

"The Takers."

Fear surged through him and he bolted up, ignoring the unsteadiness in his legs and damp clothing stuck to his skin.

"We have to go. I can't let them take you from me again." He grabbed her hand and tugged as hard as he could, but she didn't budge. "Come on, Ki."

His grasp, slick with slime, made it hard to pull her along and he couldn't figure out why she was making this so difficult. A quick glance at her expression told him all he needed to know. There was no way to escape. In her green eyes, he saw pity.

"It doesn't work that way. We can't hide from them." Kiara broke contact with him, stared into the far reaches of the cavern. She slumped down, making herself appear even smaller than she normally was.

"I'm sorry, Tyler. A part of me always wondered if I was doing the right thing, bringing you here." She shook her head. "I felt selfish. The memory . . . it was so nice there, so familiar but so painful, too. Not as painful as what you're about to go through, though. This is part of the ascension. Do you trust me, Tyler?"

He stared into her eyes, saw the sorrow and fear there and he knew no matter what happened, there was nothing he wouldn't be willing to do for the chance to stay with her. "Yes."

"Then sit and hold me before they get here. It's been so long since I've been able to touch you."

Tyler closed the distance between them and pulled her into his arms, held her as if he would never let go. Her soft skin molded against him, warm, full of life. He pushed the fear and doubt into the back of his mind and focused her. Kiara's hands traced his face, soft touches grazed his chest.

There was an intensity to the way she touched him, like she wasn't sure if she'd ever see him again.

Breathing in her scent, kissing her shoulder, he met her intensity with his own.

Minutes passed, maybe longer, before he became aware, they weren't alone. Kiara lifted her head off his shoulder and turned toward the creatures she called Takers. They stood side by side. The only time Tyler had seen them had either been on video or from a distance. That was nothing like the terror he felt as they loomed over him and Kiara.

The first figure, solid black, with an ethereal silhouette, was in the shape of man. The other one, an insectile creature, with filmy tumor-like eyes, crouched beside it. No flesh covered them. Obsidian in color and sheen, they seemed to form and re-form, as if something inside was pushing its way out. Tyler cowered under their scrutiny.

A high pitch screeching emanated from the smaller of the creatures. The noise surrounded them, pierced through them, the shrillness of it forcing Tyler to the ground. He groveled. The other creature slid forward.

As it approached, Kiara whispered, "I love you."

She let go of him, took a place beside the insect-like abhorrence. As he writhed on the spongy ground, abandoned, his eyes locked with hers.

A wordless lament echoed from the man-like creature, joined with the shrillness of the other. A deep throbbing emanated from the base of Tyler's skull and spread throughout his body. His ears vibrated, the pain building until they burst, warm liquid gushed out of them. A seizure gripped his body and although he was aware, he could gain no control. He saw the silent tears that fell down Kiara's cheeks. The convulsions stopped, but the agony continued. Were they about to kill him, to tear him apart?

The man-like creature slithered forward, closed the distance between them. From the center of the entity came a deep pulsing, and black tentacles formed, quivering as they gained shape. They snaked against Tylers flesh, burning cold, pushing against him. He tried to crawl away.

"Tyler," Kiara's called out. "Let him in. Trust me."

He looked between the creature and Kiara. She was the reason he was here, the reason he lived, the reason he died. Maybe this was the end for him. Maybe it was a chance for *them*. He didn't know. All he did know is that he trusted her, loved her, in both life and death. Taking a deep breath, he let go as the abomination pierced his flesh.

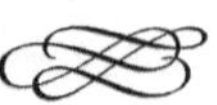

*The world was barren, empty of life, empty of creatures. Sparse vegetation appeared here and there among the dirt-formed ground. A man, naked, beautiful, opened his eyes and looked over the world. His face, radiant, caressed the earth gently, touched and admired each plant. Time passed, and the world grew, plants and animals came in abundance. The man adored each and every leaf, every creature of feather and fur, of hide and scale.*

*One day, the man stumbled across a cave and entered. There he met a woman, her fair skin calling to his soul. They became one.*

*Each son and daughter held a light and glory passed down over hundreds of generations. As they passed, their pure souls were lifted by the Takers, ascending into a bright light. All was well.*

*One day, a descendant, a young woman, curious by nature, wandered deep into the forest where she met a creature of darkness. In vengeance, the creature took the perfect creation and made her his own. Their children, half-light, half-dark would be called Humans.*

*These Humans, imperfect embodiments of both good and evil, were bound to earth, for only a perfect soul could ascend. They could not be controlled, could not be touched by those who were pure, could not be taken on. The Takers grew anxious as they watched the line of pure souls dwindle as they mated with the Humans, becoming nearly extinct.*

*The One Over All sought out the creature of darkness and cast it out of the world. The Beyond took two forms, one for good souls and one for evil. The Takers took two forms, one for good, one for evil. Yet, the Humans could not be changed. The One Over All offered them a chance at redemption, in death, when they were no longer pure mortals, but half-immortal, too. These half-mortals, imperfect creatures, would be given a chance to save their own kind, to change the fate of their world, to purify their souls—a thing in which the Takers and One Over All could not do. But many of them chose not to, not wanting to let go of the memories of flesh. They lay rotting in purgatory. Those who chose to stay and fight for redemption were the only hope for human-kind.*

TYLER OPENED HIS EYES, the image faded as he gasped for air. It had seemed real, as if he was there. He had touched the earth, the beginnings of time and watched from the eyes of the Takers as civilization destroyed itself repeatedly. He felt their longing, their hunger to carry the souls.

Kiara ran to him, placed her hands on either side of his head. "It's okay, it's okay. Look at me, baby. It's okay."

His heart rate slowed, and he sputtered, "What was that?"

"They were showing you the world, what has passed, what must come. They wanted you to know, to see what they do. They are offering you a second chance at ascension, a chance to redeem yourself."

A coldness seeped inside his skin, bruises covered his stomach and everywhere the tentacles had penetrated. "Is this what you did?"

"Yes." She brushed her lips across his forehead, whispered to him. "But you didn't. You've been trapped in purgatory. I came back to get you."

Wet droplets trailed down his face, and he realized he was crying. If what she was saying was true, then he had to consider the idea of souls, afterlife, all of it was real. The idea was almost too much to bear. "I don't understand."

"Shh . . . it's okay." Her eyes, mere inches away, studied him intently. He saw fear there. If they were together now, then why did she look so unsure? Tyler didn't know and found he was too afraid to ask.

"Did you understand what they were showing you?"

"I don't know. I think so."

She wiped the tears off his cheeks, understanding evident in her eyes. "I know it's a lot to take in, but I'll explain the best I can. When someone passes, they . . . ," Kiara waved her hands toward the Takers, ". . . take their souls on only if they are pure, but the line of pure souls no longer exists. It is rare for a human to live this life and die with a pure soul. If the soul is not pure upon death, then they offer them a chance at redemption. When the human body dies, we are no longer a part of this plane of existence, our mortal body is gone, leaving us partially immortal. During our mortal state, we cannot interact with immortals such as the Takers because our souls are bound to each other, a mix of good and bad. When we are dead, though, they can breach us, split our soul into two parts and we can choose, by our actions, to destroy one side of our own soul. Those who don't choose to accept redemption are lost to purgatory for all eternity. Does that make sense?"

"Not really." As soon as the words were out of his mouth, he realized it was a lie. Somewhere inside of him the knowledge was there. There was a thrumming of his heart that beat along with her breathing, that pulsed along with the creatures who stood a few feet away; that felt as one with the fleshy cavern around them. To deny the truth would be harder than to accept it. A feeling of opening, of unfolding, swept over him. Suddenly, he could sense everything and everything could sense him, and he was struck with awe.

He felt her, inside of him, loving him, fearing for him, touching his soul. Her eyes turned white, pearlescent, swirling with all colors of light, and he gasped. She blinked, her eyes becoming green again.

"I'm sorry, Tyler. I lost control for a second there. Feeling you like that . . . please don't be scared."

"I felt you inside of me." His words were breathless, amazed. Fear was the last thing he felt.

"And I, you." She ran her thumb over his lips. "And we can do that again, forever if you wish. But," the warmth of her thumb left his chapped lips, "you have to choose redemption first."

"What do you mean? Of course, I choose it. I choose to be with you," he shook his head, "I would never—"

She cut him off. "Redemption isn't easy. You must face what you've done, pay the debts of your sins. Then you must agree to spend the rest of eternity trying to destroy part of your own soul. Not many can do that. Some try and find it too hard to strive for good and become evil instead, anything to escape the pain caused by their sins."

He realized why she was so scared, why she acted like she might not see him again. Whatever the creatures had done to him was only the beginning. There was something else he had to go through. Fear, a deep, debilitating fear, made his skin turn cold.

*I'm not strong enough to handle anymore.*

Kiara cast her eyes down but not before he saw the doubt in them. He had a sinking feeling that she was aware of his thoughts and agreed with them.

"You said if someone goes to purgatory, they are lost. If that's true, then how were you able to come get me?"

Kiara glanced back at the creatures. "They didn't know. We're not allowed in purgatory. The chances of us finding someone, of not getting lost in their memories, to bring them back," she shook her head, "it's just not possible. Until you, that is. I'm the first to have not only traveled through purgatory but found someone and brought them back. Even then, when I found you, I got sucked into the memory. I had no idea who I was at first, no idea that the memory now embodied both the alive and dead me. The only time I was lucid was when I was sleep walking. During those moments, I was me—the me that had chosen redemption, or at least partially. That's why I kept writing, *I watched him die.* I was trying to remind myself. Except, I didn't understand until I got stronger. When I did figure it out, I did everything I could to make you see the truth, but you were so lost, you refused to see. But I still had hope. The memory, your memory, was changing, adapting to allow me in. So, I implanted a fake memory. I was hoping by doing that, you would realize it was false. It was a long shot, but it worked."

"I would have remembered meeting you." He whispered the words, tried to wrap his head around the implications of what she had done. It seemed impossible. "Wait, if it was just a memory, then you wouldn't have been able to change things."

"You're thinking about this all wrong. A memory is not something that is in your head. It is a real, physical thing. We weren't lost in our thoughts. We were reliving something that happened. It's tangible, it exists in both time and space. No one's ever been able to change one. Your perception of the memory on the other hand—that's what can be altered. The immortals have no control over what we do, they can only observe and no half-immortal has ever been that deep in purgatory. I found that, even when I knew where we were, I struggled to make the simplest changes. You were so embedded in the memory you refused to let me in."

"If you changed things, would that change the future?"

"Yes and no. The future is not predetermined. We are creatures of freewill, mostly because we are neither good nor bad, but both. Your perception of the memory adapted to the changes. What it is now is what it always was. For us, there is no other version of the memory, it simply doesn't exist anymore. What I did, though, has affected Jennifer and Henry. Which is why I can't come back if you don't choose redemption. I have to fix my mistake." Kiara looked over her shoulder. "Tyler, they are ready for you. Please, no matter what, please don't leave me again. I love you so much."

Glancing up, he saw both creatures approaching in unison and trembled. "Can you stay with me?"

"Yes." She nodded and gave him one last kiss before everything went dark.

A WAVE of pain came again. This time it was followed by an onslaught of memories, each passing as flashes, rushing by, yet he would feel the pain of each one for an eternity. He saw himself as a small child playing in a sandbox, reaching out to take another child's toy dinosaur when he wasn't looking. Suddenly, he was the other child going home, scared of his daddy because he lost his toy. His father came into the room and he screamed, huddled in a corner as his daddy pulled off his belt.

Another image. He is a teenager in the backseat of a car with a girl, kissing hot and heavy, taking her virginity, dumping her a few days later. Now he is the girl, crying in the bathroom at school, feeling ashamed and used.

Another girl, this time shooting heroine and having sex in the bar bathroom. She passed out on the sidewalk outside and he left her there. Another man approached, and he felt pain as he clawed at her body, raping her.

The images kept coming, thousands of them, so fast he could barely grasp the agony of one before the next hit. Then, when he felt he could take no more, they slowed. He saw himself as he was that morning, sitting at a table eating breakfast. Andrew approached him. He signed the man's book, gave him his pepper spray. Then he was Kiara, leaving the mall. Andrew approached her, offering to change her tire, putting his briefcase in her trunk. When he was finished, she smiled at him and he lifted the mace spraying her in the eyes before choking her and shoving her in the car. Every moment of her abduction became his. Every second of pain, every second of fear.

*He never intended on taking her, but I gave him a way.*

A scream tore from his throat. Somewhere in the distance he heard her voice, calling him back, begging him to stay. His vision wavered, shades of red, shards of pain. In the distance, a light beckoned him. Closer still, a door appeared. It stood open a crack, the world behind it a garden. Inside, the two of them laughed together, fighting over a hose. The smell of her, the taste of cold water trickling down his face was so clear—he needed only to reach the door.

As he moved toward it, claw marks on the spongy earth caught his attention. Did something else crawl through that door? Was it with them? A few more feet was all he needed to get back to her, to them. He grabbed another handful of earth and looked down. The marks underneath his nails were the same as the ones that led to the door. He stared.

*This is your second time. We will not offer again.*

Tyler realized what he was looking at.

*The marks are mine.*

Kiara's voice, muffled, floated to him from the bright light. But she was so far. There was no way he would make it to her. He was too weak to fight, too scared to move.

"Tyler, don't give up. Please, come to me. I love you."

Pushing with all the strength he had, he stood on trembling legs and approached the light, but it kept moving further and further away. He didn't know if she could hear him—if *they* could hear him—but he screamed as loudly as he could, "I chose her. I chose redemption."

The light pulsated, shimmering and growing in every direction until it shrouded him. In one moment he knew all, felt all, and understood. The light spoke to him, filled him with love and happiness. Then it was gone.

The rest of the world became dim, a mere shadow of itself. He didn't have time to grieve over the loss before the two Takers descended on him.

The pain was unlike anything he had ever experienced. Hot and cold tentacles reached inside, tearing him in half, leaving him with a gaping wound through the center of his chest. As they pulled back, his skin stitched itself back together. He tried to scream. Tried to tell them. They had left whatever was inside torn apart.

Something approached from behind them, something encased in a white light.

A voice unlike any he had ever heard sang out to him. *You may go now, Bringer.*

The pain stopped as suddenly as it came. The white light blinded him as his body moved through the air. Then, more darkness.

*T*yler?"

Her beautiful smile welcomed him back. He looked around slowly, realizing he was on his knees, in a brightly lit pasture. The colors were odd, faded almost, and the air had a sweet, floral aroma. Wisps of pale beige clouds floated overhead. Thin reeds of grass stood tall, unmoved by the slight breeze. He opened his mind to these things, storing them for a later time, one where he could process anything besides the realization that he had survived and was staring at the loving face of his wife.

"Ki? Did I . . . have I?"

"Yes." Her face lit up in a smile.

He grabbed her by the waist and hugged her tightly, a familiar ache in his chest. "I love you so much."

"I love you, too," she whispered in his ear. "I was so scared. I thought I would lose you again."

"You nearly did." The happiness drained out of him. He was the reason for the torture she went through. Each scar, every scream, was ebbed into his soul. Would she forgive him? Would he ever be able to forgive himself? The past mistakes he made flooded through him, the pain so intense his legs could no longer hold him, and he fell to the ground.

She fell with him. "Tyler, you have to relax. You can control this, I promise. You're doing this to yourself. Your soul is split in half. Focus on the good, focus on us."

He tasted her lips on his, swallowing his screams. A warmth leaked into him and he felt her inside, gently nudging, coercing him back. The pain subsided, and he opened his eyes, staring into her white ones.

"Your eyes," he whispered.

"Yours, too." Kiara sat back on her knees. "Creepy, right?"

Unable to help himself, he chuckled. "Kind of cool, actually. I still like the green better, though."

She closed her eyes and took a deep breath. When she opened them again, they were back to normal. "Better?"

"Yes." Tyler thought about his next words. He didn't want to lose her, but he couldn't keep it inside without asking. "Did you know? About me and Andrew?"

She nodded. "Not while I was alive, but afterwards, yes."

Her expression was unreadable, but a shadow of pain reflected in her eyes.

Tyler scrambled to her, grabbed her hands in his. "I'm so sorry. It was all my fault. He took you because of me. I gave him that mace and for no other reason but to get him away from me."

"No, Tyler. Don't think that way."

"It's my fault. He wouldn't have taken you without that mace."

"You don't know that." She squeezed his hands. "I let him change my tire, Tyler. I let him into my life. This is not something you could have changed. I think he would have found a way. And if not, then my life would have been forfeit anyway, because I wouldn't have met you. Please believe that."

Tyler let out a deep breath. Of course, he didn't believe that, but he would let it go for now. "I guess. If nothing else, that's why I'm here. That'll be the hardest thing for me to redeem." He tilted her head back and kissed her. "Nothing else matters right now except being with you."

They smiled at each other, held each other under the bright sun until it settled in the east. As much as he tried, he still could not erase the memory of her death, of burying her. Each time he thought of it, he pulled her closer. "You said you watched me die. Were you really there?"

"Yes. I was always there."

"Did it . . .?" He let the words drift off. He didn't want to know what his death was like, if it had hurt her to see. Maybe one day, but not now.

"Did it what?"

"Nothing. It's not important. I'm still confused about how this all happened. Did you not sleepwalk? Was it really a tumor you died of?"

"For all intents and purposes, yes. I had a tumor. I died because of it. The book wasn't real, though. There had been signs, moments when I could see you becoming more aware. In the end, after your suicide, you were already starting to ascend. That's why you kept hearing me, remembering me. There were many cracks, but it wasn't enough. Memories of the flesh draw us in, they're like vacuums.

I implanted the idea of meeting you before. During one of the times I was alert, I took the book and an old receipt and set everything up. The book was in my car after the abduction. It was Andrews. He had bought another one to read since he didn't want to mess up the copy I signed for him. It was a complete fabrication, and I was hoping you would see it for what it was. I didn't realize what I was causing."

"What do you mean?"

"You remember how I said we can't change memories, only someone's perception of them?" He nodded. "Well, I didn't realize what I was doing when I did that to Jennifer. It was only later I found out. No one's ever been able to change a human's perception after it has already happened —at least not while they are still living. The implications of that . . . ," she took a deep breath, ". . . let's just say they could be extremely bad. We're not sure yet. What we do know is that I marked her in a way that others are drawn to her."

"Others?"

"We're not the only ones out there. Like I said, some that choose redemption go bad. One has taken a particular interest in Jennifer."

"Andrew."

She glanced at his face. "How did you know?"

"Oddly enough, it just makes sense." Tyler took a deep breath. What Kiara did, she did to save him. The risks she took were as much his responsibility now as they were hers. "What do you mean by extremely bad? Are we talking dangerously bad, or end of the world bad?"

She bit her lip but didn't answer.

*End of the world? Really?*

"Oh, shit Ki." He ran his hands through the grass, feeling the brittleness of the stalks as they broke off under his palm. The sensation was odd, as if it was a fabrication. "I feel like I'm stuck in one of your horror novels."

She laughed. "It's a possibility. Maybe none of this is real."

"I will not start arguing metaphysics with you."

"That's good because I'm pretty sure the rules no longer exist for us, anyway."

From the look on her face, he decided not to ask what she meant. "So, what now? Where are we? What are we? That voice—it called me a Bringer. What does that mean?"

Kiara looked out into the distance, squinting under the odd light. "As for what we are, well, they don't use language the way we do. But the idea is they're all the same. The Takers call us Bringers, too. We no longer live on the same plane of existence humans do, but we can interact with them. Somehow, they expect us to bring them pure souls from the human world. As for where we are or what's next, I have no fucking clue."

After what he had just gone through, he figured something inside would have changed. That he would have some subconscious knowledge of what to do next, what his purpose was. Even after searching within, he came up blank and sighed. "I was kind of hoping you had all the answers."

"And I probably would if I hadn't spent the entire time since my death getting your ass out of purgatory."

"I'm never going to live that one down, am I?"

"Not a chance in hell."

The clouds floated over the sun, dimming the world around them but casting no shadows. There were so many questions. He supposed they would have plenty of time for them later. He realized he was no longer covered in pink ooze. His clothing, the same he had been wearing on the day of his death, was clean.

Curious, he pinched himself as hard as he could. The pain radiated up his arm.

*Well, I guess we can feel pain. Not sure if that's a good thing.*

Kiara hadn't moved. She was quietly observing him as he worked through all the things going on in his head.

"You keep referring to people as humans. Are we not like them anymore? Are we like angels?"

"I hope not. If we are angels, then I have no more faith for this world." She shrugged. "I try not to think too much about it. Just take it as it comes, you know?"

"I love you so much." He watched as the clouds moved and sunlight lit up her face. "You're so beautiful."

As the sun caressed her shoulders, it highlighted a small scar and the pain and guilt overwhelmed him again.

"Don't, Tyler." His face must have shown his thoughts, or maybe she was better at feeling them than he was. "I have my own guilt, too, my own sins. You realize that you killed yourself because of me? I had to watch you suffer, watch you take your life? At one point, I even tried to convince myself to leave you, make you *not* love me. I understand how it feels, what you're going through, but we can't let that get between us. I don't blame you and I'm hoping you don't blame me."

"No, of course not," he said, surprised. "I'm sorry, Ki. I didn't realize."

"I know." Her lips found his, and they became lost in each other.

The sun crawled toward the horizon as darkness descended. Together, they watched the first sunset of their new lives.

"We should probably start walking." Kiara stood and stretched, more from habit than from necessity.

"Where are we anyway?" Tyler asked.

"It appears to be the woods behind our house. My

guess is that things just look different to us. If we walk east, we should be home in half an hour or so."

"Walk? Well, that sucks. I was hoping we would sprout wings or something." Kiara gave him an incredulous look, and he grinned. "They could have at least dropped us off on the side of the road with a sign that said, 'redemption this way'."

"Baby, where we're going, we don't need roads."

"Did you seriously just quote *Back to the Future*?"

Kiara gave him a mischievous smile and started walking. He chased after her. "I don't know if this is going to work out, Ki. Death has made you lame."

She pushed him and ran, her giggles fading into the night as he chased her down. Their forms entangled, two shadows becoming one as he grabbed her by the waist and planted a kiss on her forehead. Together, they took their first steps toward eternity.

## THE END